BOND OF FLAMES

DARK MAGIC SHIFTERS 2

EVERLY FROST

Seven series. One world.

Suggested Reading Order:

Bright Wicked
Storm Princess
Assassin's Magic
Soul Bitten Shifter
Supernatural Legacy
Dark Magic Shifters
Kingdom of Betrayal

Come on in, Darkness.
Make yourself at home,
but don't get too comfortable
because...

CHAPTER ONE

$\mathcal{N}$ames have power.
Too much power.

My enemy lies on the cold floor with my claws at his throat.

One downward cut will end him, and yet...

He calls me *Daughter*.

A week ago, I escaped the cell in which I was imprisoned for my entire life. My mother gave birth to me in that darkness and raised me until she died in my arms.

She taught me many things while she was alive, but none more important than the reason why I was born in a supernatural prison: I was the heir to a powerful empire that others would kill to control. My father had been murdered, my mother betrayed, and everything had been taken from me.

I was only thirteen when she died. It took me another ten years to escape the prison and seek revenge.

Now, I'm here to kill this dark angel because I believed he was the one who murdered my father and stole my empire. I believed he was my uncle—my father's jealous brother.

He's lying beneath my claws and drawing breath at my mercy and yet...

"Daughter?" That single name carries so much power that it propels me away from him, compelling me to let him go.

I leap backward across the cold, stone floor of this small, dark space, feeling like the inky-black walls are closing in around me.

"No," I whisper, shaking my head rapidly. "You died."

He jumps to his feet with a *swoosh* of black wings. His skin is as pale as a distant star, his face framed by black hair, both of which make his golden eyes glow even more brightly. He is tall, lean, and gaunt—a perfectly beautiful dark angel whose smirk makes my blood run cold.

"Yes," he says. "The man I used to be... He died and is no more."

His gaze tears at me, as if he would peel me apart, dissecting me layer by layer. He gives a soft laugh, his posture relaxed. "Why did you stop fighting me, Daughter? You came for revenge, so take it!"

He moves in a flash, leaping toward me in a flurry of wings, his hard-as-a-rock fist crashing toward me.

I dart out of his path, narrowly avoiding the crushing blow he would have landed across my jaw.

I have nowhere to go.

The whole space is only fifty paces from side to side, although it stretches high above me, so far that I can't see the ceiling. The dark walls sparkle, as if little stars have been painted on them, and the only piece of furniture is a pedestal that sits in the middle of the room.

There's only one other person here with us: the dark angel named Lucian, who huddles against the far wall, his sporadic breathing telling me how badly injured he is. He hasn't willingly involved himself in our interaction, and I don't expect him to jump in now.

I can't see an exit. There's no outline of a door. No way out, as far as I can tell.

I barely have the chance to recover my balance when the man who claims to be my father comes after me.

"Take your revenge for the years I left you to rot in prison," he snarls.

I throw myself backward, desperately trying to stay out of his path as both of his fists smack into the stone wall one after the other, sending cracks through the surface.

"Take your revenge for the years of darkness and starvation I inflicted on you!" he shouts.

His speed would be awe-inspiring if he weren't my opponent. Instead, it's simply terrifying.

A split second after his fist crashes into the wall far too close to my face, he drops and sweeps his left wing low, attempting to knock me off my feet. In my effort to evade the move, I don't miss the fist he aims at my bare stomach. I'm wearing nothing more than a black bra and long, black pants, leaving much of my torso exposed.

My back hits the wall, pinned there by his left hand, the air *whooshing* out of my chest in a painful rush.

"Take your revenge for everything I took from you," he whispers, his other hand snapping out, reaching for my throat.

My claws descend, but I turn them toward the wall at my back and ram them into the stone. With every rasped breath, I fight the need to strike him, but by fuck… I can't.

Not yet.

Because if he's really my father…

If he's really my family…

How can I fight him when I came here to avenge him?

It has to be a lie. A deception of some kind.

It can't be true.

"You're lying—" My voice becomes a rasp, my speech cut short when his right hand closes around my throat and blocks my air.

"My blood can't lie." His wings push into my shoulders,

joining the hand he keeps around my neck to pin me to the wall. "Just as *your* blood can't lie."

I focus on the black liquid dripping from a gash across his jaw.

His blood is black, not red.

I gave him the wound from which it slides.

He's healing quickly. The cut is sealing up. The fluid is merely obeying gravity as it continues its downward motion.

"Your mother must have told you that the heir to the Nostra Empire is always born with two traits: golden eyes and black blood," he continues. "As you can see, I have both."

It's undeniable proof that this man is the firstborn and rightful heir to the empire, a powerful underground organization made up of supernaturals who have sworn allegiance to the Nostra family.

Just as my own black blood and golden eyes prove that I'm *his* rightful heir.

He has to be my father.

Not dead, after all.

Not murdered.

Everything I believed is crumbling down around me. My foundations have shifted and an abyss is opening at my feet. It's filled with questions, each of them slithering like a venomous snake.

How could this man hang me from my feet for hours in this dark space and still call himself my father? How could he goad me into fighting him?

We are dark creatures. We aren't known for our empathy or compassion, but even creatures of the dark understand loyalty and hierarchy and, in a family like the Nostra family, the need for a strong heir.

I was brought to this place wearing an illusion that disguised my true features, but he would have known I was his daughter from the moment he saw my blood.

Why is he trying to make an enemy of me?

My voice remains a rasp, the barest sound since he's squeezing my neck so tightly that breathing is painful. "You can't be my father."

"Why not, Daughter?" he asks, his lips twisting. "Because I was supposed to be dead?"

Well, that too. And I have a million questions about it, but my reasoning is more painful than that.

"Because my father loved me."

I didn't think it was possible for his face to become paler than it already is. His eyes widen and his hand loosens around my neck, although he doesn't let me go.

There's a question in his voice as he says, "Galeia didn't raise you to hate me."

Galeia is my mother's name. It was only a short time ago that I heard it for the first time. Until then, she'd been *Mother*. And while she was alive, I was *Daughter*. Because names, well, they have power and my relationship with her was my whole world.

"She raised me to love you," I say, making it sound so simple and uncomplicated.

His forehead creases, his eyes widen and then quickly narrow, and his lips press tightly together, a quick sequence of reactions.

I sense my vocal cords healing now that he's no longer squeezing my neck so tightly. I can't keep my own confusion—or pain—from my voice. "I came to claim your empire in your name and destroy the one who took your life. I came here to avenge *you*."

Even with that declaration, he doesn't let me go. His wings dig painfully into my shoulders, his left hand presses against my abdomen, and he doesn't remove his hand from my neck.

His expression wipes clean. "That means nothing to me."

My eyes widen at his cold response. I retaliate against the

sudden pain in my heart in the only way I know how: with violence.

Ripping my claws out of the wall, I knock his wings wide and strike both of my hands across the space between us.

I snatch at his shoulder with one hand and drive the claws of my other toward his throat.

The deadly tips once again meet his skin, making him freeze.

Now, he's pinning me to the wall while I'm pulling him toward me, my claws drawing little pinpricks of blood across his throat.

He could snap my neck. I could drive my nails through his neck.

Neither of us moves.

I try once more to reach him through the cold mask he's wearing. "I didn't come here to steal your empire," I say, in case that possibility is the cause of the fear I glimpsed briefly in his eyes. "I'm here because I believed you had been wronged and it was my duty to seek justice on your behalf."

He remains frozen where he stands, even as his blood trickles to the neckline of his black shirt. "Your need for vengeance is misplaced, Daughter."

His whisper only adds to the turmoil within my heart—a heart that beats in my chest but isn't fully whole.

If I'm truly honest, it never has been. There has always been something missing from my heart. But I chose to widen that chasm when I gave away my heart's power to the keeper of dark magic in exchange for his loyalty.

The keeper is out there somewhere right now, and so are my panthers. Only three of them now that one was killed.

Hot tears fill my eyes because losing that panther—the one I called "Anarchy"—is the hardest loss I've experienced since my mother died.

"Stop calling me *Daughter*," I whisper back. "You *can't* be my father. Because my father wouldn't say things like that to me."

I loosen my grip on his shoulder and draw back my claws from his neck. It's a dangerous move, and I prepare for him to strike me now that I've given up any advantage I had.

He surprises me by leaping backward, his shoulders hunched, his wings curved around his body as he lands lightly a few paces away.

"What did your mother tell you about me?" he asks.

She told me he was powerful, commanding, a strong leader. But most importantly…

"She told me that you loved her." My throat constricts as I lower my hands to my sides. "She said you loved *us*."

His jaw clenches before he takes a shaky breath.

"Once," he says quietly. "I didn't think a dark creature like me could feel that sort of love, but I did." His gaze is suddenly far away. "For a few perfect months."

In the next moment, his expression hardens. "Then the truth was revealed to me."

My forehead creases. "What truth?"

His mouth pinches, and a look of disgust falls over his face. "That a creature like you has no right to exist."

A creature like me?

I would stumble if the wall at my back weren't keeping me upright.

My skin is suddenly crawling. The sensation is all over me, but it's especially intense along my spine, a tingle that runs from my lower back up to the base of my skull.

I try to steady my breathing as I yearn for the abhorrence in my father's eyes to fade.

When it doesn't, a cold anger rises within me and a shield I've long held over my heart and body lifts back into place.

"What could you possibly mean, Father?" I ask, sounding nonchalant in the face of his contempt. "Do you mean a creature like this?"

I focus on the prickling sensation in my back that increases beneath my shoulder blades. I draw on the strange sensation that I've taught myself to ignore because this aspect of myself doesn't fit with who I am.

With *what* I am.

Or maybe more accurately, with what I *should* be.

Hunching my shoulders, I allow the sensations within my shoulder blades to take control, gritting my teeth as a part of my spine tears apart and my back bursts open.

CHAPTER TWO

I scream with pain as ragged, black wings burst from my back.

They extend for a full five paces to each side of me, every feather long, jagged, sharp, and misshapen.

My wings are not beautiful. They aren't flowing or majestic.

They're the kind of wings that belong in a nightmare.

My fists clench reflexively, the tips scraping my palms before I force my fingers to relax.

Well, not exactly *relax*.

I draw my lips back, letting my teeth sharpen and the shape of my face to change, elongating and becoming more wolfish.

And there I stand, a wolf with golden eyes that see perfectly in the dark, indestructible black claws that can cut through anything, and deadly-sharp teeth that can rip out another creature's throat as easily as snapping at air.

Oh, and wings.

I'm a wolf with fucking wings.

A mash up of a dark angel and a hellhound. A strange combination of the two. The keeper hasn't seen this part of me. Nobody but my mother has.

Until now.

My father's jaw drops. His throat visibly constricts and a strangled sound leaves his lips.

I'm not sure why he seems so surprised when he was the one who asserted I have no right to exist, as if a creature like me is so abhorrent, I don't deserve life.

As he stumbles back a step, I'm once again aware of Lucian where he huddles on the other side of the room.

His father, who is *my* father.

Lucian must be my half-brother—my younger half-brother —although exactly when he was born isn't my greatest concern right now.

My larger worry is the way he's looking at me as he rises to his feet. His wing is broken and it unbalances him, making him wobble and then press back against the wall as if for support. I didn't break his wing. Our father did.

Lucian's eyes are wide, and his lips are pursed into an "Oh" as if he's had some sort of revelation.

There's no way I have a hope of guessing what it could be.

So far, I've badly misread this entire situation.

"Dad," Lucian says, seeming transfixed by my feathers before he focuses on my face. To my shock, he smiles. Not a cruel smile, but a strangely relieved one. "She has wings."

Our father snaps back at him. "It changes nothing." His voice rises. "None of this changes anything!"

Lucian's smile disappears, but his whisper is clear. "But... it changes everything."

I'm not sure exactly what it's supposed to change.

Our father turns his back on Lucian, returning his attention to me. His eyes are cold and once again, his expression is so hard, he could be made of ice.

"You are an impossibly dangerous creature," he says to me. "Your mother's claws were always a threat, but you have the blood of dark angels running within your veins, and now I see that you have the power of flight."

Well, it might look that way.

In reality, these wings are useless to me. I don't know how to fly because I grew up in a cell with a low ceiling and flying was an impossibility. I had no chance to learn and I'm not even sure, with the way these wings are structured, that they are built for flight.

He takes a step toward me. "It was my responsibility to ensure you were removed from this world, and that you never returned to it. That was my burden." He thumps his heart with his fist. "That was my sacrifice."

My lips part in surprise.

Can I really believe there's now pain in his eyes?

"Why?" I ask, incredibly confused. "What could possibly make you judge me before I was born?"

I should have been prepared for him to play games with my emotions. To lie and cheat as dark creatures do. But the walls of my heart are suddenly cracking and my insides are hurting because with every word he speaks, there is no guile in his voice.

No subterfuge. No pretense.

He speaks only with conviction.

"I am Taiven Nostra, the Ultima Nostra," he says, announcing the title to the empire I came to claim. "I'm responsible for the lives of countless dark creatures who follow me with unquestioning loyalty. They live or die according to my commands. For millennia, we have fought the forces of light for our place in this world, a battle that rages beneath the awareness of humans."

He takes a step toward me. "But *you*..." His jaw clenches, his lips drawing back from his teeth. "You will fill the streets with blood."

My eyes widen at his words. "I'll... what?"

Declaring me unworthy of life is one thing, but telling me with so much certainty what I will or won't do in the future…?

That's fucking bullshit.

"You will incite a war among dark creatures that even the forces of light would never wish for."

There's an emptiness in his eyes. No longer do they gleam. There's no triumph. Only a deep nothingness that, if I peer into his eyes too long, appears driven by fear.

It hits me hard that this dark angel, who commands an army of vicious, bloodthirsty, vile creatures, is afraid… of me.

"I gave you life," he says. "Now, it's my duty to end it."

"But—"

I don't have time to react.

He strikes far faster than I anticipate and this time, his attack takes a different form.

He hits my face open-handed. It's barely more than a slap and shouldn't hurt me and yet—

Bright, white light bursts from his palm, searing my cheek.

A shocked scream wrenches from me.

The scent of my own burning skin fills my chest and suddenly, I'm pulled back into the past when I faced my jailer's light magic. He was a Sentinel—an elite angel capable of wielding the purest soul light. There aren't many Sentinels, but their light can cause extreme damage to dark creatures.

My father shouldn't be able to wield anything like soul light. His power stems from darkness.

It shouldn't be possible. It can't be possible!

But the danger is very real.

I need to move. I need to evade him. I need to retract my wings because they're an awful liability, giving him more surface area to attack. Even as my scream tears from my throat, I'm trying to pull them in.

His other hand shoots out, grabbing at the disappearing tip of my right wing.

He manages to pluck two long feathers from it before I can fully retract it.

Pain bursts through me again, far more intense than I was expecting.

Holy fuck! I've never lost a feather. I didn't think it would hurt so damn much.

Desperate to get out of his path, I spin to my left, my clawed right fist aiming for his chest as I whirl past. My intention is to push him away from me, but if I cut him in the process, so be it.

He angles his body at the last moment and my claws miss him by a hairsbreadth, slicing only through his shirt, shredding the material instead of his skin.

He doesn't let go of my feathers to defend himself, keeping hold of them as I follow up with my left fist and then my right. I deliver a flurry of near-hits that sends him backpedaling across the room, evading me by what feels like a mere sliver each time.

My goal is to beat him backward, unbalance him, and unsettle him enough that I have a chance to get out of here.

I need to find the keeper, return to my panthers, and regroup. I have to come to terms with what I've learned and re-examine my path. I have a thousand questions, but I won't get answers in this place.

But how can I escape if the only exit is high above me?

When Taiven and Lucian appeared, they dropped from the ceiling. Since I don't see any other openings, it's possible that the entrance is way up there. High, *high* up there. If I knew how to use my wings, that might not be a problem, but I don't know if they're even functional.

My father's evasion takes him to the pedestal in the middle of the room, which he has to sidestep in his effort to avoid my next punch.

I anticipate his move to his left and drop to sweep my leg across the floor in an attempt to knock him down.

I picture him taking a few seconds to get back up, during which I'm sure I can make it to the side of the room.

Since I can't be sure I can use my wings, I'll use my claws to climb instead. After all, they can impale anything. I'll ram them into the rock and use them as leverage to somehow make it to the top.

In response to my attempt to put him on his back, my father extends his wings. They catch the air and lift him from the danger of my sweeping leg.

My wings might be a liability to me, but by the hottest fires of hell, he uses his wings to their full potential.

Twisting where I crouch, my hands planted on the floor, I extend my body and kick upward with my other leg.

This time, I connect.

The impact is lessened because he was already mostly out of my reach, but it knocks him a little off-balance.

I shove at the floor with my hands, leaping upward, using all of the strength in my arms, legs, and stomach to move in a flash, throwing myself through the air at him.

One more hit and I'll knock him to the ground.

For a split second as I sail past the pedestal, I can finally see its slanted top. I'm surprised that there's nothing on it. Only a white scorch mark and a film of gray ash, as if a small fire burned on it at some point.

Opposite me, my father's wings shiver. He sweeps them to the front in what looks like a struggle to drive himself backward and away from me.

My fists are outstretched, one aimed at his neck, the other at his ribs.

Two strong punches.

But then his stance shifts midair. It's the smallest movement and the slightest flex of his biceps and stomach muscles, which are visible through his torn shirt, but suddenly…

Oh, fuck, no.

I realize that his midair wobble was a ruse. He wasn't off-balance or out of control. And now I'm right where he wants me.

My weight is forward, making my body a perfect target and allowing him to use my momentum against me.

He collapses his wings and drops to a crouch.

As my claws fly over his head, his left arm swings up, and the *thump* he lands against my side sends a cracking vibration through my torso.

Burning light blasts through me. There's a sickening *crunch* as several of my ribs break. And then the force of his punch knocks me across the air and into the wall.

I hit the cold stone, unable to scream despite the pain.

One of my broken ribs must have punctured my left lung. My clothing is scorched, and the skin across my midriff is red and raw.

I can't… breathe…

And I can't get my feet under me fast enough.

He shoots toward me, one of my own feathers in each of his hands, the sharp ends pointed toward me.

I've never plucked out one of my feathers—*why the hell would I?* But I'm suddenly confronted with the realization that the ends of them—the ends that were embedded in my bone—have the same metallic sheen as my claws.

Move, Veda!

I've made it only inches away from the wall when he rams one of the feathers into my left shoulder, knocking me back into the stone surface.

The feather impales me all the way through to the other side of my body, stopping only when his closed fist bangs into my chest.

Agony shoots down my left arm, but the pain isn't all.

Somehow, he's driven the feather through a spot that's pinching the nerves, instantly immobilizing that arm.

I can't bend my elbow. I can't get my left claws up.

I swing my right fist instead, a desperate defensive move, but that, too, was a mistake.

He drives the other feather through my oncoming palm, using its length to avoid my claws as he rams my hand back against the wall. The feather travels through flesh and sinew and into the stone, pinning my hand between the rock and his fist.

I don't have breath to scream.

I'm gasping, trying to get enough air, desperate for my body to heal the puncture wound in my lung before I pass out.

I can't pass out or it will be the end of me.

His weight is on his hands, where he continues to grip the feathers and press them into me.

I want to ask him how he could possibly loathe me this much when he doesn't even know me, but I can't catch enough air to speak.

He's taking a risk remaining this close to me, and if I could just catch my breath, I might be able to use my legs. Maybe ram my knee into his stomach. But it's taking all my effort to remain conscious.

A sudden despair fills me because, for the first time since I woke up in this dark place, I wonder if this is where I'll die.

CHAPTER THREE

"Before I kill you, there's one thing I want from you, Veda," my father says.

At this point, I don't really care what he wants from me. I only have regrets. Mostly, I regret not driving my claws through his throat when I had the chance—assuming I could have. For all I know, he allowed me to get the upper hand in that moment and would have easily repelled me.

Then there are other regrets. Deeper ones.

Not seeing more of the world beyond my cage when I had the chance.

Not asking the keeper to take me to every beach where I could look up and drink in the beautiful darkness of the night sky.

Not trying every food that could possibly be eaten.

Not letting myself lose control when the keeper offered me the chance.

My voice wheezes between my gritted teeth, an exhalation that somehow forms discernible sound. "What... do you... want?"

Taiven's lips twist. "You will tell me where your mother is."

I can only blink at him. *Does he mean her grave?*

Somehow, I manage to make intelligible sounds, although my words are barely more than forced whispers. "I don't... fucking know."

"Oh, come now, Daughter." He *tsks* at me. "She may hate me for abandoning her—not that I would have been able to find her in the veil even if I'd wanted to—but she can't hide from her destiny."

He's talking about her as if...

My face falls as a shocking possibility occurs to me. "You think... she's alive?"

His brow puckers. "Of course she's alive. Galeia walked with gods. She was over a thousand years old. The closest to an immortal that any dark creature can be. Two decades in prison would have been a mere blink of an eye to her."

I continue to stare at him in disbelief.

My mother was over a thousand years old? A near immortal? *Fucking bullshit.*

I can't possibly reconcile his description of her with the starved, frail woman who gave me her share of the scraps our jailer fed us and who died in my arms, gasping for breath just as I am now.

A terrible, horrible laugh bubbles between my teeth. "You're... deluded."

My laughter only seems to enrage him. His right hand rams the feather further into my shoulder and he roars at me. "*Where is she?*"

I scream as the weapon travels all the way through my torso and into the wall at my back. Warm blood pools across my shoulder, but it's a mere trickle of feeling compared to the pain of the feather's stem raking through my body.

The hurt makes me angry.

So, too, does Taiven's sickening belief that he didn't kill the woman he claims to have once loved.

Well, I can play on that.

Why the hell should I insist on the truth?

"Oh, she'll come for you now," I whisper. "She'll destroy you for what you've done to me."

It dawns on me then that my voice is clear.

The air no longer wheezes through my lips. I may be in terrible pain and can't move my left arm, but at least I can breathe again.

His response is to roar at me again, but this time, it's a wordless shout, a scream of sound, his lips so twisted and his eyes so full of hatred that they make his beautiful face look perfectly ugly.

Quietly, I bare my teeth back at him, letting them sharpen, wishing only for the chance to sink them into his throat.

He wants me dead, and he has claimed responsibility for my mother's imprisonment and, as a consequence, her death.

Any reservations I had about killing him are now gone.

Without a sound, I propel myself forward, tearing my right hand through the feather, damaging my palm but leaving the stem embedded in the wall. At the same time, I shove so hard with my left foot against the wall that I dislodge his hold on my shoulder and rip the end of that feather out of the stone behind me. The feather remains embedded in my shoulder, and my left arm is still immobilized, but my right hand is free.

I drive my right claws at his throat, desperate to end him.

He's faster than me.

Oh-so-much fucking faster.

All I feel is a cascade of pain as he strikes in a blur, every hit bursting with light magic that burns across my vision and sears my body.

He snatches hold of my oncoming hand, twists, and the bones in my wrist, thumb, and forefinger shatter. His other fist smacks my left cheekbone with a *crunch* and suddenly, I can't see out of that eye. So quickly it seems to happen at the same time, his foot hits my outstretched left leg and the bone in my calf snaps.

I can't even scream.

I can barely process what happened as the onslaught of light stops and I plummet to the cold, stone floor, my broken leg bent at a horrible angle and my other leg folded beneath me.

His shadow engulfs me and it feels like death.

A cold, inevitable death.

I try to look up, try to make sense of what he's saying because he's speaking, but it's a wash of noise garbled by the pain ravaging my body.

"Do you think me cruel, Daughter?" he asks. "I could have broken every bone in your body from the moment you were brought to me, unconscious. I held off because I wanted to know where Galeia is, but you've failed to provide that information. I'll give you one more chance and if you answer my question, I'll kill you quickly."

Somewhere in the midst of the chaos within my mind, there's a cold version of myself quietly cataloging my injuries.

I've lost vision in my left eye. My cheekbone is broken. So are many of the bones in my right hand and wrist, along with the bone in my left calf. My left arm remains immobilized with my feather still jutting from my shoulder. Blood pools in my mouth, making it difficult to breathe again, even though my ribs have repaired themselves. Where he hit me, I can see burn marks across my leg and hand. There are also scorches that stretch from one side to the other, as if the light splashed across me. The burns are easily visible since I'm wearing nothing more than a bra up top. I'm sure there are more burns across my face.

I've never experienced wounds like this. Not even at the hands of my jailer. He never broke my bones while using his light magic.

It's clear that my healing power is struggling to cope because my bones aren't knitting together and my vision isn't clearing.

As for what is still functioning: my right leg, my right eye, and my hearing to some extent.

My heart is beating.

I'm breathing, but it's difficult.

With a hateful sense of finality, I acknowledge to myself that I don't have a hope of beating him. He's fast and strong. But I suppose he has hundreds of years of fighting experience to draw on while I only had a short time learning basic combat from my mother.

My father approaches my broken leg, retracts his wings fully, and crouches beside me.

I have to turn my head to keep him within sight of my good eye.

As my labored breathing bubbles in the silence, he flicks my blood off his hands. "I was hoping you would come to me with anger in your heart because it would make this so much easier." He sighs. "Galeia must have hoped I'd let you live if you came to me in good faith. Trust me—I never wanted to be the one to kill you."

The fact that he's stopped to talk, instead of snapping my neck already, gives me hope that there's still some conflict within him about what he plans to do.

"Then don't be." I spit out the blood pooling in my mouth. "Don't be the one who kills me. Let me go. I came here to avenge you. You're alive. My purpose is spent. I can disappear from your life."

He shakes his head, the corners of his mouth turned down. His hair is so inky against his pale skin that it's like black lines slashing across his features and separating the pieces of his face.

One piece conflicted. One piece resolved. Another piece indifferent. A final piece cold.

"Have you ever seen true darkness, Daughter?"

I've seen it in many forms.

I saw it in the light within my jailer's hands. He was an

angel of supposed purity who used his power to cause pain and subjugation. Surely, darkness masquerading as light is evil.

I've seen it in the eyes of a beautiful man, the keeper of dark magic himself, who stood at my side for the last week and to whom I gave the power in my heart. *His* darkness is a thing of beauty and carries endless possibilities, a darkness that forms a shield between me and the rest of the world, a not-so-quiet protection.

But true darkness...

I see it now, crouched in front of me.

Fathers should never hurt their daughters. No matter their reasons.

Any father who hurts his child is a fucking monster.

"I've seen darkness," I say.

"Then you will understand why I must do everything in my power to end you."

His words send a shudder through me.

Yes, I am darkness, but I had a purpose that was not unjust.

I thought I would come here to avenge a father who loved me, even though, as dark creatures, we rarely love anything other than power and control and pain.

I believed I was destined to take back the Nostra Empire in his name and as retribution for the life that had been stolen from my mother and the childhood that had been stolen from me.

But now...

The hatred in his eyes leaves me empty.

"You fought well, Daughter," he says.

Unable to move, I can't do anything more than snarl at him. "If you're going to kill me, stop talking and get the fuck on with it."

Ignoring the taunt, he bends and takes hold of my left wrist —the unbroken but immobilized one. His fingers and thumb dig into my limb in a configuration that feels incredibly deliberate, but his intent is confusing and unclear.

He increases the pressure and suddenly, my claws are forced outward as far as they can go.

I can't retract them.

Which wouldn't be a concern, except that he's pressing them toward my own chest.

Sickening pain streaks through me the moment he compels my arm to bend in a way it currently doesn't want to, but it's nothing compared to the fear that bursts through me.

"What are you doing?"

"Your claws and feathers are made of an extremely rare metal," he says. "A dark substance. One of the few metals that can kill you."

Fuck no.

"I would use one of your feathers," he continues, glancing up at the feather embedded in the wall, "but your claws will shred your heart in a single strike. A much more efficient death."

I try to push back with all of my strength, needing to control my arm and hand while at the same time afraid that he'll break those bones, too. Panic floods me when I sense the pressure between the feather in my shoulder and the angle of my arm working against me.

Bones, please don't break.

I moan with pain and fear, trying to get my right leg out from under me so I can kick him—assuming I can even reach across the space between us, since he was clever to crouch on the more heavily injured side of me.

He glances once more up at the feather in the wall, and I imagine he's starting to think that my claws are becoming more effort than he was counting on.

Beads of sweat break out across his forehead, and a snarl rises to his lips.

That's when a soft swishing sound registers in my hearing,

and I become aware of movement in the darkness behind my father.

Lucian appears in the gloom, his broken wing dragging across the floor, his face pale. Like Taiven, his skin is fair, his hair is black, and his eyes are golden, but his blood is red and his wing isn't healing quickly.

He carves a ragged, unsteady path toward the pedestal and kicks its wooden base hard. Once, twice.

It snaps near the bottom and topples to the floor with a clatter. The little platform that sits on its top breaks off upon impact, so that what remains of the pedestal is a plank of wood with two jagged ends.

I'm not sure what Lucian intends to do with that plank until he hoists it upward and carves another ragged path, this time in our direction.

As he comes closer, his other injuries become more apparent. There are bruises across his face and neck and on his arms where his sleeves don't cover them. A thick ring of reddened skin is visible around his neck, the kind that might be made by a rope.

Lucian had none of those injuries before he brought me here and all of them when I woke up.

His golden eyes flash over me and I can't decipher his expression—other than to register a hatred as cold as our father's.

He isn't my friend.

If he hits me over the head with that chunk of wood and knocks me out even for a second, it will all be over for me.

CHAPTER FOUR

"Do it, Son," Taiven says without turning to Lucian. "Make me proud for the first time in your life."

"Proud?" Lucian's voice is an angry rasp. "Why would I give a fuck about making you proud?"

Taiven's eyes widen.

Lucian swings the wooden plank.

It cracks across the back of our father's head so hard that I'm sure a chunk of his scalp will fly across the room before his body follows.

Taiven barely flinches.

My stomach sinks low and bile rises to my throat.

Dark saints, what will it take to defeat him?

Taiven turns his angry eyes up at Lucian while managing to keep my claws pressing toward my chest.

"Oh… fuck." Lucian backs away, the plank slipping between his fingers.

"Pathetic." Taiven spits before returning his attention to me. "As weak as his mother."

Lucian stops backpedaling, catching hold of the plank before it can drop to the ground. His fingers tighten around it, his knuckles turning white. "You're the weak one."

Taiven's lips draw back from his teeth as he turns his head to side-eye his son. "What did you say to me?"

"I said, you're a coward," Lucian snarls. "Hiding behind powerful supernaturals like Jonah and Vanguard. Using their loved ones as leverage to get what you want."

Jonah and Vanguard were my way in to the empire. Vanguard promised me that if I completed a mission for him, he would give me access to the inner circle of what I thought was my father's usurper. That mission involved taking Vanguard's five-year-old son to safety.

I didn't realize when I first met them just how powerful Jonah and Vanguard are. Jonah is a rare fire Jotunn, capable of burning any living creature to ash within seconds.

James Vanguard, well, I thought he was a snake shifter, but it turns out he's an old god: Jormungandr, the World Serpent, to be exact.

I later met his delightful sister, Hel, the Goddess of Death and the Underworld, who goes by the name Halle now.

Vanguard's son had been the leverage my father had been using to keep Vanguard in line. It'd been Lucian's job to make sure the boy didn't escape, and our father was clearly unhappy Lucian failed.

Now, Lucian stands his ground, barely stopping to take a breath as he continues to accuse our father. "You promised my mother safety and then you used her as a shield to protect yourself against your enemies." He hits his chest with his free hand. "*I* am the leverage you use to keep her people from taking revenge for her death. You hide behind children and the powers of others. You're a fucking weak coward!"

My eyes widen at what Lucian says.

Another woman was destroyed by this man who dares to call himself a father?

My blood boils and a surge of energy strikes through me.

The muscles of my good leg tense, ready to propel me to the side. My right arm is already bent and if I can just twist and ram my elbow into his neck, maybe I can dislodge him without impaling myself on my other claws.

Before I can try, Taiven lurches away from me.

He releases me so suddenly that my left arm swings back in the opposite direction, traveling even faster because I was trying to push in that direction. My limb moves at a *snap* and I swallow my scream of pain.

But I'm free.

At least… I *feel* free…

It takes me what feels like horribly long seconds to leverage my right shoulder against the wall and push myself upright with my right leg.

In the meantime, Taiven has reached Lucian. The crack of his fist across his son's face splashes painfully bright light across the room. It obscures my already-diminished vision, but I make out Lucian dropping to the ground.

He won't be able to withstand the burning light magic in our father's fists for long. Lucian's healing power is far weaker than mine.

I need to get over there. I need to do something. Lucian isn't my friend, not even my ally, but he's… my brother.

And right now, he and I have a common enemy.

I have to move.

But how can I make it to him?

This wall at my back is the only reason I'm upright. Without it, I'll topple over again.

Fuck that. If I have to hop across this room like a damn bunny rabbit, I fucking will.

My vision clears enough to now see that Lucian is on his knees, but his eyes are open. Taiven grips the front neckline of his shirt, as if he'd yanked Lucian up into that position, his fist raised over his son's face.

Lucian should be worried about our father's threatening fist, but his focus is on me. "Fly, Veda! Go up! It's the only way out!"

I'm so unused to counting on my wings for anything—and, hell, I don't even know if they'll function—but I'm willing to give them a try.

What I'll do if they work is another matter. Although my hands and arms aren't functioning, if Lucian can somehow hold on to me, maybe at least get the feather out of my left shoulder and free up my left arm, then maybe I can get us both out of here.

Reaching for the crawling sensation in my spine that I've taught myself to ignore, I brace for the pain my wings cause when they tear out of my back.

It's far worse than before.

Only my right wing extends.

My left wing sticks, halts, then makes a shrieking sound as it rips—

Fuck!

The feather rammed through my left shoulder must be preventing it from extending.

In a rush of panic, I retract both wings, folding them away again, sensing my left wing tearing even further as it disappears.

Oh, damn.

My gasp of pain is drowned by the *thump* of Taiven's fist on Lucian's face. A cut opens above the younger angel's eye, but he doesn't go down. His focus is still on me, although only with his uninjured eye.

He must have seen my wings extend and retract because his focus moves briefly to the feather in my shoulder. I'm sure he will have understood why I can't try to use my wings after all.

He returns his attention to our father. "Do it!" Lucian screams. "Kill me! If you get what you want, you'll have no children left. Nobody to challenge you. But there'll be plenty of supernaturals who'll come after you now that Vanguard isn't standing at your si—"

Smack.

Lucian falls silent, his head lolling.

I catch sight of the burn across his face before our father drops him to the floor, where he ends up crumpled forward over his knees. Lucian's uninjured wing drapes across his back and side while the broken one stretches out across the floor.

Now that Lucian's unconscious, I assume Taiven will come back to finish me off, but he remains standing over his son.

The light glimmering around his fists grows brighter.

"I will finish you now, boy," he spits. "Just as you wish."

Oh, no, you fucking won't.

As quietly as I can, I push away from the wall, desperately trying to get my balance by bending the knee of my good leg a little. I don't look at my bad leg, conscious only that it's a big problem and will probably be my downfall.

If I'm going to die, I'll do it with a tiny bit of honor, trying to protect my little brother.

I may be a dark creature with fucking ugly wings, and I may have no right to exist, but I have rules.

Number one: Some bonds are worth dying for.

Like my bond with Anarchy.

She was family to me, and she died to protect me.

Hot tears burn my good eye, but my anger gives me strength.

I manage a painful but not terribly quiet hop and my lips draw back from my teeth in a grin at my success.

Hop, bunny rabbit, hop.

Taiven seems too busy focusing on the light magic growing in his palms to pay any attention to me.

Which is a shame, because holy fuck, I must be a sight right now.

I make it two more hops while his power increases until it's so bright that large specks form in my vision.

The specks expand and then I'm fighting to see anything at all, since my good eye seems to be failing.

Not now!

A soft haze falls across my sight like a gentle mist, swirling in ribbons all the way to the floor.

The mist seems to touch everything. *Blur* everything.

I squint harder, trying to see through the haze to my brother, wondering if maybe, actually, I'm…

Dying.

If I think about my situation for more than a heartbeat, it's incredible that I've remained alive at all.

When creatures of magic die, their power is collected by one of the four keepers of magic, whose task it is to tether their energy so it doesn't contaminate the world, which happened in ancient times. There are four keepers, one for each kind of magic: light magic, dark magic, old magic, and elemental magic.

My magic should be collected by the keeper of dark magic, except that I freed him from the realm within which he was caged. Given that, I'm actually not sure what will happen to my magic now.

Of course, my soul is another matter and, as a dark creature, there's only one place it's headed.

A smile grows on my face because I like the idea that, if I'm dying right now, my untethered energy might spill out across this room, wrap around my father, and drag him to hell with me.

But my body is still moving, and I'm going to keep moving until my body gives up, even if my mind is already gone.

I manage another hop before the ribbons of mist around me begin to swirl in a growing tornado that quickly envelops me. The rushing air plucks me up off the floor, although it doesn't toss me around. Rather, it's as if I'm being held upright in the quiet center of an equally silent storm.

I can't hear a thing now.

I can barely see the brightness of my father's magic across the room—a power that a dark angel like himself shouldn't be able to summon.

The pain in my broken leg eases. It seems to be cushioned on the air beneath me and, oh, dark saints, it's a relief.

Still, I struggle against the growing mist, trying once more to get to my brother, grunting with effort, spitting blood in the process.

The mist won't let me go.

My forehead creases when it quickly expands, stretching far into the distance in front of me—much farther than the walls.

Two silhouettes form within it, both running toward me at a startling pace.

One of the figures is tall and distinctly male with broad shoulders and a heavily muscled physique.

The other is feline. A big cat.

My eyes widen and my heart leaps.

My sob is snatched from my mouth by the increasingly intense rush of air around me. *"Diavolo."*

Devil.

The one with my heart. My keeper.

He's here.

He storms into view, his features crystal clear despite my one-eyed vision. He can change his appearance at will, and now he's wearing his most muscular form. His eyes are the darkest brown, his jaw is sharp, and his cheekbones are high. His skin is light brown and his lips are as beautiful as a god's.

He wears a crown-shaped ring on his left hand. It's an object of immense power. When I first met him, he wore that crown around his eyes, his sight constrained by it.

His crown contains all of the dark magic he's collected over thousands of years from dark magic creatures who died: the power of dark shifters, warlocks, witches, fae, elves, vampires, goblins, trolls, sirens, and every other kind of dark creature that ever walked this Earth. So much power. But the rules of his creation meant he couldn't use it for his own benefit.

Until I freed him.

We are both escapees from the cages we were placed in.

Even though his brown-eyed form is one of his most intimidating, it's also his calmest, most confident persona.

Though he doesn't stay calm for longer than a few seconds.

His gaze flashes across my broken body, racing from my busted face to the feather in my shoulder, to my broken arm and hand, down to my mangled leg, and then up across all the burns and bruises that must be visible across my torso, neck, and face.

Murder fills his eyes.

His countenance changes in a heartbeat.

His hair is instantly inky black and his eyes become the deepest, darkest blue, like a stormy sea. His body becomes leaner, although it remains muscular, and his clothing changes, becoming all black.

This is the face that stops my heart and fills me with both fear and anticipation.

"Veda." He speaks in a low, broken snarl as his arms close around me, his hands cradling my back and supporting me. His voice tears at my soul. "My dark Veda."

"You're here." I can't keep the sob from my voice as I close my good eye and let him hold my suddenly trembling body.

I'm not sure how he found me, but right now, I don't care.

His hands are so gentle that his touch doesn't hurt me.

But his voice is tight with fury. "Tell me who I need to kill."

CHAPTER FIVE

I inhale the mist in the air, tasting Diavolo's magic on my tongue.

I want nothing more in this moment than to ask him to kill the dark angel who gave me life.

After all, that was what Diavolo promised me. In return for giving him the power in my heart, he vowed to help me kill the man who'd murdered my father, imprisoned my mother, and stole the empire that should have been mine.

Of course, if I think about it, that promise is now fragile. My father is alive, and I have no right to claim his empire while he lives. So the first and third parts of the promise are void.

My father did imprison my mother. Or at least, he ordered it to happen. But what if Diavolo chooses to interpret that part of the promise more literally?

It wasn't my father who held my mother in a prison, but the angel who took her into the veil and kept her there. That angel is already dead, so Diavolo might consider that part of the promise already fulfilled.

What if Diavolo is no longer bound to me?

Dark saints, what then?

All of these thoughts rage through my mind within a heartbeat and I can't stop my increasing trembles.

In response to my shiver, Diavolo's hands slide across my back in soothing strokes.

"Don't be afraid," he murmurs. "I'm holding my translocation power in place. It can whisk us away within a heartbeat. I've created an illusion on this side of the room so the mist isn't visible. It will look as if you're still alone…" His voice hardens and his snarl returns. "And hurt."

The corners of his mouth turn down. "You may not be able to see past the power I've placed around you, but I can see clearly the two dark angels on the other side of this room. So help me, my Veda. I'm fighting the impulse to set them alight and watch them burn."

His beautiful lips are twisted with fury.

His rage on my behalf calms some of my fear, but a new anxiety is replacing it.

Diavolo may want to lay waste to this place, but my father controls light magic of a strength I never expected to encounter.

If that light magic burned me this badly, it could hurt Diavolo, too.

My throat is tight with emotion, and speaking is painful—but not impossible.

It would be so easy for me, as a dark creature, to lie to him, but I choose not to.

He would find out the truth soon enough.

"My father is alive," I say.

Diavolo stiffens. He takes a brief glance at the mist behind him and I can only assume that he can see beyond it to Taiven. He knows that the Ultima Nostra is a dark angel with golden eyes. He will recognize those features in my father. But no doubt he will have mistakenly assumed—like I did—that Taiven was my uncle.

"Then that angel is not your uncle, after all."

"He is not." My throat is tight as I dread the possibility that Diavolo will abandon me now.

His arms only close more tightly around me. His facial features morph for a moment, becoming wolfish, before he inhales deeply. "I can smell your blood on his fists. He's the one who did this to you."

The muscles within his arms are coiled, the tension in his body intense. His dark eyes consume my vision as he says, "I will end him for you, my Veda."

If I could hold on to Diavolo, grip him and make him listen to me, I would, but all I have is my voice. "Please don't fight him."

Diavolo's eyes widen, and I try to continue as quickly as I can, although fresh blood bubbles between my lips. "He's controlling light magic. It's stronger even than the magic used by the angel who caged me."

Diavolo's brow furrows, but his wary expression grows. "That should be impossible."

His focus flashes once again to the burns on my skin.

Burns that aren't healing.

They're worse than the injury I experienced when I fought Jonah, the fire Jotunn. Because Jonah is a creature of old magic, his magic can hurt me—and pretty much every other supernatural. That was before Jonah became our uneasy ally.

Diavolo's gaze flows across my face and I wish I could decipher the shadows growing in his expression.

"Fuck," he whispers, squeezing his eyes shut for a moment. "There has to be a world beyond vengeance."

He said something similar when we stood together on the first beach I'd ever seen and looked up at the infinite night sky.

At the time, I'd replied: *"Not for me, there isn't."*

I wonder now if I was wrong.

Vengeance hasn't worked out so well for me so far.

Diavolo opens his eyes and they flash with new fury.

"Striking now carries great risk." A cold smile touches his lips as he seems to reach a decision. "Retribution must be planned and vengeance carefully extracted to achieve the greatest pain. Our vengeance on your father will wait."

"But my brother's life cannot," I say.

Diavolo's dark-blue eyes narrow at me. "Your brother?" His forehead pinches before it clears. "You mean Lucian."

Diavolo peers back again, as if he's reassessing what he can apparently see on the far side of the room. "Your father is preparing to kill him, but it seems he likes the sound of his own voice too much to do it quickly."

"Yeah." I sigh. "I noticed."

"A lot of threats. Significant belittling," Diavolo murmurs, as if he's recounting what he's hearing. Then a sudden, deep fury enters his eyes again. "Now, he's talking about you." His jaw clenches. "Your father is conflicted. But it's clear that ending Lucian will be easier for him than ending you."

I give a snarl of disgust. "As if one child's life is worth less than another's."

Diavolo considers me carefully. "I feel your hatred, my Veda, but saving Lucian may not be wise."

Diavolo isn't wrong.

Until Lucian hit our father over the head, I believed he was as much my enemy as my father has become.

I could be making a terrible mistake.

"You are my concern," Diavolo says, as if the decision is made. "Not your brother."

With that, he pulls me into his arms, gently supporting the back of my thighs as well as my shoulders while the rest of my body is cushioned by the mist.

Sapphire light glows at the edge of my vision as he says, "I can mask most of your pain until I'm able to heal you properly, but be warned—it's an illusion."

He once explained to me that the simplest use of his power is to create illusions. He can change my physical appearance, give me any clothing I like, even create food and objects. His illusions feel very real, but they aren't. The illusion wears off and, in the case of food and objects, they would be without any actual substance.

It doesn't bother me so much that he plans to use his magic to trick my body into believing I'm not in pain. Hell, any method is fine with me right now, but... "Why will you only mask *most* of my pain?"

"Because pain is useful. It will remind you not to put weight on that leg or try to use your hands. Both of which would cause further damage."

I exhale my disappointment that his reasoning is sound.

"I would remove the feather from your shoulder, but I don't want you to suffer greater blood loss," he continues.

His magic must have already begun working because my pain lessens significantly.

The relief of not having to fight through the agony is huge.

I try not to sob at the respite, but fuck it, I let the tears fall. They're only trickling from one eye anyway.

With the easing of my pain comes a new determination. "Diavolo," I say, firmly fixing my good eye on him. "Please save my brother."

His jaw clenches and he doesn't make a move toward Lucian. "You're hurt badly. The pain I'm masking is unbearable. Let me take you where I can heal you properly. We can leave this place, and the supernaturals in it, far behind us."

It isn't lost on me that he described my pain as unbearable. My heart must be causing him to feel my physical injuries, too.

I want to shake my head, but it still hurts too much. "My brother has answers." I remember the way Lucian looked at me when I revealed my wings. "I *need* answers."

Still, Diavolo hesitates.

"Please." I'm struggling to keep the urgency out of my voice now. "If you don't try… then I will."

I attempt to wriggle out of his firm hold, even though the pain surges back at me.

He holds on tightly but exhales heavily, a mask of resignation falling across his face. "As you like."

I slump with relief.

His arms slide out from under me, leaving me cradled within the fog.

As he turns away, his eyes become completely white, smoke churning within them. His form expands, growing taller within the space of seconds. His skin turns a deep, dark gray, and the acrid scent of smoke rises off his body.

The last time he took the form of an enenra—a demon of smoke and ash—he ripped his clothes to shreds because his body expanded so fast.

This time, his transition is smooth.

The control he has over his powers is growing exponentially.

The fog parts where he walks, and I can finally see the other side of the room.

My brother is still on his knees, although his head lolls now and his eyes are barely open. There's new blood dripping from his mouth.

Bright light gleams over him from our father's hands, seeming to lick like flames across the air, a light that's hungry for death.

Diavolo pauses at the edge of the still-churning tornado.

As his presence clears a path in the fog, I can finally make out the shape of the animal that was racing toward me before.

The big cat must have decided to stop and hang back because it's only now that I can discern its features.

I assumed it was one of the male panthers, but my heart leaps.

Anarchy!

A cry of happiness leaves my lips, and I'm grateful that we're concealed within the mist so my cry doesn't draw my father's attention. "Anarchy, you're alive!"

She closes the gap between her and me, snarling a greeting, her big, silver eyes turn up to mine. She's big enough that if I were standing upright, instead of floating on my back in the mist, her backbone would reach my hips.

Right now, she's baring her deadly silver claws and her silver teeth, but if she closes her eyes and retracts her claws, she can fully camouflage in dark places.

She and her three brothers are the only shadow panthers in existence, although most supernaturals don't know about them. I wouldn't, either, if my mother hadn't told me about them.

I make a snarling sound back at her, then smile at Diavolo's back.

He saved her when I couldn't.

He will save my brother, too.

Diavolo glances back at me, every muscle in his body tense. "Anarchy will stay beside you," he says. "Be prepared for me to move fast."

In response, Anarchy snarls. She turns to face in my father's direction, her body straining forward as if her impulse is to attack.

Diavolo bursts through the edge of the mist, sounds from the other side of the room break through, and all I catch of my father's voice is "fucking disappointment" before Diavolo races toward him.

The keeper speeds across the short distance in a whirlwind of smoke, his left hand extended toward my father, who barely has the chance to startle at Diavolo's sudden appearance.

The air pulses.

Black light blasts from Diavolo's outstretched hand into my father's form, colliding with his light.

I feel the impact of the collision all the way inside the mist, the blowback washing across me and jostling me within the fog.

My father is thrown against the far wall, but the light around him doesn't diminish. If anything, it only grows stronger, expanding and spreading like a shield around him until I can hardly make out his features.

The keeper's hand remains outstretched, dark magic pouring from his palm, burning across the air and spilling toward the light.

The two powers spark and explode against each other and I wonder if this is what fireworks or maybe bombs look like when they go off—a chaotic mess of light and dark clashing against each other. A volatile mix that seems to create an increasing pressure in the air around me.

It's so intense that my ears hurt. I whimper, afraid that my eardrums might burst.

Beside me, Anarchy yowls softly. Her ears are pinned back and she drags a paw across one of them as if she's in pain.

The pressure increases. And *increases*.

I fight the impulse to squeeze my eyes closed because all this pressure can only mean the real explosion is yet to come.

Diavolo darts toward Lucian and wraps his fist around the back of Lucian's shirt, wrenching him into the air before my brother can give a startled shout.

Still pouring dark magic into the wash, the keeper races— facing partially backward—toward me, dragging my brother so fast that his feet bounce against the floor.

The dark light shuts off, the keeper spins to face me, and now his free hand is extended toward me, reaching for me.

Behind him, the mess of dark magic and light magic seems to become still. A fucking scary calm.

The keeper's face is pale.

His fear, so unexpected, makes my heart squeeze with anxiety.

I struggle to move, only to realize that I don't need to because he's pulling me toward him through the air. Pulling Anarchy too, lifting her off her paws.

Then his free arm closes around me and the pressure around me shifts.

The mist implodes toward all four of us, a tornado of white that fills my view.

But it doesn't block out the storm behind it.

White light, dark light, ribbons of energy explode through the air toward us.

A scream rises into my throat as I brace for impact.

The keeper's shout roars in my ears as the blast knocks into his back and then everything goes dark.

CHAPTER SIX

ilence.

It blocks my ears and fills me with fear.

I can't see anything, not even with my good eye. I can't seem to feel anything except a pressure that encompasses my whole body and forces me into a ball, my knees drawn to my chest, although my broken leg is somehow still cushioned and pain-free.

I can't smell anything except maybe the scent of... *burning...*

A light flickers at the edge of my vision. It's a little flame dancing across a surface that shimmers with... scales?

There's a creaking sound for which I struggle to find an association. Maybe a little like a leather belt creaking. It groans louder, the darkness around me moves, and then—

Whoosh.

The darkness parts.

I make out the edges of two enormous wings opening on either side of me. Great, big, shimmery, leathery... *massive...* black wings.

Dappled sunlight rushes in as they recede. The hushed

sounds of leaves rustling in the breeze are like whispers compared to the boom of the explosion.

I catch a glimpse of trees, leaves, and forest, but it's impossible to pay attention to my surroundings when I realize that I'm nestled in the crook of a dragon's arm.

A fierce, nightmarish dragon with black horns on top of its head, jagged teeth, fiery eyes, and a jaw that looks powerful enough to treat my head like a little snack.

My voice sticks in my throat. "Uh...?"

Falling to the ground in surprise would be a very bad idea in my current state of health, but I'm tipping back all the same.

Emerald light gleams across the dragon's nearest claws and wraps around me before I can slip backward. The light is soft around me, supporting my broken limbs as it lowers me gently onto what seems to be mossy earth. I've never seen—or felt—moss in real life before, so I can only guess that's what I'm now lying on.

The dragon growls at me. "My Veda. I'm happy you're alive."

I peer up at the beast. "Diavolo?"

I mean... I've never seen this dragon version of him before, but... *Who else could it be?*

He inclines his head, his eyes twinkling at me, beautiful in the way that only a dark creature can be in the moments before it eats you.

I'm suddenly aware that his left wing is still unfolding.

As it opens, I make out Lucian cocooned within it. So too, is Anarchy. She's nestled against Lucian's chest, her head in the crook of his neck and her front paws pressed to his shoulders.

She startles, squints into the light, and then leaps away from him. Landing lightly on the ground, she spins and hisses up at the dragon first and Lucian second—even though my brother appears to be unconscious.

Judging by the tone of her hiss, she's more disgruntled than angry or afraid.

The dragon allows Lucian to slide to the ground but doesn't seem to care that he lands in an undignified heap. His knees meet the ground before he falls forward onto his face, a soft landing in the thick moss, upon which his head somehow glides a little farther forward and turns to the side so that one cheek is smooshed against the earth while his butt ends up in the air.

The dragon huffs at him.

There's certainly no love lost between them.

My greater concern right now are the flames licking along the edges of one of Diavolo's wings and rising up at his back—which would explain the scent of burning when I regained consciousness.

"Fire!" I gasp. "You're on fire!"

Dark saints, the fire can only be from the explosion before he brought us to this place. His body must have taken the brunt of the flames to protect the rest of us.

"I *am* the fire." He growls, rolling his shoulders, at which a shiver travels through his wings and body.

The fire immediately disappears, but astonishingly, it doesn't seem to extinguish. Rather, the tendrils seem to suck inward—toward his hide.

In the next moment, his lips part, revealing a mouth full of flames before he gulps them down. Then they're gone.

Well, nearly.

One little flame dances on his right foreleg—possibly the flame I saw when I regained consciousness moments ago.

He sees it, swipes a claw across it, and catches it in his closing fist.

When he opens his paw, the flame is gone.

"Fuck," I whisper, staring up at him.

He looms over me, blocking out much of our surroundings before his form changes again, slowly morphing back into his dark-haired, blue-eyed persona.

His stature may be smaller now that he isn't a dragon, but he isn't diminished. If anything, it feels like his power is even more concentrated. I wasn't sure if he might choose his calmer demeanor, but I guess he's still angry.

He kneels at my side and leans over me. "Let me see your wounds," he says, "so I can be sure to heal them all."

His hands move across the air above me—starting at my face, then traveling down across my arms and chest.

"How did you find me?" I ask.

He can only travel to places he's seen. And he's only seen places where dark creatures have died, since he has access to their final memories and therefore knowledge of the circumstances of their deaths.

Of course, that dark room felt like the kind of place my father might take enemies to end them, so maybe many dark magic creatures have died there.

"I will always know where you are." Diavolo's voice rumbles softly as he returns his focus to my face, assessing my cheekbone. "Your heart will always lead me to you."

At this angle, with my left eye sealed shut, I can't really make out his expression. "Even if you've never seen the place before?"

"Even then."

Good to know. "And this place? Where are we now?"

"This is a vast forest in Portland, Oregon. Many dark witches have died here, so I know its layout very well." He leans back on his heels. "Most importantly, the life force in a single one of these trees will give me all the energy I need to heal you."

While he studies the trees around us—presumably to pick one—I'm finally able to pay attention to our surroundings.

They're enormous, their trunks so wide that they can only be hundreds of years old. Maybe even older.

I've never seen anything like them.

Neither have I felt anything like the moss at my back, which is soft and spongy and damp, but not in a bad way. More cooling than anything else.

I add it to my list of 'soft as' comparisons. *Soft as moss.*

There's so much of the world I've never experienced. My mother taught me as much as she could, described as much to me as she could. Much of my recognition of the world around me now comes from the images I saw in whatever books our jailer deigned to bring us, from children's picture books to random encyclopedias.

There's so much I don't know.

Mere days ago, I discovered that humans like to ride waves using rectangular-shaped boards, that pizza is delicious (second only to burgers), and that teenage human girls think fluffy, little doggies are so cute that they'll risk losing a finger to pat one.

Now, I'm surrounded by trees so colossal that I feel like a bug lying on the forest floor beneath them.

Diavolo's expression has changed, a kind of serenity coming over him, and it makes me wonder how much of a cage he keeps around his power every second of every hour.

Black light glimmers at his fingertips, sparking briefly around the crown-shaped ring on his left hand.

I shiver at the cold emptiness of that light.

It's pure, dark magic.

Even though it's the power that forms the very fabric of my being, it's a frightening force for one simple reason: Dark magic feeds on life. Using it means taking life from the living things around us.

Usually, the keeper chooses not to access his dark magic. After all, we can't have things falling dead wherever we go. Drawing that kind of attention would be very unwise.

Which is why he instead chooses to use the power in the ring to create illusions. He described that process as simply rearranging what's already there, no draining of life required.

His crown allows him to access every kind of dark magic there is: sorcery, witchcraft, shapeshifting. It gives him the knowledge to use that magic and harness the energy in the environment around him.

But he also made it clear that there are limits to what he can do without accessing true dark magic. Like healing me when particularly dangerous magic has hurt me. In the first instance, that was when Jonah's old magic burned me.

Now, suddenly, I'm startled to realize that Diavolo was using enormous amounts of dark magic against my father... but I don't know where he sourced it from.

That level of dark magic would have instantly drained life from any number of living beings nearby.

But... whose life did he take?

I'm fine. Anarchy is clearly full of wrathful energy because she's prowling back and forth between me and Lucian... who has remained in an undignified position but is finally showing signs of waking up.

So... who or what did the keeper kill to produce that dark magic?

My eyes have flown wide. "Back in my father's lair, whose energy were you draining?"

"Your father's."

My panic fades. "Oh." Then I'm filled with confusion. "But he didn't die. He didn't even stumble."

Diavolo's jaw clenches and he blows out what sounds like an unhappy breath. "I should have clarified: I *attempted* to drain his energy. What I actually took was the energy from the light magic he was producing. As much power as I drained, it simply replenished, as if it were coming from a limitless source."

I can't stop my shudder. *Is my father's power limitless?*

"How can that be?" I ask. "He's a dark creature. He shouldn't be able to control light magic in the first place, let alone a limitless amount of it." A possibility occurs to me, since my great-grandfather was originally a Sentinel, able to use his pure soul light before he turned to the dark. "Is it something to do with his ancestry?"

Diavolo is aware of my father's family history because I told him about it. He chews his lip, a troubled crease forming in his forehead. "All I'm certain of is that that much light magic can't possibly belong to one creature."

I quail a little. "Is he somehow siphoning it off others? Some sort of… dark magic draining off light magic."

I'm not sure if that even makes sense.

None of it makes sense.

"We'll figure it out," Diavolo says. "My concern now is healing you before the numbing illusion wears off and you start to feel pain again."

The black light intensifies around his hands and a look of deep concentration falls over his face.

Across the clearing to my right, one of the trees groans, and its lowest hanging branches turn slowly black as if it's rotting at an exponential rate.

My broken leg begins straightening out and a blissful sense of relief comes over me.

At that same moment, Lucian groans.

His butt sways in the air before he slides all the way down onto his stomach.

At the contact of his chest with the ground, his eyes fly open, but his shout is muffled against the moss. "What the fuck?"

He rolls onto his side and jumps to his feet, dragging his wings up with him, and then he stands there, swaying unsteadily.

When I first met Lucian, he was completely in control. A menacing figure full of deadly threats. His hands were covered in golden rings, he was wearing an expensive-looking suit, and he didn't hesitate to make his power and status known, but now…

The mask he wore has cracked wide open to reveal all of his vulnerabilities.

I've seen his fears. Probably, more accurately, I've seen him *face* his fears. I've watched him stand up to our father's cruelty.

Now that we're in a brighter place, I can make out the edge of the tattoo on one of his biceps. I can also see a strange glint across the tops of his wings and the edges of his feathers, a sort of sheen that catches the light.

The shadow he casts is once more like a dark aura around his form, dragging at the light around him.

I can also clearly see the burns across his face and neck. The scorched sections of his shirt.

He looks beat-up and downtrodden and painfully unsure of himself.

And yet…

He looks more powerful to me now than he did before he faced our father.

"What happened?" he asks, swaying when he tries to look around, his unsteady assessment coming to a stop on Anarchy.

She snarls up at him, a threatening sound, although the brightness in her eyes speaks to a continuing curiosity. When she first met Lucian, she was very restrained in her reaction to him. Her nostrils flared as if she were assessing his scent, but if anything, she seemed confused. I wonder now if that's because she sensed what I didn't at the time: that he was my brother.

"We're safe," I say.

"Speak for yourself," Lucian grumbles, continuing to eye Anarchy, whose snarling only grows louder and silver eyes, brighter. She seems to be taking great delight in his discomfort.

Diavolo's magic halted abruptly when Lucian stirred, and I understand why. Any break in the keeper's concentration could cause him to drain life from an unintended target like Anarchy or Lucian or even, harmfully, from me.

Before he can resume healing me, Lucian's focus shifts to the trees around us and he gives a sharp exclamation.

"Wait!" His eyes have widened and his speech is rapid. "Where are we?"

"Portland," the keeper says, calmly, not reacting to the sudden, clear panic in Lucian's voice. "West of the city."

"West? You've got to be fucking kidding me." Lucian shakes his head rapidly. "No, this can't be happening."

He stumbles toward me, even though he's too unsteady to make it far. In fact, I'd wager he's about to fall on his butt. Which would be fine, except that his panic is becoming contagious.

"We can't be here!" he exclaims. "We need to get the fuck out of here. *Now.*"

I glance nervously at Diavolo, whose lips are pursed. He doesn't look worried, exactly. Maybe more peeved than anything else…

"Nobody fucks with the wolves who control this forest," Lucian rushes on, nearly bumping into Anarchy as he stumbles another step in my direction. "*Nobody.* Not my father, not Vanguard, not Jonah—"

"Which is why it's the ideal place to be," the keeper says, his voice still calm. "Nobody will try to follow us. If they're tracing our path, it will break here."

Lucian stares at the keeper. "Yes. Because nobody messes with the pack that runs in this forest. Ever."

Now, any threatening panic fades and a shiver of anticipation runs through me.

Yes, I'm not in a good place to face any kind of powerful pack, but this would be the first wolf pack I've ever encountered, and by fuck, I need to meet them.

Diavolo, on the other hand, doesn't seem to be listening to Lucian anymore. His ears have taken on the shape of a wolf's while his nose has elongated and thickened like a bear's. His nostrils flare and he inhales deeply as he twists toward the forest behind him—the direction I'm facing.

I can't hear or smell what he can.

Normally, I should be able to sense any threats from a distance, but my abilities are all messed up—numbed, it seems, along with my pain.

Lucian suddenly spins in the same direction the keeper is facing.

"Oh, fuck." His face is deathly pale. "Too late."

CHAPTER SEVEN

Three wolves prowl toward us through the trees, their forms glowing an unexpected blood-red color. Their lips are drawn back from their sharp teeth, and their crimson-colored eyes are filled with what I can only interpret as anger.

The ethereal red hue of their fur is nothing like the color of my own pelt, or for that matter like the fur of any natural wolf, as far as I know.

What really surprises me is that their bodies seem to be insubstantial, a bit like ghosts. I can see through them to the trees and greenery behind them.

Yet they seem very much alive.

Dark saints, how would anyone kill them?

The keeper rises slowly to his feet, moving at a pace that tells me he's warier than he let on before. He retains his blue-eyed, black-haired, dangerous persona while he places himself in a protective position in front of me. Thankfully, he doesn't block my view.

Lucian surprises me by stepping in front of me, too, positioning himself in front of my feet, his movements faster and more controlled than before. He must be regaining his coordination, which can only be a good thing in this situation.

Anarchy jostles past him, nearly upsetting his balance, but her glares and snarls are aimed at the approaching beasts.

All three crimson wolves stand at hip height, their bodies possibly slightly larger than Anarchy's, but as they draw closer, I can make out subtle differences between them.

The middle one is taking the lead, a sleek beast, while the one on its left is a little bulkier, its jaw a little wider. The one on the far right has more bounce in its step and, even though it's growling like a hound of hell, there's a bright curiosity in its eyes that gives me hope these beasts won't launch an immediate attack on us.

Lucian makes a strangled sound as if he's about to speak, but Diavolo shoots him a warning look and my brother falls silent again.

The three wolves come to a stop a few paces into the clearing—about ten paces away from us.

That's when three other figures become visible through the trees, these ones humanoid in shape.

One of them is a woman holding a little girl on her hip. The woman picks her way through the undergrowth while the remaining figure—a young boy—walks at her side, holding her hand.

The woman's hair is as crimson red as the wolves' fur and her eyes are a bright blue. She's wearing a flannel shirt and jeans. Not exactly the garb of a warrior and yet...

Fuck me.

Even though my senses are dulled, the power radiating off this woman hits me with an intensity I can't ignore. It's reminiscent of the power I sensed in Vanguard, the old god. Which definitely makes me wary.

The little girl on her hip can't be more than two years old, dressed in pink shorts with frills at the hems and a white T-shirt that has "wolves are fun" written on it in curly, pink letters. She watches us with big, bright, green eyes that remind me of the color of green apples I once saw in a book. Her hair is as crimson red as her mother's. She may be little, and the blue ribbon tied in her hair might be slipping off, but the power she exudes is no less intense than her mother's.

Likewise for the boy walking beside them. Unlike the two females, he has raven-black hair, but he shares the same crisp, green eyes as the little girl.

He reminds me of Elijah, Vanguard's son—the son of an old god. Judging by this boy's facial features, he's a little older than Elijah. His quiet confidence as he calmly surveys us sends shivers down my spine.

The mother's power may be frightening, but once those children are fully grown, I would not want to come up against them.

The woman draws level with the three wolves and it's intriguing to me that one of the animals—the more masculine one—steps closer to the boy, while the two apparently female wolves stand nearer to the woman's other side.

"You don't have my permission to be here." The woman doesn't raise her voice, but her growl carries authority, the kind of calm shown by those who know they have the upper hand no matter what.

"You will tell me who you are and why you're here," she continues. "Then I will decide if I allow you to live."

My eyes widen at how peacefully she uttered her threat. She could be speaking of the weather, not of death.

Diavolo returns the threat in kind, equally serenely. "Our business is our own. I would advise you not to get in our way."

As he speaks, his form changes, becoming smoke and ash once more, the insubstantial demon that defied even Vanguard's power.

The woman doesn't seem concerned. She turns to the male wolf and then leans toward the little boy.

He looks up at her. "Mom, what's on his hand?"

The woman has taken her eyes off us—a move that could be dangerous except that the wolves are keeping us in their sights.

"What do *you* think, Theo?" she asks the boy, her voice equally quiet.

Theo's serious gaze washes over us again. "He's the dark keeper we heard about."

The woman nods. "Yes, I think he is."

She continues to give her son her full attention, even though the gray smoke swirling around the keeper is thickening and Anarchy's growls are intensifying.

"He is the keeper of dark magic, escaped from his realm," she says. "A being who was created from the *oldest* of old magic." She arches an eyebrow at her son. "And what does that mean for our chances of survival against him?"

The little boy doesn't flinch. "Well... He's old magic." Once more, his serious gaze washes over us. "Which means we can kill him."

"Yes." The mother straightens. "We are some of the few who can."

The central wolf hunches a little lower to the ground, its body language indicating that it's preparing to strike. It's uncanny how that wolf seems so in tune with the woman's own body language. Also uncanny how the masculine wolf seems intensely connected to the boy—like when it looked at the woman as if it had a question and she replied to the boy instead.

There has to be some sort of mental connection between them, but I can't quite figure out what it is. They certainly aren't like any kind of wolf shifters my mother ever mentioned. But then, these children were most certainly born after my mother was imprisoned, so maybe she didn't know they existed.

As for the woman, well, who knows how old she is?

She sighs into the tense silence, speaking at a murmur that sounds genuinely unhappy. "It's a terrible waste to end other old magic creatures when there are so few of us left."

She said 'us'.

Which means the woman and her children must be old magic.

Of all the things my mother did teach me, my paramount lessons were about survival. Knowing who the real threats are is crucial.

Any old magic creature is a serious threat, without exception.

Old magic creatures can kill every other kind of creature: light, dark, elemental—it doesn't matter how powerful they are.

Old magic is at the top of the food chain.

This woman's two-year-old daughter could pulverize me.

Which is a humiliating fact, for sure, but a fact all the same.

And as for the harm they could do to the keeper…

Despite what the woman said, he seems intent on fighting. So does Anarchy, whose magic is the purest of dark magic. And… so does Lucian, who is angling his body so that his broken wing must be less visible from the front, even if all his other wounds are on display. Even though he, too, must be aware that his chances of surviving this fight are the slimmest of all.

And… *dammit…* he's grown on me.

All three crimson wolves have hunched low to the ground, as if they're preparing to leap forward, their growls ringing through the air.

"We're here because of me." My voice rises above the snarling and growls and draws the woman's attention immediately to me. Of course, I'm under no illusion that she didn't notice me before now. "Because I'm hurt."

It seems like an obvious thing to say. I mean, she has eyes, and I'm lying right here, all busted up.

But what she might not have figured out is what I'm forced to admit next. "Because I can't heal these wounds on my own."

The tension around me now is so thick, it would take my claws to cut through it.

The woman purses her lips while the little boy looks up at her again, this time with his eyebrows raised, seemingly for instructions. At the same moment, the little girl snuggles closer to her mother's side.

Whatever communication passes between them, it isn't spoken aloud.

But the three wolves stop growling and stand a little more upright, indicating a reprieve from their murderous intent, however short that reprieve may end up being.

"Ask your protectors to stand aside," the woman says to me. "You and I will decide how this is going to end."

CHAPTER EIGHT

one of my "protectors," as the woman calls them, look happy about her proposal that they should step aside, but already, I can feel the illusion of painlessness wearing off. Not horribly. Just enough for me to notice and decide I really don't like the resurgence of pain.

I want to believe I'm tough enough to withstand any agony endlessly, but, fuck it, I'd rather not.

The keeper is already kneeling to me, as if he knows I'm about to agree.

"No," he whispers. "You should not allow this wolf to get close to you."

"We don't have a choice."

This brings a glower to his face and increases the whiteness of his current demon form's eyes.

But he doesn't argue further. "At the first hint of danger, I will step in," he says, loud enough that the woman will certainly have heard him.

Anarchy takes her cue from Diavolo, both of them backing off to either side of me.

Lucian continues to surprise me when he stands his ground

for a moment longer. "I risked my life for my sister today," he says to the woman, squaring off with her as she steps toward us. "I won't hesitate to do it again."

"I understand and respect your position." She acknowledges him with a nod before the three crimson wolves spread out ahead of her, the two females positioning themselves between her and the keeper, while the masculine wolf approaches Lucian, urging him away from me and toward Anarchy.

The boy—Theo—hangs back a few steps while his mother kneels beside me, still holding the little girl on her hip.

Both of them consider me carefully.

The feather in my shoulder is within their reach and I consider for a moment if I should be concerned the mother will try to use it against me. I quickly dismiss that possibility. She has far more power at her disposal to worry about retrieving a weapon that's dug deep into my torso. Especially when she doesn't even glance at it.

"You're a creature of darkness," the woman says, her focus on my face.

Strangely, what she said doesn't sound like an accusation.

In fact, if I didn't know better, I'd say there was a hint of curiosity in her tone.

The press of her lips softens. "And yet you appear to have gained the loyalty and protection of other dark creatures. That is a very rare thing indeed."

She can only mean the keeper and Anarchy. I'm a little surprised when her focus flickers to Lucian, too.

I counter with a curiosity of my own. "You must be very sure of yourself to bring your daughter so close to me."

A smile flickers around her lips. "Like my son, my daughter inherited her father's power as well as mine. You're no danger to her."

I'm about to reply when a bright-blue, fluttery thing darts across the air above my face, startling me.

It flits so quickly past me that I can't immediately make out its shape.

I recoil—which knocks my head into the moss since I'm lying on the ground. I wince. "What is that?" I demand to know. "Did you bring that with you?"

The woman blinks at me, as if she's surprised by my question. "Uh… no… it's just a—"

"Flutterby!" the little girl exclaims. She's focused on the fluttering creature and, as the woman spoke, both of her arms stretched out so far that she nearly tips herself out of her mother's arms.

"Whatter-by?" I ask, perturbed.

"Butterfly," the woman says.

"Oh." I squint at the creature, trying to take another look.

The butterflies I saw in illustrations were always flat, their wings outstretched. I assumed they glided through the air. All majestic-like. This one is beating its wings so fast, I can't follow the movements, and it's darting around so much that it's making my head spin.

Just a butterfly.

In my defense, I'm one-eyed right now, so my perception is a little skewed.

The butterfly evades the little girl's hands and lands on her nose.

"Flutterby," she whispers. "Hello."

Her big, green eyes swivel to her mother's and her little lips press together as the butterfly's wings slow down and *now* it looks like the butterflies I saw in books.

"Okay, then, Tori," the woman murmurs. "Go play."

She eases the little girl to the ground—butterfly on her nose and all—and that's when I make out another swarm of the blue-winged critters gathering on the low-lying leaves of a nearby tree. They're increasing in number by the second, forming multiple blue clouds in the air and across the surrounding branches.

As soon as Tori's feet touch the ground, she bounces away toward them, which takes her directly past the keeper.

He glowers down at her from his great height as she dances past.

"Happy little creature," he grumbles, his nose wrinkling when her giggles fill the air.

At the same time as she passes him, one of the female wolves—the one with more bounce in its step—follows her, pouncing and leaping at the butterflies. It doesn't jump at them in a way that looks like it's trying to catch them, rather like it's dancing with them as they move through the air and pour toward the little girl.

Almost as if the wolf wishes it could fly too.

I want to warn it that wings are a fucking nuisance.

Even so, it's a curious thing to watch because every move the wolf makes, the little girl seems to make *first*.

These wolves are definitely connected to the minds of these beings.

The woman is quietly studying me, and I don't miss the way she's watching me watching her daughter. "These are light magic burns," she says, startling me with the change of topic and bringing me back to my unhappy reality.

"Yes."

And I would like them healed already. Please and thank you.

But first I have to convince this woman not to finish me off.

Her forehead puckers, the first hint of real concern. "They're far worse than any I've ever seen."

"Trust me, I know," I mutter. I narrow my good eye at her because surely she can't be feeling sorry for me. She's probably worried about the supernatural who is strong enough to have delivered these blows.

"The magic has extended right down to your bones." She

draws back a little, her shoulders tense. "It should have killed you." She chews on her lip as she contemplates me. I'm gratified that her expression becomes wary for the first time since she approached us. "And yet you're still alive."

"I guess I'm hard to kill."

She makes a humming sound in the back of her throat that's difficult to interpret. "Who did this to you?"

"My father."

Her expression changes so rapidly that it's like a storm rushing in, as powerful as the churning sea the keeper once showed me. All that lightning striking across a beautifully dark sky.

Her growl is dangerously low. "Fathers should never hurt their daughters."

My thoughts exactly. It's a shame she's my enemy. I might otherwise like her.

"Who is he?" she demands to know.

I don't lie, even though I maybe *should*. "My father is the Ultima Nostra."

"Of New York," she says, her lips twisting angrily. "I'm aware of him. I have friends who would like to see him eliminated."

"As would I," I snarl, my own anger rising. "He doesn't deserve his title or his empire. I loved him once."

Damn. I didn't mean to blurt out that last bit. My throat constricts and my good eye burns with tears. Hot, angry ones. Tears I wish weren't threatening to fall right now because I don't want this woman to see my vulnerabilities or know my deepest hurts.

But I can't stop my rising rage and, damn her, she stays silent and lets me talk.

"I loved him so much that I would have died to avenge him. But not anymore."

Slowly, the woman exhales into the silence, as if she's breathing her own tension out and dragging clean air in. The silence extends as she breathes, as if it's a deliberately controlled action on her part.

She exhales a fourth time and the anger in her demeanor finally fades.

I can only stare at her, watch as she deals with whatever anger she was feeling—whyever she was feeling it.

Oh, to be able to release hatred so easily from my body.

Not that hatred is bad for a dark creature like me. Just that blind rage could lead me to make reckless decisions that don't do me any favors.

She leans a little closer to me, the strands of her hair cascading over her shoulder and brushing my bare stomach.

Her expression hardens again, a steely glint in her blue eyes that brings to mind the sharpest blade. "The critical question is: What will you do if I let you live?"

CHAPTER NINE

y voice sticks in my throat. "I..."

It should be an easy answer, but it isn't.

Where does my vengeance lie now?

Where is my dark justice?

If I vow to end my father and take his empire from him, am I not repeating a cycle of the past?

My father killed my mother and then tried to kill me, all because he wants to retain power. Oh, he framed his murderous intent in terms of stopping me, as if he has some kind of altruistic purpose because I'm supposedly some incredibly dangerous creature. But his actions have ensured he retains power.

If I kill him, am I not the same as him, killing a family member for the sake of that power?

Does the element of vengeance change the nature of my intentions, even though the outcome is the same?

Can the thin line of justice make me different than him?

"I don't know," I whisper, answering perhaps more honestly than I should. "I don't know what I'll do."

All she does is give me a quiet nod. "You're angry."

Yes. I am.

Again, I speak my thoughts truthfully, even though I can't be sure it's in my best interests not to lie. "I'm filled with rage. Deep, terrible rage. I want him to *burn*." My throat squeezes again with the fury I've been keeping caged, but I gasp for breath, forcing myself to continue. "I want vengeance for my mother's life. I want justice for the years that were stolen from me. I want him to feel the pain I've felt."

Much of that won't make sense to this woman since she doesn't know my history, doesn't know that my mother died in a dark prison or that I was kept there for most of my life. But it's the best I can do.

My snarls fade into the silence around me and, when the woman remains quiet, an emptiness fills my chest, growing greater the longer she considers me without any kind of judgement in her eyes.

"But he will never feel what I've felt," I say. "Because he doesn't love anyone. He can never feel the pain that comes with that kind of loss."

She leans back and folds her hands in her lap. "You're a creature of darkness," she says again. "Yet you speak of love and loss."

"Dark creatures *feel*," I snap. "We feel more than most other creatures. It's our feelings that turn us to the dark in the first place."

"Some, yes," she says. "But others are born into it and they are the darkest of all. They are the most dangerous because they know nothing else, and it was never a choice they made for themselves."

"Just as a creature of light will always believe their actions are righteous, simply because that's the magic they control," I counter. "It doesn't make it so."

She tips her head in a small, acknowledging nod. "True."

I wait for her to continue, finding myself holding my breath, but it doesn't do me any favors. My pain is returning in full force now, and the ache in my leg is threatening to jumble my thoughts. The bone had started to knit before, but it's nowhere near fully healed.

I don't want to wait for her decision any longer. "Will you let me live?"

She meets my eyes. "You are a dangerous, *wounded* being, which makes you even more of a threat than the man who stands at your side." Her lips press together, forming an unhappy line. "Your wounds are not only physical. In fact, it's the invisible wounds, the emotional scars, I sense in you that worry me the most. Every instinct in my body is telling me to end you right here, right now, and yet…"

She glances back at her son.

He has stayed in the background, quietly watching over his sister. The male wolf turns its head in unison with the boy's as he returns his mother's gaze.

She continues. "And yet my son believes you need to live." The corners of her mouth dart up as her focus shifts past him to the shadows beneath the far trees. "As does my mate."

I startle. My gaze flashes to the trees.

Her mate?

If there's someone else here, I can't see or smell them, but again, my senses are dulled. Even though my pain is returning, which means the illusion is wearing off, I can't unjumble much of the sensory input around me.

I take my cue from Diavolo, who has stiffened. The tension in his shoulders and the way he's suddenly studying the trees tells me he can't see whatever mate she's referring to. His features once again morph, giving him a wolf's ears and a bear's nose. He tilts his head and inhales deeply at the same time.

His eyes widen.

Which is my cue to worry.

Then he glowers, as if he's annoyed at himself.

Which is my cue to stop worrying. Well, maybe *as much*.

Anarchy, too, has lifted her nose to the air and is making soft, hissing sounds, hunching low to the ground before she becomes very subdued. It may be the most subservient body language I've ever seen her exhibit. She certainly didn't sink as low when she met me for the first time.

Okay, now I'm worried again.

Lucian, like me, appears perplexed. I guess we're both missing out on those predatorial instincts right now.

Safe to assume, this woman's mate is someone we don't want to mess with. Although the more I consider her, I have a feeling *she* is the truly deadly one. She's just hiding it behind a calm, motherly demeanor and a casual-looking flannel shirt and jeans.

Without another moment of hesitation, she turns to the keeper. "One tree," she says. "But not that one."

She points from the tree that the keeper's magic had been curling around when he started to heal me, to another tree on the opposite side of the clearing. The only real difference between them appears to be that the second has more space around its trunk.

"That tree is acceptable," she says. "When it dies, its woody pieces will nourish the earth and provide homes for the little creatures that live in this forest, and soon new life will grow."

She arches an eyebrow at the keeper. "Life will always spring from death, dark one." Her expression softens. "Even when all hope seems lost."

A crease forms in his forehead and his head tilts slightly, as if he's both surprised and puzzled by what she said.

She rises to her feet and quickly scoops up her daughter, who continues reaching for the butterflies for a moment before she settles back into her mother's arms.

"Our dark wolves will remain here until you leave," the woman says. "But we will continue on our walk."

She reaches for her son's hand, and he takes it immediately.

Then she pauses and turns back to me. "Consider your choices carefully, and when you decide on your path, remember that you don't have to walk it alone."

With that, she steps into the shadows of the trees, and within seconds, she and her children are gone.

The crimson wolves remain in the shadows. They seem to blend into their surroundings now, which makes me think the color of their fur is changing, camouflaging them against the foliage, but it's becoming hard to tell.

I should feel relieved that the threat is over, but weirdly, my strongest emotion is envy.

The connection the woman has with her children, and apparently with her mate, is beyond anything I ever imagined possible.

Family.

It's a little word that means a lot.

Right now, a member of my biological family is sliding to the ground.

"Fuck me," Lucian whispers, his knees buckling and his butt meeting the moss as he drops onto it. "That was close."

"Stand clear," Diavolo snaps at him. "Veda has suffered for long enough."

Lucian isn't exactly close to me, and he's certainly not in the keeper's path, but he won't want to be anywhere near his magic.

He scrambles to move farther away, taking himself off to the side of the clearing while Anarchy hurries along close behind him.

The keeper is already spinning to me, his right hand held out toward the tree the woman gave him permission to use while his left arm is outstretched toward me.

Dark light pours from the fingertips of his right hand, shooting across the air, curling around the tree's trunk in a single ribbon that splits into many threads, each one wrapping around a different part of the tree from its base, up its trunk, and out to the ends of its branches.

The nearby butterflies scatter and fly away.

The keeper's attention is only on me.

Black light rushes back to his right hand in a loop that intensifies in strength, making the air tingle and the hairs across my body stand on end.

Glorious, dark magic, more powerful than he's shown me before, pours from his right hand to his left, winding around his crown-shaped ring before it streams toward me in a single ribbon that splits into a multitude of threads once it reaches me.

Each thread wraps around a different part of my body, sliding beneath me and curling around my legs, torso, arms, neck, and head, lifting me off the ground.

Every hint of pain in my body vanishes in that instant.

My back gently arches as the dark magic Diavolo's pouring into me fills my mind.

As *he* fills my mind.

When the keeper healed my shoulder after Jonah left a hand-sized burn on it, the keeper's magic only descended skin deep, healing the scorch and leaving the rest of my body alone. But as the wolf-woman said, the light magic I was attacked with this time struck to my very bones.

The keeper's power descends beneath the surface of my skin, coursing through my flesh from my head to my toes and it's only getting stronger. The ribbons of dark light become a continuously moving coil, looping back to the keeper, connecting him and me in a whirlwind of sensation. Pleasure. Pain. And suddenly, it feels like breaking, even though I know I'm healing.

His eyes meet mine, the color of his irises shifting through a myriad of colors, from the deep brown of his in-control persona, to the dark blue of his angry soul, to the fierce bronze of a dragon, to the dark amber of a wolf, to the pure black of a demon, and finally... a color he's never shown me before: a gentle green. Not bright green like the eyes of the children who were here only minutes ago, but a soft teal. It reminds me of the palest green leaves.

As his eyes settle into that color, his hair color also changes, bleaching of color until it looks like strands of silver. Just as quickly, it darkens again, becoming black once more.

I can't tear my eyes away from him, the tension pouring from him hitting me hard.

He's healing me, but... it's costing him.

Sweat beads on his forehead. His chest is heaving. He drops to his knees on the ground beside me, the dark light filling the air around him with shadows.

They engulf me, blocking out the forest. Blocking out Lucian and Anarchy.

Until the world is just the keeper and me.

It's as if we're back in his realm and the darkness will never let us go. I feel it pulling at me, tugging at my body, threatening to cage me again.

My chest hurts and it feels exactly like the sharp pain I experienced when I gave him the power in my heart.

It's pounding in my ears now. A rhythm that threatens to destroy me.

And him.

I fight the pressure around me, struggling to turn toward him, reaching out across the distance between us, stretching my fingertips toward his chest.

I need the contact, the connection beyond the dark light twining around us both.

I need it desperately or I fear I'll break.

CHAPTER TEN

The keeper's gaze burns me like the flames he consumed when he took me from my father's lair, a hint of fire once more licking across his skin.

His focus flashes to my hand a second before I brush his chest, the tips of my fingers meeting the location of his heart.

In that moment, I experience the vastness of his power, the limitless energy he controls, and then, something unexpected: a sharp twist of fear.

It's gone as suddenly as I felt it.

He catches my hand in his and just like that, the dark light vanishes. The power he was conjuring disappears, the black ribbons are no more, and silence falls.

My body lowers slowly to the ground while he keeps hold of my hand, lifting my fingers away from his chest but clasping my palm firmly in his.

The dark magic that had been rushing around me was so intense that I wasn't able to feel anything else while it continued. It's only when I touch the ground again that I can sense what's happened to my body.

My broken leg has knitted and reformed, my left eye is

opening easily, and my cheekbone has healed. My right hand and wrist have most definitely been repaired because that's the hand I reached toward him.

The feather that was embedded in my shoulder must have lifted out of it at some point—although I didn't feel it happen—because it's now resting in the air beside me.

When I sit up and run my free hand over my face, I find all of the swelling is gone. My skin, where I can see it from my torso down to my feet, is no longer bruised.

A small worry nudges at the back of my mind. My wings were damaged in the fight with my father. I can only hope that the dark magic reached them as surely as it reached my bones.

Actually, now that I think about it, Diavolo may have sensed the existence of my wings, since his power was streaming all the way through me.

I'm about to ask him, but through the act of asking, I could reveal their existence when he might not otherwise have become aware of them.

Argh.

I shouldn't be worried about him finding out about them. It's just that they're a part of myself that I have never loved, and the thought of showing him makes me feel all kinds of vulnerable.

I'm not ready for that yet.

I remind myself of what my mother taught me above all else: Always stay in control. Well, I've lost enough control in the last twenty-four hours—or however long it's been since I was taken to my father. I don't need to lose anymore.

The keeper releases my hand to pluck the feather from the air.

A curious light grows in his eyes as he studies it briefly. "Your father's, I presume."

Before I can confirm or deny his assumption, the tree that he was draining gives a groan. It appears just as it was before, completely unchanged in appearance. Then a gentle breeze wafts across the clearing, and the entire tree crumbles.

Its fine pieces fall in a large heap onto the ground, scattering at the edges and blowing upward. Fine dust sparkles in the air before it settles.

At that, Anarchy rushes toward me, pouncing so quickly that she nearly knocks me back to the ground.

I can't stop the laughter rising to my throat, or my groan of relief. "Finally, I can hug you!"

I guess she had the same thought.

She nudges her head into my shoulder, purring loudly.

I close my eyes, bow my head over hers, and wrap my arms around her. I wish I could make the purring sound that she makes to tell her how much I welcome her nearness. "I'm so glad you're alive. It hurt me when I thought you'd died."

"She did die," the keeper grumbles. "I brought her back from death."

Tears fall down my cheeks and I'm not at all worried about letting them flow now. "You did it for me."

He looks disconcerted. "I did it for your heart." Anarchy hisses softly at him, and he rolls his eyes at her. "Fine. Maybe I, too, would have missed you a little."

Her purring resumes in full force, muffled against my shoulder when she turns her head into my chest again.

We stay like that for another few moments before I force myself to focus on what needs to happen next. I don't want this moment with Anarchy to end, but there's a growing tension in the air around me that I can't ignore.

My wounds may be healed, but I haven't forgotten where we are or that the crimson wolves are watching us.

Neither, it seems, has Diavolo, who has re-focused on a spot past the edge of the clearing. Or, for that matter, Lucian, who is edging toward me.

"We need to leave," he murmurs urgently.

Now that my sharp eyesight has been restored, the wolves appear to me as glowing forms of pure energy where they stand within the trees.

I can finally glean their characteristics and personalities from the nature of that energy, in a way I couldn't before.

The wolf who danced with the butterflies is younger than the other two, a lightness in her energy that feels innocent. Free from the knowledge of pain and loneliness.

The masculine wolf is far too wise for its young energy, but his demeanor easily reflects the young boy's solemn personality.

As for the oldest of the three—the mother's wolf, no doubt—well, I don't want to focus on her too long because it's hurting my eyes.

What's more, I can smell them now.

I inhale deeply, at which my blood stirs in a way I never expected.

I can't keep the intrigue from my voice or stop myself from leaning in their direction. "What is that scent?"

My heart is suddenly pounding and an intense need to run to the wolves is overpowering me—

Diavolo's arms swing around me and that's when I realize that I was already rising to my feet.

"Stop, Veda," he says, pulling me close, my shoulder pressed to his chest as I struggle to close the gap between me and the wolves.

"But—"

"No." His harsh order draws my focus back to him.

I narrow my eyes, ready to snap at him, but he says, "Your pupils are dilated."

I don't know what that's got to do with anything, and nor do I particularly care. My arms are free to move, even if Diavolo is keeping the rest of me anchored to the spot and I stretch them out like the little girl reaching for the butterflies. "Okay, but what about that scent?"

It's intoxicating. Magnetic. Irresistible.

"It's calling to me," I say.

"Blood and war," he snarls at my ear. "The power of old wolves."

Still holding me tightly, he lifts me off my feet and hoists me up into his arms before he rushes toward Lucian.

I gasp with surprise and indignation, but before I can utter a stern rebuke, he snarls, "It's time to go before you either fight those wolves or join them."

Weirdly, I'm not sure exactly which I'd prefer to do.

Fighting wolves so powerful and so unexpectedly dark as these would be a glorious way to die...

Across the distance, the wolves' ears have pricked up and I'm fully aware that they must be listening to every word we say.

I wonder, for a moment, what they would think if I didn't fight them and joined them instead.

I need powerful beings at my side if I'm going to have a hope of seeking justice for what my father has done.

At the exact moment I consider that possibility, the mother wolf gives a *yip*, and for the briefest heartbeat, I think she's going to run toward me—

Instead, she turns and races away. The other two immediately follow and within seconds, they're gone.

The scent of blood and war recedes with them and it's like the life drains from the air around me.

My heart slowly sinks.

I don't know why, but the fact that they turned away from me feels like some sort of rejection.

Maybe it's simply because they're the first wolf pack I've encountered since I freed myself. It's the first time I've witnessed a wolf pack in action. The first time I've had a glimpse of what it would be like to grow up in a pack like that.

The first time I could see the family I never got to have.

Diavolo has reached Lucian's location and he's still speaking, but his voice washes over me and through me, as if I'm suddenly an empty vial.

"Your heart is hurting." His tone is strained. I imagine he'd press his hand to his aching chest if he wasn't holding me with both arms. "We're going home."

Home. It's what I called the little apartment that became our base over the last few days.

I barely have time to give him a nod, an acknowledgment that I accept his actions before mist forms around us.

The haze builds within the air and quickly becomes a churning tornado of power. It sweeps inward, scooping up Anarchy, snatching Lucian off his feet, and pressing in on me so intensely that I'm plastered up against Diavolo's body.

Accepting the pressure, I turn toward his chest and slip my legs around his waist, tipping my head back to see his face.

The mist plucks at my voice, but I'm sure he hears me. "Thank you for healing me."

He is a storm in my vision, as violently churning as the mist around me. One of his hands rises to the nape of my neck, his fingers tangling in my hair even as it billows in black waves around my face.

For a moment, his lips part, and I think he's going to say something. There's a spark in his eyes, once more a hint of metal.

But then his lips press together, his chest rises and falls deeply against mine, and I don't have a hope of interpreting his thoughts.

There so much I don't know about him, and so much I don't understand, and for the first time, I wonder if what I don't know could destroy me.

CHAPTER ELEVEN

moment later, the keeper's power steals the breath from my chest and I'm disintegrating...

And being put back together.

We arrive in the same state of suspension as when we left the forest.

The keeper's arms are around me, my legs hooked around his waist, his presence consuming my vision. But he must have turned during the journey here because I'm now facing Anarchy and Lucian once more.

A short distance to my right, Anarchy drops from her airborne position and lands lithely on her feet, as cats can do.

Lucian, on the other hand, doesn't fare so well. The translocation power lifted him off the ground and gathered his wings around him. He drops heavily from two feet above the floor and stumbles backward, his wings dragging across the floor and catching on one of the kitchen chairs before he finally hits the edge of the kitchen table and stops there.

The apartment isn't big. There's a bedroom with an attached dressing room and a bathroom around the corner from that bedroom—both located on my right. We're currently standing

in the larger living space that contains lounge chairs at one end
—all behind me—and a little kitchen at the end I'm facing. The
kitchen basically sits in the corner, consisting of a countertop
and cupboards on the far wall with more cupboards and a sink
against the wall perpendicular to the left. The table sits in the
space between them. It's a nice, neat, square-shaped, little
kitchen.

When we first arrived here, the keeper pinned blankets over
the windows since my eyes were very sensitive to light then. It's
difficult to tell what time it is without seeing outside, but I
assume it must be around mid-morning now.

I don't have time to say anything more to the keeper before
my ears fill with soft, chirping sounds, the likes of which I've
never heard before.

A second later, multiple furry bodies collide with mine,
knocking the keeper and me to the floor. With a flash of
sapphire energy, a large rug appears beneath him, along with a
plush cushion positioned perfectly behind his head—both
materializing a moment before he hits the floor on his back
with me on top of him.

My view fills with massive, black, chirping cats.

"Panthers!" I exclaim, a second before the three male
panthers knock me off the keeper and onto the rug, piling
around me, their chirps turning into purrs so loud that it feels
like the room is vibrating around me.

"Happy panthers!" I make it up onto my knees and hug them,
one by one, while the other two take turns nudging their heads
across my back and shoulders.

"Riot. Rumble. Strife," I greet them each in turn. It hasn't
been all that long since I last saw these three, but... "Oh, I
missed you."

They purr and purr while I scratch their chins and the soft
fur beneath their ears.

Anarchy sits on her haunches a few paces away grinning

happily at us. I'm vaguely aware of Lucian sliding across the table and dropping onto one of the kitchen chairs.

But it's the keeper who demands my attention next.

"Move." He's on his knees, pushing the panthers aside as he makes his way toward me. "It's my turn."

"Oh." I turn into his arms once more.

The panthers back off, but their purrs only become louder as they mill around Anarchy, nudge their cheeks to hers, enforcing their bond with her.

The keeper manages to tower over me even when kneeling as I am. I guess it helps that he can change his height at will. At some point while I was hugging the panthers, he changed back into his brown-eyed persona, now wearing a soft-feeling T-shirt and sweatpants, both a gray color. Despite how snuggly the material feels up against my stomach when he pulls me closer, and how gentle his hold on me is, his voice is a harsh contrast.

"You pushed yourself out of my magic and made yourself vulnerable to capture."

I bite my lip as I look up at him, trying to quell my regret. There's no denying it. "I did."

Our mission was to deliver Vanguard's son, Elijah, to his new home. We were to escort the boy on the train trip from New York to Boston, where Vanguard had arranged for powerful supernaturals to keep Elijah safe.

Vanguard promised me that successfully completing the mission would get me in to the Ultima Nostra's inner circle, which I knew would get me closer to the Ultima Nostra. Of course, at the time, I thought the Ultima Nostra was my uncle, a murderer and a usurper.

Along the way, it became apparent that the mission wasn't for the Ultima Nostra, after all. It was for Vanguard. The Ultima Nostra was using Elijah as leverage to control Vanguard. By taking his son out of the equation, Vanguard would gain his freedom. The keeper and I were intended be his scapegoats. He could claim that we kidnapped his son and by doing so, he could pretend to remain the Ultima Nostra's ally.

He didn't count on Lucian coming to check on him. It seems my father was clever enough to know that something might be afoot.

Then came Halle, Vanguard's vengeful sister, who blasted her way onto the train and threw everything into chaos. She tried to kill Elijah—for reasons that are still unknown to me—and pretty much everyone else who wasn't on her side. Including me and the keeper.

In the battle that followed, I had two goals: first, to get Elijah to safety because there's no freaking way I'll ever let a kid be used as leverage; and second, to get myself closer to the Ultima Nostra.

When the keeper was conjuring a translocation spell to transport Elijah to safety, I'd feigned going with them, only to push myself away from the keeper's magic at the last moment.

He was gone and I was left to Lucian's mercies. Lucian demanded to know where Elijah had been taken, and I told him I'd only speak with the Ultima Nostra. He had no choice but to take me to our father, who, after all that, never did ask me where Elijah ended up.

I guess he was too focused on killing me to care at that point.

Now, the keeper's ire only grows, the rebuke in his voice a harsh reminder that I'd taken a massive risk. "You thought you would get what you wanted, but it wasn't what you needed."

Unfortunately, that's true.

What I wanted was vengeance and closure.

What I *needed* was justice for my family… But it's a family that never existed in the way I thought it did.

I know this, and yet I grip his arms, putting a little distance between myself and his snuggly body to challenge him. "What is it that *you* think I need?"

His voice lowers, becoming just a little softer, although not much. "Your heart tells me what you need, Veda, and it wasn't to be hurt by someone you should have been able to trust."

My eyes widen. The truth of his words impales me so deeply that my only response is to lash out. "Don't tell me what I *didn't* need!"

"Okay, then." He is calm now in the face of my anger, all reproach vanishing from his voice. "You need your family."

There's a new darkness in his eyes as he speaks. Shadows and anger and a hint of empathy—only the briefest hint, but the kind that could only be felt by someone who understands my pain.

My shoulders hunch and it takes me closer to his chest, where I want to sink my head. "My only living family hates me."

He cups the back of my head, sliding his fingers through my hair, easing the tension in my neck. "As much as it pains me to say this, because that boy grates every fucking nerve in my body… Not all of them hate you."

He twists a little so I have a clear line of sight to Lucian.

My brother's shoulders are hunched where he sits, his hands folded in his lap. His wings are drooping on either side of the chair, even the uninjured one hanging low. He still wears a burn mark across his cheek. Blood has continued to trickle from a cut above his eye. Not to mention the rope burn around his neck or all the bruises across his arms and face that are turning a nasty purple color.

Since I woke up in my father's lair, Lucian's demeanor has transitioned and now it's nothing like the arrogant façade he presented when we first met him on the train with Elijah. In fact, Elijah was terrified when Lucian first approached us. The little boy gripped my hand so hard, his knuckles turned white.

My brother may have stepped between me and our father, but he is no saint.

I have no idea the things he might have done at our father's bidding.

The keeper's hands slide away from my neck and back, and I miss the firmness of his touch, but it's also time to make decisions.

"What you do in regard to your brother is entirely up to you," the keeper says, most certainly loud enough for Lucian to hear. "Kill him. Don't kill him. Ask me to heal him. Don't ask me to heal him. Interrogate him. Don't interrogate him." The keeper gives me a resigned look, although it's clear he would prefer the interrogation-followed-by-death approach. "Whatever you decide, I'll respect your decision."

I chew the inside of my lip as I rise to my feet. I made it clear to Diavolo that I want Lucian alive because he has answers. But... just because I need my brother alive right now doesn't mean I always will.

When we were in our father's lair, Lucian and I were both fighting for our lives. We had a common enemy. Joining forces made sense.

We aren't in that situation anymore.

And... well... Even if I could trust that Lucian hadn't done anything I'd find despicable, my relationship with him is tenuous at best.

He could end up being an enemy I can't afford to have. He could end up being a spy in our midst.

He could have defended me just to gain my trust. After all, our father took his sweet time acting on his supposed intention to kill Lucian. It could have all been an act.

My brother could lie to me, betray me, and run back to our father.

Lucian is, after all, a dark creature like me.

And now I need to decide if I can trust him.

CHAPTER TWELVE

Rising to my feet, I make my way to Lucian.

The panthers stay close, although they give me space to move.

Lucian eyes them uncertainly but doesn't stand or try to back away.

I stop in front of him. "How can I trust you?"

He shakes his head. "Trust between dark beings is impossible."

Too true.

"Did you know about me before we met?"

He nods. "I knew I had an older sister." He points to the red blood on his face. "The firstborn has black blood. It was obvious I wasn't the firstborn, and it wasn't like anyone tried to keep that a secret from me."

I want to ask him why he looked so surprised and weirdly relieved when he saw my wings, but again, I'm not ready to bring them up yet… Even though I know I'll need to speak of them eventually and possibly sooner than I want to.

"What *did* you know about me?"

His forehead puckers. "It was more what I was told about

your mother than about you—because nobody ever saw or met you."

"Well, then, what did you know about my mother?"

He takes his time answering me, more hesitant than I would like. *Cagier* than I would like. "Our father referred to her as a hellhound. So did Vanguard and Jonah. Somehow, they all omitted to tell me about her claws. The same claws you have. Or I might have made the connection earlier."

"What else did you know about her?"

His forehead creases. "They said she disappeared when she was pregnant with you."

"And?"

"And what?"

"Did you know our father betrayed her?"

Lucian looks away.

I lurch forward but stop myself before I grab him. "Did you know?"

His focus flashes back to me. "It wasn't hard to guess! Okay?" he snaps. "Dad rarely spoke about her, but when he did, he got this fucking awful look on his face. Knowing what he's capable of, the chances that he *didn't* do something to fuck her over were fucking slim!"

His voice has risen. His lips are drawn back from his teeth as he takes sharp breaths. If he were a wolf shifter, I'm sure he'd be accessing his incisors right now. As it is, his fury is evident in the paleness of his cheeks and the way his eyes narrow at me.

"Look, if you're going to kill me, then get the fuck on with it," he says. "I can't tell you anything that could be worth something to you because our father didn't trust me with information that was worth having."

My response is a low growl. "I think you know more than you're telling me."

He shakes his head, a slow, side-to-side motion, the corners of his mouth turning down and his shoulders hunching again.

"If I am, what are you going to do about it, Veda?" he asks. "Beat it out of me?"

I rub my hands over my face, my voice losing its growl, my thoughts becoming quiet. "I'm not going to kill you, Lucian."

At my declaration, the anger drains from his face and he looks at me with a deeply furrowed brow.

The air *whooshes* out of my chest in a defeated sound. "I didn't free myself from a dark prison so I could destroy my family." I dare to look away from Lucian, even though I'm standing close enough for him to strike me while my back is turned.

I take in the panthers and the keeper, the way they're all standing close enough to back me up, no matter what happens.

"I came here *for* my family," I say.

When I turn back to Lucian, he gives a heavy sigh that sounds a lot like my own defeated exhalation.

"Yeah," he says. "But you can't trust me."

I wish I could tell if he's lying from listening to his heartbeats. Some supernaturals give away their lies when their heartbeats jump—that is, according to my mother. But dark creatures are very good at masking their lies, aided by a general lack of guilt that means their actions don't affect their emotional state.

There are a few supernatural species with the ability to instantly detect lies, no matter who is telling them. Creatures like the Valkyrie, Keres, and of course, Avenging Angels. They all had that ability, but they're extinct. Even if they weren't, it's not like I could convince one of them to help me.

Keeping Lucian at my side is a huge risk.

It's true that I need family, but I have a pack. The panthers are my pack. So is the keeper. I need to protect *them* now.

So I make a decision: I will ask the keeper to heal Lucian, but after that, I don't have much choice but to send my brother on his way. The keeper will need to find us another home base, since Lucian has seen this one, but I hope it won't be too hard.

Already, I'm cataloging in my mind the things I want to take with me, all of them having a personal meaning to me—my mother's old shirt and the strip of material from her old skirt, the sash of black material I took from the angel's cathedral when I first escaped, and the torn-out page from *The Book of Dark Magic* that I retrieved from Central Park.

I'm turning to the keeper when Lucian speaks softly again.

"You asked me what I *knew* about you, which pretty much amounted to nothing until I met you, but I can tell you what I *know* about you."

I consider him carefully before I ask, "Which is?"

"You have what no other dark creature I've ever met has."

Oh, he'd better not mention my wings.

Or repeat that bullshit our father was spouting about me filling the streets with blood.

Before I can speak, he continues. "You have an internal moral code."

It isn't anywhere close to what I thought he might say.

He exhales softly into the silence. "That mother-wolf back in the forest described you as a dangerous, wounded creature, but when she asked you what you would do if she let you live, you said you didn't know."

I stare back at him warily, uncertain where he's going with this.

He continues softly. "There isn't a dark creature on this planet who wouldn't have immediately said they wanted to tear our father apart. But you hesitated."

He peers at me with an intense gaze, as if he can't really understand what he's looking at. "There also isn't a dark creature on this planet who would have let me live this long— no matter that I hit our father over the head with a useless plank of wood. But you haven't killed me, and you've said you won't. Despite the fact that I probably shouldn't believe you, I do."

He finally rises off the chair, although his wings hang even lower than they did before and he reaches for the table to keep himself steady. "So, yeah, you can't trust me. Not at all. But maybe you can trust this: I'm not going back to our father. I'd rather fucking die. And the chances of dying at your side are way higher than anywhere else, so this is where I'd like to stay."

I blink at him, mentally replaying what he said and trying to process it. "I can trust you… because you have a death wish?"

"Yeah. I guess that's what I'm saying."

Huh.

I can't stop the slightly crooked smile forcing itself onto my face. "I can't promise you a *glorious* death at my side," I say. "But death is highly likely."

He shrugs.

I shrug back.

I let the moment settle a little before I consider the panthers and, finally, the keeper.

Each of the panthers tips their head in a nod.

The keeper exhales heavily before he gives me a nod.

I guess we're in agreement.

"Okay, then," I say to Lucian. "You can stay."

A hesitant smile flickers across his lips. "It's nice to meet you, big sister."

"Yeah, you too, little brother." But I quickly follow up with a dark scowl. "I'm not hugging you. You busted up my face."

Before he took me to our father, Lucian tried to beat Elijah's location out of me. I'd healed fast, but even so, I didn't appreciate the treatment. Lucian had exclaimed at the time that his father was going to kill him for losing Elijah. As it turns out, he anticipated our father's reaction precisely.

Lucian suddenly looks a little defensive. "Don't worry. I'm not a hugger."

Well, now I'm tempted to hug him just to spite him, but that's my dark nature.

"Are you sure you're not a hugger?" I ask, edging toward him.

He said his mother was killed, but not when it happened, so I can't be certain he ever experienced affection from her. I certainly can't imagine our father ever hugging him. So maybe he just doesn't know what hugs feel like?

I may have been deprived of a lot of things growing up in a cell, but in the first decade of my life, hugs from my mother kept me alive.

Lucian edges away from me. "I'm sure."

"Well... who hugged you?"

His jaw clenches and he snaps at me so suddenly that I freeze where I stand. "Affection either comes with strings attached or it's followed by a fist you don't see coming," he snarls. "I've had enough fists for today."

My hands rise, but I don't back off. I mean every word when I say, "Lucian, I'm sorry I pushed it. I won't hug you if you don't want to be hugged."

At my promise, he stops inching away from me.

"Okay," he says, wiping at the beads of sweat that appeared on his forehead and rolling out his shoulders, as if he's trying to rid himself of tension.

Fuck.

The idea of being hugged really caused him anxiety.

I consider him carefully, trying to fight the sudden bleakness rising within my mind.

He may be even more damaged than I am.

Well, at least I can do something about his physical wounds.

I turn to the keeper, intending to ask him to heal Lucian, when Anarchy takes a step toward my brother.

In his bid to evade me, Lucian ended up right beside her.

She must not have understood the *no touching* agreement—

or, to her panther thinking, it doesn't apply to her—because she nudges her head against the palm of his hand.

It's the sort of gesture she would give me to show solidarity.

He flinches at her sudden touch and his hand flicks past her nose. It's the same hand he used to wipe the sweat from his face and his fingers leave a smear across her nose.

Her tongue darts out, and she quickly licks the moisture away.

But then she suddenly freezes.

I pause, half-turned to the keeper, peering back at the female panther. "Anarchy?"

She inhales a sharp breath that sounds like a hiss.

Then she lets it out with a blood-curdling shriek.

CHAPTER THIRTEEN

"Anarchy!" My cry mixes with Lucian's shout as he leaps away from the female panther.

"What the fuck?" he cries.

She turns on him, her teeth bared and claws slashing the space where he was standing a moment before.

He leaps up onto the table, even though she could easily follow him up there, and wildly searches around—probably for higher ground, given that his focus lands briefly on the tops of the cupboards against the wall to his right and then flies to the open space above the refrigerator on his left.

All three of the male panthers have startled at Anarchy's scream and are hunched low to the ground, as if they aren't sure whether or not to leap forward or stay put.

When I first met these panthers, they were the vicious predators I expected them to be, but I knew from that very first moment that Anarchy was in charge. The most vicious of them all. The one who calls the shots.

Why the fuck she's suddenly intent on taking a chunk out of Lucian is a mystery I intend to solve—once I ensure she doesn't succeed.

I put the full force of my wolf's growl into my voice. *"Anarchy, stop!"*

She barely reacts to my cry. Barely glances in my direction. But the quick look she gives me is enough for me to assess her intentions. Her lips are drawn back from her teeth and her nose is wrinkled with threat, a clear indication that her predatory instincts are controlling her choices.

I won't be able to break through to her.

She won't be able to listen to me.

I try to step in front of the other panthers. *"No, stop!"*

They don't listen to me until Anarchy spins and snarls at them, a harsh sound that I interpret all too well: *Lucian is hers.*

Her brief pause to snap at her brothers gives me a heartbeat to react.

My first thought is to fully shift into my wolf form and tackle her, but it will call forth my wings, too, and they'll be a huge liability in this already small space. When we fought an angel after escaping from the prison, Anarchy proved just how efficiently she can take down a creature with wings.

My second option has already stepped up to my side. "Diavolo!"

His hands have lifted toward Anarchy. Energy sizzles around him, crackling in the air so close beside me that the hairs on my arms stand on end.

Sapphire light shoots across his crown-shaped ring and out from his fingertips.

It's his illusion magic. He's used it on the panthers several times before, multiple times to turn them into Doberman Pinschers, and once to turn them into fluffy, little puppies. I'd love to say they were harmless in that form, but their teeth were sharp enough to bite off fingers.

His light bursts across the distance and smacks into Anarchy's back, flooding her form.

Her body instantly shrinks, her snarls becoming strange huffing noises.

Huh?

I follow her shrinking form down to the floor, my eyes widening at the fluffy, little creature she's become.

She has two floppy, black ears, a snuggly-looking body, and the cutest button tail.

"A rabbit?" Lucian cries, now poised in the center of the tabletop, his weight on his left leg, as if he's decided the refrigerator is his best bet. "How is that supposed to help? Rabbits chew through carrots, for fuck's sake!"

Indeed, Anarchy doesn't seem the least perturbed by her new shape. She bounces up onto the table in a single leap, her very sharp teeth snapping at the air as she lands a bare few paces from Lucian.

He backpedals at an astounding speed. He can't fly with his still-broken wing or I'm certain he'd be up near the ceiling by now.

Not that Anarchy couldn't reach him there. Along with taking down winged creatures, she's proven she can jump to extreme heights.

Lucian's good wing shivers, lifting him lopsidedly, while his broken wing drags.

It just reinforces my belief that wings are a huge fucking liability.

Diavolo doesn't waste time with talk.

Light flashes once more around his fingertips, but this time, it's an alarming black.

Dark magic.

I'm worried about what life Diavolo might be draining to feed it, but my more immediate concern is my brother—and stopping Anarchy from doing something she might later regret.

At the same time as the dark light flashes, bunny-rabbit

Anarchy leaps across the table at Lucian, gaining enough air that she's level with his chest.

He recoils backward, his good wing beating wildly at the air, his legs moving. His foot hits the far edge of the table while his good wing propels him awkwardly through the air.

Except that the table isn't anchored to the floor, so the impact of his foot against its edge causes it to slide right out from under him.

In that heartbeat, he's airborne within the space between the sliding table and the stationary countertop. Anarchy is soaring toward him in all her graceful bunny-rabbit glory, her mouth about to close around his outstretched fingers. And Diavolo's dark light splashes across Anarchy's back, as if he threw a bucket of black paint at her.

The dark liquid disappears instantly into her fur and then there's a *thud*.

Everything ahead of me slows, as if time has halted where the magic hit.

I'm already reaching forward, preparing to throw myself across at Anarchy, but I'm suddenly aware that the keeper's hand has wrapped around my arm and he's just as forcefully wrenching me backward.

His voice rises to a shout. "Veda! Get down!"

Get down?

Ahead of me, the ripple of energy that seems to have frozen both Anarchy and Lucian in place appears to be rippling right back at me, the keeper, and the male panthers. It's a shimmer of black light and it's originating from Anarchy.

What the fuck is that?

I may not know the answer, but I know it can't be good.

Even though my muscles are responding and I'm leaping backward, I'm not going to be fast enough.

Darkness explodes across Anarchy's body, the blast

throwing me and the keeper and the panthers across the room, all of us tumbling through the air, head over heels.

Thump.

I find myself on my back, my ears ringing as I stare upward at the black smoke billowing across the air above me. It smells weirdly like lavender, both the smoke and the scent so thick that I can't see more than a few feet in any direction.

I didn't land on the floor, I know that much.

Once more, I'm cushioned in a dragon's wing, this time not wrapped around me so much as forming a hammock beneath me. As I twist to the right, I discover that the keeper kept his humanoid form while dragon wings must have shot out on either side of his torso. I'm caught in one wing while the moving shapes on the other side of him indicate that the three panthers landed in his other wing.

The keeper's dark eyes flash in my direction as the panthers and I roll out of his wings and into the black smog.

As safe as we are, I'm terrified for both Anarchy and Lucian right now.

I don't know what that blast was or how they could have survived it.

As fast as I can, I find my feet and launch myself through the smoke, a cry on my tongue. "Anarchy! Lucian!"

Riot, Rumble, and Strife are right beside me as I plow across the room, waving my arms and trying to clear the air so I don't crash into anything.

The explosion must have flung us all the way back across the living area, because the first furniture I reach is the lounge chairs. All are upturned, their upholstery singed, as if a flash of fire blazed across them.

I dart around them while the panthers leap over them, but we've only made it a few more steps when there's a rushing sound from behind me. An impossibly strong drag of air sucks me backward, my bare feet sliding on the floor for several paces until I skid right into the keeper's chest.

"What are you—?" It takes me a glance upward to understand that he's inhaling, pulling the black smoke into his chest to clear the air.

Despite the frustrating and panic-inducing delay, I understand why he's doing it. Without visibility, I'm racing into dangers unknown and it's not as if I can use my sense of smell right now—the only scents I can discern are lavender and burning magic.

What's more, we can't exactly open a window and let the smoke out. I don't know nearly as much about humans as I need to, but smoke billowing from a window means fire and I'm sure they won't like fire. I learned that much from all the knights-killing-fire-breathing-dragons fairy tale books that my jailer brought me.

Even so, the panthers fight the pull, extending their claws and catching hold of the lounge chairs, ripping partway through the cushions in their effort to retain their progress across the room.

The keeper's left arm has wrapped around me, holding me against his chest. His dragon wings have disappeared, but his skin has a sheen to it, as if he's wearing translucent scales.

He stops inhaling, at which point the air settles around me and the panthers drop to the floor.

Even though the keeper's breaths have cleared most of the smoke from the room, it's still hazy up ahead.

"Stay close," the keeper rumbles in my ear before he releases me.

Up ahead, I can make out the kitchen table where it's tipped on its side, its top pressed to the cupboards on the left side of the kitchen. But where the haze is the thickest, I can only just make out the silhouettes of two figures lying on the floor in front of the far kitchen cupboards, and... something doesn't look right.

I move cautiously forward while the keeper remains on my heels and the male panthers join me on my way, their steps slower now, as if they, too, are wary of what lies ahead.

My heart remains in my throat.

I don't understand why the keeper's dark magic exploded so violently, and I don't understand why the silhouettes ahead of me look so wrong...

I pull to an abrupt stop as the haze of energy finally disperses and the scene ahead of us becomes clear.

My lips purse in confusion.

All I can manage is a soft, "Huh?"

Lucian lies on his back on the floor, his broken wing pushed up against the cupboards, while his good wing is spread out across the floor in our direction. His arm on this side is lifted off the floor, his palm facing up, hovering as if he doesn't know what to do with it.

Straddling him, her naked legs on either side of his waist, is one of the most beautiful women I've ever seen.

CHAPTER FOURTEEN

*L*ong, pale-lilac hair cascades down the woman's back in waves that roll past her narrow waist. She's tall and slender and she's holding Lucian's other hand in both of hers.

She brushes the tips of his fingers across her lips while her mouth curves into a sultry smile. Her focus is entirely on him, and in fact, she seems oblivious to our presence.

Until she looks up, I won't be able to see clearly the color of her eyes, but her chin is delicate, her cheekbones high but softly rounded, and her skin is pale like the moon in a beautifully dark sky.

Beside me, the male panthers have skidded to a stop, their eyes wide, their claws retracting, and their nostrils flaring. Rumble makes a soft, chirping sound that gives me some reassurance, since it's a sound I associate with the panthers' happiness, but then he falls silent again.

The keeper, too, has stopped in his tracks, but instead of focusing on the scene ahead, he's studying his hands, turning them back and forth, his forehead deeply furrowed.

Barely able to peel my eyes away from the woman, I whisper to him, "What did you do? What magic is this?"

He shakes his head before he looks up from his hands. "I have no fucking idea."

Well, while he may have gained complete control over his power in some respects, it seems there are still some aspects of his power he's yet to master.

"Could this be another illusion?" I ask.

"No," he says. "Of that, I'm certain."

Up ahead, the woman's mouth closes over the tips of Lucian's fingers, her tongue darting out as she licks every drop of sweat and blood off his hand.

"You're tasty," she says before her mouth closes over the side of his palm—the fleshy part beneath his thumb.

Lucian seems to have lost his ability to speak. "Uh…"

She leans down over him, her pale-lilac hair brushing across his chest as she draws his left hand to her shoulder and presses it there. She catches his other hand, which she presses to her other shoulder. After which, she lowers her face to his.

He appears to hold his breath as she drags her tongue across the wound on his forehead and down the side of his cheek where the light magic scorched him.

"So very tasty," she says before she leans back and licks the last smears of his blood from around her mouth.

He stares up at her, his eyes wide. To his credit, he's focused on her face and not on her naked body.

It seems she isn't done with him when she leans across to his broken wing—the one on the far side. I can't see exactly what she's doing because the curtain of her hair falls forward and pools across his chest. All I'm certain of is that she seems to have lowered her head to the location of the break near his shoulder.

He flinches, visibly pulling away from her as if he could

scooch across the floor with her still on top of him. "What are you...?"

I step forward, ready to intervene, but then he visibly relaxes.

A sigh passes his lips, the tension leaves his shoulders and chest, and his eyes slowly close.

They stay like that for a long moment while I hover uncertainly and the panthers watch warily and the keeper continues to take unhappy glances at his hands.

Then the woman sits slowly upright again and her voice is gentle as she says to Lucian, "All better now."

He opens his eyes, a serenity in his expression that I never expected to see on his face. His cheeks have regained their color and, if I look closely enough, it appears that the wound on his forehead and burn across his other cheek are gone.

The flutter of his broken wing and the way he lifts and lowers his shoulder on that side indicates that his wing may not be broken anymore.

My jaw has dropped. Even the keeper seems surprised, his eyebrows now raised.

Lucian's hands have remained on the woman's shoulders where she put them and he seems transfixed. "How did you do that?"

"Heal you?" She slowly bares her teeth, revealing two pointy canines. They aren't as long or as prominent as a vampire's fangs, and it's not immediately clear to me if they can extend or retract, since they don't grow longer or shorter as I watch.

She runs her tongue over the tips of them. "My teeth secrete a healing solution. A little is good. A lot is bad."

"You bit me?" His voice is startled, but then his forehead creases. "I didn't feel you bite me."

She gives a soft laugh. "Biting isn't necessary. I just need to lick you."

His eyes are wide and his voice is a whisper. "Fuck me."

A slow smile grows on her face. "It's been a while, but I'm sure I can remember how."

"Uh... No... I didn't mean..."

She shrugs. "Your loss, gargoyle boy."

I'm not sure how it's possible for my jaw to drop lower than it already has.

Gargoyle boy?

"What the fuck is going on here?" I whisper, at which the woman with the lilac hair rises swiftly off Lucian, revealing how tall she is when she stands at her full height—certainly as tall as Lucian, if not taller.

She doesn't seem to care that she's completely naked. She gives herself a quick once-over, casting her gaze at her legs, arms, and hands before giving a laugh that sounds like a far-off melody, pulsing with magic.

"*Two* legs." She reaches up to her ears, pushing her hair back to reveal what I couldn't see before: elven ears. "My beautiful pointy ears!"

She gives a groan of apparent happiness before she promptly tries to see her butt. "Where is my tail?" She stops. "Oh, that's right. No tail. Ha!"

"Okay," I say, more loudly this time. "What the actual fuck?"

She plants one hand on her hip as she turns her gleaming smile on me. "Well, hello there, Darkness."

"Uh..." I squint back at her. "Hi?"

Now that she's facing me, I can see all of her facial features. Her eyes are the palest blue, a color that looks otherworldly in contrast to her hair, and her cheekbones and chin are as delicate as they first appeared.

Behind her, Lucian rises to his feet, pressing his hands to his apparently healed face and testing his wings, both now seeming to be functioning normally. I'm not sure how she healed him, but my more immediate concern is her identity.

I direct my question at the woman. "And you are…?"

She bows her head briefly but solemnly. "I'm Anna-ve-shaleia of the House of Dark Dreams, but I prefer the name you gave me."

My forehead puckers. "Anarchy?"

She tips her head, and the male panthers suddenly grin up at me, their eyes bright, each of them chirping softly.

I don't know what question to ask first. "How…? Why…?"

"*What*," she replies, tapping her ears. "I'm a dark elf."

She turns to the keeper, bowing her head briefly to him. "Keeper of Dark Magic," she addresses him as solemnly as she acknowledged me. "I am not prone to gratitude, but it would be dishonorable of me not to thank you for breaking the curse that was placed on me."

He clears his throat. "I assure you it was completely unintentional."

She acknowledges his response with another brief bow. "Naturally. You could not have known that your dark magic would break a spell that had caged me for nearly a thousand years."

She continues before he can respond, although her voice sounds more cautious now. "A curse that was particularly painful to me because I had already cheated death and prolonged my own life for nearly a thousand years before that."

"You're two thousand years old?" The keeper immediately stands more upright, his lips pursed as he looks at her with renewed interest.

"Yes, keeper," she murmurs, her eyes glimmering darkly. "I was a youngling when you were created. My people felt the force of your creation all the way into the heart of our domain. Whatever terrible power was used to make you, I can't imagine the devastating cost to your creator."

The keeper is now frozen. He told me once that he doesn't

remember his creation or who he was before he became the keeper. The panthers were present for that conversation, so they're aware of it.

"What do you know of me?" he asks, and I sense the stillness of his chest, the way he's holding his breath.

She shakes her head, a hint of regret in her voice. "I apologize, Keeper, if I gave you hope. My brothers and I felt the impact of your creation, along with the creation of the other keepers, but your identity was a mystery that nobody seemed able to answer."

"Oh." He withdraws a step, his expression closing off.

"Your brothers and you?" I ask carefully, feeling the need to take the focus off the keeper while latching on to the way Anarchy didn't refer to herself alone.

"These are my brothers," she says, holding her hand out to the male panthers, who nudge up against her. "They, too, are dark elves of the House of Dark Dreams, cursed at the same time I was. I would tell you their elven names, but they are very difficult to pronounce in your tongue." She smiles at me. "They won't mind if you don't use their original names, though, because like me, they prefer the names you gave them."

"Riot. Rumble. Strife." I murmur each in turn as the male panthers bow their heads to me.

Seemingly in unison, they all turn to the keeper, staring up at him expectantly.

He blinks back at them for a long moment.

Then his expression darkens.

"No," he says, seeming to regain his spirit as he glares down at them. "One explosion was enough. I don't care if you're all cursed. I'm not doing that again."

They huff and roll their eyes at him.

I can imagine how badly they want to return to their original forms. Being trapped in the body of an animal would be like being trapped in a cage. But I also understand why the keeper wouldn't want to cause three more explosions like the one we just endured.

I reach out to press my hand to his arm, drawing his attention to me. "Maybe when it's safe?"

He capitulates. "Of course."

"Soon, then." Anarchy sighs as she drags her gaze away from her brothers to take in the room and all of its disarray. "Now that we've got introductions over, what are the chances that the humans in this building will have been alarmed by the explosion of power?"

"None," the keeper says, sounding confident now. "I contained its impact. They won't have felt a thing."

"Good," she says. "Why don't we clean this up, and while we work, I can answer any other questions you have?"

I clear my throat, squinting at her. "How about I get you some clothes first?"

Her forehead creases. Then clears. "Oh, that's right. I need clothing in this form, don't I?"

"You certainly do." I nod my head firmly and gesture toward the bedroom. "Hopefully, something will fit you."

She may be taller than I am, but she isn't as skinny. Until I ate my first proper meal, the first in my life, my stomach had been caved in from malnourishment. It's rounded out now and I'm loving it. I've eaten as much as I could since then and I'm hungry again now, but I tell my stomach to wait just a little longer.

As I move to step away from the keeper, he sweeps his hand across his chest and I'm not sure what he's doing until the feather he removed from my shoulder materializes in his hand.

"You may want to put this in a safe place," he says.

It's only then that I remember, with a shudder, that I left the other feather in the wall of my father's lair. I'd ripped my hand through it to free my arm.

Damn.

My stomach sinks to my toes.

That feather can be used to kill me, and I've left it in my father's hands.

CHAPTER FIFTEEN

"Veda?" the keeper asks quietly.

My voice is strained, but I force myself to speak. "That feather is very dangerous to me. But there was a second feather that I left behind."

"Do you mean this one?" He moves his fingers, adjusting his hold on what I thought was a single feather, revealing that he is, in fact, holding two feathers.

My heart leaps to see them. "When did you retrieve that?"

"While you were trying to convince me to save your brother." He smirks at me. "Since one of these had been rammed into your shoulder, I assumed your father enjoyed using them against you. I also smelled your blood on the feather in the wall. I wasn't about to leave a weapon like that behind for your father to use in the future."

I slip my hands around the keeper's waist and rest my head against his chest. "Thank you."

His arms rise around me, warm and strong against my back, and his voice rumbles in my ear. "I'm a little insulted that you underestimated my determination to protect you, my Veda."

With an enormous feeling of relief, I step back and accept both of the feathers from him. "Never again."

Even though... at the back of my mind... there's a question about whether or not he's still bound to me.

But by asking that question, I could trigger a realization on his part that he might not yet have had. Just like revealing that the feathers are actually mine, I'm not ready for that yet. Maybe it's deceptive, but I need to stretch out these moments as long as I can.

Besides, deception is in my nature.

I swallow my fears and focus on the task at hand.

Clasping the feathers closely, I lead Anarchy into the bedroom and then to the dressing room at its side.

I head to the drawer where I previously laid out my treasured items—the remains of my mother's clothing and the page from *The Book of Dark Magic*. These feathers aren't precious—far from it—but they're a part of me, so I place them alongside my treasures.

Ragged material. A ragged page. And now ragged feathers.

Anarchy immediately sets about rummaging through the racks of clothing. This apartment once belonged to a witch who was killed by an assassin. The assassin kindly cleaned up her body and left her apartment in pristine condition. The keeper saw the witch's memories when he collected her magic and, as he said, she liked to shop.

Now that Anarchy's standing closer to me, I inhale the lavender scent of her elven skin. It explains the perfume in the air when the curse was broken. I have a lot of questions for her, but most of them need to be asked when the keeper and Lucian can hear the answers, too.

She pulls out a pair of black pants and a low-cut purple T-shirt. She tries on a few bras before she settles on one she seems to like and I help her clip it up at the back.

She grumbles about corsets being easier to latch together

before she puzzles over the drawer filled with string-like underpants. She's seen me wearing underpants, but nothing like those ones.

"Do I need these?" she asks, dangling a triangle of lace from her fingers.

"Not those, you don't." I'm sure there must be some point to underwear like that, but I can't for the life of me figure out what it is.

I quickly retrieve a pair of underpants from a different drawer. They're made of a softer material and will cover her butt. "These are more comfortable."

Her comment about corsets and the fact that she seems as much in the dark about the string-like underwear as I am makes me wonder how much experience she has with this modern world.

Handing over the underpants, I ask, "How long were you imprisoned in the veil?"

With a sigh, she throws the lacy item into the drawer and takes the other one from me. "We lost count of the years we spent in that dark place. Probably several centuries." She thinks for a moment. "We'd survived for nearly 1500 years when the Sentinels caught us. It was the 1700s and we'd made our way into France, where the humans were in the middle of some sort of revolution. Death and war always called to us, but I suppose it made us easier to track."

As she pulls on the underpants, she muses, "Say what you will about dark magic creatures, but we barely make a mark compared to what humans do to each other."

"If you were in that cage for hundreds of years, then this world must be as strange to you as it is to me."

"Very strange." Her eyes brighten again. "Although I'm happy there's basic sanitation. I don't miss the piss and shit that caked some city streets."

She shudders and shakes out her hands and feet one after the other. I can't help but imagine her in her feline form, picking her way along a filthy street and trying not to get any sludge on her paws. Cats, after all, are clean creatures.

She pulls on the long pants and shirt and turns to me. "I'm ready." She wrinkles her nose at me. "You have blood in your hair. I'd approve if it were someone else's blood, but the fact that it's your own..." Her expression darkens. "Your father will answer for what he did."

My voice sticks in my throat. Gratitude shouldn't be in my nature, but I've felt it multiple times today. "Thank you for coming for me."

"Not just me." Her anger fades and her voice lowers. "That dark king needs you, Veda." Her focus flickers in the direction of the living area. "He won't let you die."

It sounds a little like a warning, but I can't be sure because she's already turning away.

If I didn't sense a rising tension from within the living area, I'd ask more questions. I'd also indulge in a good wash. I never thought I'd wish for a shower after my first disastrous experience with them, but I desperately want one now.

However, I've left Lucian alone with the keeper and the panthers for long enough that I can sense the rising friction seeping through the walls.

I promise myself I'll grab a wet cloth in the kitchen to clean off my hair as I hurry after Anarchy.

Emerging from the bedroom, I stop just outside the door when I find the living area awash with emerald light.

The keeper's power *whooshes* around the room, ruffling the male panthers' fur and blowing through Lucian's feathers. The lounge chairs appear to have been whisked back into place and now their upholstery is stitching back together and smoothing out. Within seconds, it looks like they were never torn in the first place. The scorch marks on them appear to have been dealt with already.

At the other end of the room, the contents of the cupboards are clattering—presumably a sign that the crockery was smashed during the explosion and the keeper is now mending it —while the kitchen table slides back into place.

Finally, one of the kitchen chairs rushes across the floor right into the back of Lucian's legs.

"Take a seat, boy." The keeper smirks at him.

"I'll stand, thanks," Lucian snaps, rapidly sidestepping the chair and fully retracting his wings before he takes up a position near the kitchen sink.

The panthers are huddled against the left of the living area, their fur sticking up at all angles and their expressions disgruntled. As the emerald light recedes, they resume their usual positions, draping themselves over the lounge chairs.

"All done." With a pleased look on his face, the keeper nudges Riot aside to claim the armchair.

Riot hisses at him before finding a spot on the rug.

Anarchy is a step in front of me, but it seems she's quickly taking stock of the keeper and Lucian.

"So tense," she mutters before she glides across the room and pulls up the very chair that the keeper had nudged into Lucian's legs.

She casts Lucian glances from beneath her dark lashes as she sits down, her head held high, appearing for all the world as if she's claiming what he gave away.

His forehead crinkles at her.

I head straight for the sink and the drawers I've previously ascertained contain kitchen cloths. Dampening several of them, I drag one through my hair, doing my best to clean off some of the blood before I hand Lucian one of the damp towels.

"Anarchy missed a spot," I say, gesturing to his arm.

He takes the cloth but doesn't use it, holding it as if he doesn't trust it.

"It's just a cloth," I say. "No strings attached."

Hanging the rest of the cloths over the faucet, I turn away and allow him to make his own decisions.

Reaching the lounge chairs, I nudge myself between Rumble and Strife where they laze on the largest seat, squeezing myself between them.

"Are you really shadow panthers?" I ask, all of my questions suddenly burning. "Or simply cursed to look like them?"

To my surprise, Anarchy looks affronted.

"Of course we're shadow panthers." She gives a little sigh. "All of the original shadow panthers were other creatures cursed into that shape by a malevolent being."

I lean forward, curious. "Okay? How did that happen?"

"Let me start from the beginning," she says. "And I'll tell you all about it."

CHAPTER SIXTEEN

narchy's fingers curl around each side of her chair as if she's anchoring herself before she begins.

"Over a thousand years ago—and remember, I was already nearly a thousand years old by this time—humans became a significant threat to supernaturals. They had started to develop all sorts of weaponry that they could use against us, the worst of which was black powder that caused massive explosions."

She gives a heavy exhale. "It is indeed unfortunate, but there were whispers at the time that the black powder came about because it was inspired by a similar explosive powder belonging to dragons." She grips the chair tightly. "Regardless, supernaturals found themselves vulnerable. The *bright* elves had the idea to go into hiding. They decided to create a new world for themselves where humans would never find them.

"But in doing so, they were vulnerable for the first time in the history of our enmity with them, and my queen saw her chance to annihilate them. It was my duty, as the leader of her army, to obey my queen's every command."

Anarchy pauses and I remember very clearly the sense of

rebellion I'd felt around her and her brothers when I was deciding what names to give them.

At the time, I hypothesized that they'd done something incredibly unruly to get themselves locked up in a prison in the veil, but now it seems their insurrection may have occurred long before the Sentinels captured them.

"You rebelled against your queen," I say, a calculated guess on my part. "You didn't attack the bright elves as ordered."

Anarchy drags her fingernails along the edge of the chair's wooden seat. Her nails have retained the same silver sheen that was the color of her claws, and they flash in the dim light.

"Oh, it wasn't an act of mercy," she says. "Our actions were purely self-serving. Humans were a threat to us all. As long as their focus was on the bright elves, their eyes weren't turned on our people. The bright elves were a buffer that, once gone, would leave *us* vulnerable. For once, we should have joined forces with them." Her shoulders sink. "Possibly even gone with them into hiding."

"I take it your queen didn't see it that way?"

"She did not. No matter what I said, she was not dissuaded from the path of war with the bright elves. She said to me: *'Light and dark, we will all burn together.'* It became clear that she had given up any hope of our survival and craved only a glorious death."

Now, Anarchy casts a long glance at Lucian, since a magnificent death seems to be his wish also. Once again, his forehead crinkles in response, but not so deep a scowl this time.

"So she turned you into panthers?" I ask Anarchy.

"No, actually, it wasn't her." Anarchy gives a huff. "The bright elves had formed an alliance with gargoyles, whom we thought might be more receptive to our warning, since there wasn't such a long history of enmity between us and them.

"But upon delivering our information to one of their warriors, who was a gargoyle with an unusually dark heart—

which, by the way, is why we thought we could get through to him…" She gives another disgruntled sigh. "Well, he repaid us by cursing us."

On either side of me, Rumble and Strife hiss with indignation and on the floor, Riot adds his snarls to theirs.

"That gargoyle was so delighted with the beasts he turned us into," Anarchy continues, "that he vowed he would create more shadow panthers. We stayed long enough to witness him curse three of his own warriors before we escaped.

"But it seems he did pass on our warning to his people because our queen didn't get her wish. We watched from afar when she attacked the bright elves' stronghold, but they and the gargoyles had already gone."

"Not all of them," Lucian says, speaking up for the first time since Anarchy started her story.

She inclines her head at him. "Indeed. One gargoyle clan remained behind, surviving by concealing themselves in the stone monoliths that humans create." She inclines her head at Lucian. "A clever plan to hide in plain sight."

"Is that why you attacked me?" Lucian asks. "For revenge because of what that gargoyle did to you?"

"Revenge would be a good reason, but no." She catches her bottom lip between her teeth and gives him a sudden smile. "It was your blood."

Lucian presses back against the sink. "What about my blood?"

Her canine teeth flash as her grin grows. "The gargoyle who created us took great amusement in adding a little extra factor to our curse: We crave gargoyle blood."

I can only blink at her. "Why would he do that when it means you might attack his own people?"

"He had a dark heart. I don't think he liked his people very much. If I had to guess, he may have had a little dark-elven blood in him." She shrugs, as if it doesn't matter to her. "I'll never know for sure."

Lucian's brow furrows and he eases away from the sink. "I was bleeding the whole time in the forest. Why didn't you attack me then?"

She lifts her hand up in front of her face and holds her thumb and forefinger very slightly apart. "Because you only have a *little* bit of gargoyle in you. Your dark angel energy dominates your gargoyle side and overpowers it. I could easily resist your scent until you slathered your blood all over my nose."

Lucian scowls and folds his arms across his chest. "I didn't *slather* my blood across your nose."

She lowers her hand and gives him a wide-eyed look. "I'm not sorry you did. Licking you satisfied my cravings."

Lucian doesn't seem to know how to react, half-frozen, forehead crinkled, his cheeks flushing a little.

She gives him a soft smile, her pale-blue eyes twinkling.

One corner of his mouth rises, just a little reminiscent of the confidence he conveyed when I first met him. "You're welcome?"

"Maybe I'd like to be welcome again sometime."

I clear my throat to get their attention.

Now that Anarchy has answered my questions about her curse and why she attacked Lucian, my focus is on him.

What happened to his mother has clearly driven his decisions, and I need to understand his motivations—especially as it seems that both of our mothers were destroyed by our father.

"Your mother was a gargoyle," I say quietly. "Can you tell me about her?"

His smile vanishes and his expression immediately closes off, so I'm surprised when he gives me an answer. "Her name was Jalinda. She belonged to the clan Anarchy spoke about.

They were all brutal gargoyles who, over time, earned a reputation for solving problems that eluded other methods of resolution."

"You mean you could hire them to kill your enemies," I say, drawing conclusions from Lucian's guarded speech.

My brother inclines his head. "For the right price."

I blow out an exhale. When I was negotiating with James Vanguard for a way in to the Nostra Empire, I used that same language. The right price. But as I discovered, sometimes the price is too high.

"Well, my mother was hired to take out our father," Lucian says. "That was how they met."

I'm surprised. "So your mother, like the other members of her clan, was an assassin for hire."

"At that time, Jalinda was *the* assassin-for-hire. She was the clan's leader and the only one with an impeccable track record of kills." He grimaces. "But unbeknownst to her, our father was already negotiating with one of her rivals in the clan. He knew the attack was coming, captured Jalinda, and gave her a choice: death or a life with him. Either way, her rival took control of the clan and our father forged an alliance with them so they'd never come after him again."

Damn. "Her clan betrayed her," I whisper.

Lucian falls silent. He's told me more than I thought he would, and I give him a moment, not wanting to push it, but it seems he isn't done talking when he continues.

"You might be surprised to learn that Dad treated Jalinda like a queen," he says. "He showered her with gifts. Gave her everything she asked for. Never raised his voice to her or belittled her. Not that I saw, anyway. But he had two rules. The first rule: He had the right to discipline *me* however he saw fit."

I flinch at how coldly Lucian speaks about discipline, but he continues before I can say anything.

"And Jalinda was never to pick up a weapon again." Lucian's

eyes meet mine. "I can't forget the way she would fixate on dinner knives… or on the guns that the human mafia would bring to meetings… or the katana that James Vanguard carries on his back. It was like she was searching for pieces of herself."

"You can't take a warrior and turn her into an ornament," I murmur.

Lucian nods. "Over time, Dad grew complacent about Jalinda's safety. When I was seventeen years old, which was only four years ago, she went to a restaurant for dinner and her body came back riddled with bullets."

Lucian's expression is scarily blank. "A rival family—an emerging one—arranged the hit. I expected Dad to rage after them. Seek retribution. Take them out. I expected *war* and I was fucking ready for it!"

He sucks in a sharp breath and suddenly, his gaze is piercing. Angry. "Instead, Dad had Jalinda cremated without a funeral and that was that. When I dared to question him, he told me that his rivals killed her to draw him out. They wanted to make him so emotional that he'd make mistakes. He said he would not be so weak."

Lucian turns on me now and I'm stunned by the way he seems to direct his anger at me, the way his golden eyes burn.

"I told you before that I knew nothing about you and hardly anything about your mother, Galeia. But today wasn't the first time I heard her described as nearly immortal. James Vanguard said Galeia was like a sister to him. He called her a ferocious warrior, practically unkillable."

Lucian's jaw clenches. "*My* mother was murdered. I watched her dead body be put into the flames. But *your* mother disappeared. There is no body."

He barely takes another breath before he shoots a question at me. "Is Galeia really dead?"

I'm still trying to process everything he told me about his own mother, and I stumble over my response.

"Yes," I manage to say. "She died in my arms."

He shakes his head at me, a hint of disbelief in his voice. "Are you sure?"

A cold anger rises within me. "Of course I'm fucking sure. She died. *In my arms.*"

"How do you know it was her?"

"I… What?"

I'm frozen. *Why the fuck would he ask me that?*

He takes a step toward me and asks again, more quietly this time, "How do you know that the woman in the prison with you was your biological mother?"

CHAPTER SEVENTEEN

*A*narchy rises to her feet and turns on Lucian so fast that she nearly tips her chair over. "How could you ask Darkness such a thing? How could you stab at the wound in her heart?"

Lucian swallows visibly but stands his ground. "It isn't my intention to be cruel. But something doesn't add up here."

He dares to take his eyes off her and focus on me. "Veda, think about it. Dad is sure that Galeia's alive, even though it would be better for him if she were dead. He said she's thousands of years old. He said she walked with gods. Well, Vanguard and his sister, Halle, must be the gods she walked with. Why else would Vanguard describe Galeia as 'like a sister'?"

I'm swimming in the questions he's directing at me—questions I can hardly hear because the pain they're inducing is unbearable.

I press my hand to my chest and he falls silent.

I'm aware that the keeper was sitting stiffly in his seat but now he leans back, his forehead quietly creased.

The male panthers were hissing at Lucian, but now they've

fallen quiet. On either side of me, Rumble and Strife are both studying me, their whiskers twitching.

Anarchy turns carefully back to me, a wary light in her eyes. "Galeia was as old as me?" Her gaze flickers to Diavolo. "As old as the keeper?"

I don't know how to answer that. I would have said my father was lying if Lucian hadn't heard it from other sources.

My brother takes a step toward me, a brave move, since I'm in danger of lashing out right now.

"What *if* the woman in the cell wasn't your biological mother?" he asks again.

I can barely speak. "Not possible."

"Nothing's impossible. Not when it comes to dark magic." Lucian shakes his head stubbornly. "How could someone like Galeia die so easily?"

"Easily?" I push past Rumble's and Strife's furry bodies and lurch to my feet, anger burning within me. "You think starvation is easy? You think struggling to breathe is easy?"

"No." Lucian shakes his head, a look of regret washing across his face. "That's not what I meant."

It's only when Anarchy's hand closes around my arm that I realize I've made it all the way across the rug, prowling toward my brother like the predator I was born to be.

I'm acutely aware that the keeper has risen to his feet behind me and there's now a tinge of power in the room, a white haze, as if he might whisk me out of here before I hurt Lucian.

Anarchy's hand is gentle, and her voice is soft. "Darkness, I know you don't want to consider this… but is it possible that the woman in the veil prison wasn't your biological mother like you believed?"

I immediately shake my head. "She had the same claws as me."

Anarchy glances at the keeper. "Could the claws have been an illusion?"

He rumbles a quiet reply. "Veda was in prison for twenty-three years. An illusion, or a similar kind of glamour, couldn't have been sustained that long."

I close my eyes with relief, but then Anarchy asks, "What about a curse, like the one that was placed on me and my brothers?"

My eyes fly open. The curse that was placed on Anarchy lasted a thousand years.

Diavolo is slow to respond. "It's possible."

"No!" I shake free of Anarchy's hold. My breath is suddenly coming fast. I've never wanted so badly to believe that my mother is dead because the alternative…

"If Galeia died, you would have collected her magic," I say to him. "That was your job as the keeper of dark magic. So… did you?"

He is once more like stone as I prowl toward him.

I search his eyes, needing answers, even though I'm afraid of them. "Diavolo, you have the power to clear this up, once and for all. Did you tether Galeia's magic?"

He barely moves. "If she died, then I tethered it."

"*If* she died?" I'm trying to catch my breath, trying to comprehend the possibility that the woman who fed me and cared for me and taught me everything she knew…

I advance on the keeper, my claws extending and clashing against each other. "If Lucian's correct, then Galeia was practically immortal. Surely, you would remember tethering that much power."

The keeper stands his ground, his expression unreadable. "I don't."

"Don't what? Remember her?"

"I don't recall tethering that much power," he says.

"Which means?"

His jaw clenches. "I didn't tether it."

I stop still in front of him, my voice suddenly a bare whisper. "Which means…?"

He exhales heavily. "I don't want you to be hurt, my Veda."

I close my eyes, trying to squeeze my feelings into a tiny box and close them away, but it's impossible. "The woman who was in that cell with me… She was with me from the time of my first memories. She never left the cell. Not once."

I take a shaky breath. "If Galeia is alive, then it means she gave birth to me and at some point before my memories began, she left me in that prison. She might have given me up willingly or under duress, but either way, she knowingly left me in that place."

Opening my eyes, I wait for Anarchy or Lucian or even the keeper to refute my logic, but none of them do.

Their silence presses in on me.

"She gave birth to me and then she left me to die in that place."

Maybe she made a deal with my jailer to secure her own freedom. After all, I'm the one who is hated and feared. Maybe she planned all along for me to be imprisoned. Maybe she believed, as my father clearly does, that I'm too monstrous for this world and I belong in a cage.

I want to believe there's an explanation. I want someone to convince me that she was forced to give me up. Maybe she was separated from me and put in another cell in the veil prison… except that, when I escaped with the panthers, all of the other cages were empty.

Or maybe she's out there somewhere right now fighting to get back to me. Fighting with all her might…

Even if all the evidence points to her being an incredibly strong, incredibly clever, nearly immortal supernatural. If she wanted to get back to me, surely, she would have found a way.

I'm trying to breathe, trying to come up with possibilities. "She abandoned Halle and Vanguard too. Halle was drowning her sorrows in drink when I first met her. Halle believes that Galeia's gone. If she's really alive, why wouldn't she return to the people who treated her like family? Why would she disappear on them, too?"

The keeper's voice washes over me. "We have no answers for that."

"No," I say, backing away from him. "She died in that prison."

"Veda—"

"No!" I hold up my hands, warding him off. "She wouldn't abandon me. She wouldn't leave me to rot in that place."

He reaches for me and I shove at his arms. "She wouldn't do that!"

The keeper's arms slip around me, warm and comforting, but he doesn't say anything as my hot tears soak into his shirt.

My emotions must be hurting him. All my turmoil. All my anger. All my disbelief. All my questions.

You were loved.

That's what the woman who raised me—the woman who cared for me and kept me alive—whispered to me over and over.

If she wasn't my biological mother, then who was she? Why wouldn't she tell me the truth? And how could she care for me if she was cursed to look like someone else and forced to live in a prison because of me?

Unless... the curse *made her* care for me. Compelled her to go through the motions of child-rearing.

Because who could love a monstrous child like me unless they were forced to do so?

Suddenly, there's only a deep, dark pit of nothingness within me.

"It was lies," I whisper against the keeper's chest. "It was all lies."

His voice rumbles in my ear. "I'm taking you away from here."

The scent of his skin becomes fiery a moment before dragon wings form smoothly at his sides and he wraps them around me.

"I'm taking us all away."

The now-familiar pressure of the mist envelops me, and I wish it could fill the cracks in my heart.

CHAPTER EIGHTEEN

The keeper's warm wings part, one of them remaining wrapped around me, supporting me as I open my eyes.

I see my new surroundings as if I'm far away and removed from them.

My bare feet settle onto the wooden boards of a wide porch that overlooks a pristine beach and a vast ocean. It was morning back at the apartment in New York, but it's nighttime here. The air is salty and the sky is clear, a deep darkness that's sprinkled with stars.

I'm aware of Lucian, Anarchy, and the three male panthers arriving at different points along the porch, the mist clearing from their bodies as they find their feet.

There's a sense of space within the building behind me. Diaphanous, white curtains swoosh softly where they billow at wide windows and multiple wide doors, but the sound they make may as well be a million miles away.

"Where are we?" I ask, my voice wooden. "Are we back in Australia?"

The keeper's arms remain around me as he shakes his head.

"This is an uninhabited island off the coast of Japan. Dark creatures once lived, fought, and died here."

Nearest to me, Anarchy shivers and the panthers are on alert as they edge toward the front of the porch in the direction of the vast beach.

"What kind of creatures?" Anarchy asks, her head tilted and her nostrils flaring, as if she's trying to access the sharp hearing and sense of smell she must have possessed as a panther.

"Dead ones," the keeper reiterates.

Her eyes narrow at him.

Without further elaborating on the creatures that once lived here, he says, "There's a jungle at the center of this island. Your brothers will enjoy hunting in it."

She sniffs. "It's true. They're hungry. As am I." She continues to glare at the keeper. "We need to hunt and eat." Her expression softens as it passes across me. "But we won't go far."

"As you like," he replies.

I'm not exactly sure what food Anarchy will consume now, but I'm certain that the panthers are in need of raw meat.

I expect them to take off immediately, but they all look at me, quietly approaching to nudge up against my legs.

"You don't need my permission," I manage to say.

With a final nudge each, the strength in their bodies pushing me harder into the keeper's side, they leap down the porch steps and disappear along the white beach. Their black bodies are like shadows as they run like I've never seen them run before—like they haven't had a chance to run since they were liberated—all sleek and elegant as they stretch their legs.

Anarchy gives me a determined glance. "If there are any threats on this island, we'll take care of them."

The keeper huffs. "I placed a protection spell over this entire island the moment we got here."

"Very well." Some of the tension leaves Anarchy's shoulders before she leaps off the porch and onto the sand.

Landing smoothly, she races away down the beach, her feet flying, moving at an impossibly fast pace even in her dark elf form.

Within seconds, she and her brothers are gone.

The keeper immediately turns to Lucian and says, "Farther down the beach that way, you'll find a path that leads about a hundred paces inland. At the end of the path is a furnished hut. It contains a bountiful supply of food that should be suitable for your consumption. There should also be a place to bathe and sleep." He gives my brother a pointed stare. "I'm sure you'll be comfortable there."

Lucian hesitates, his expression filled with the same regret that washed over him when he insisted Galeia was alive. "I'm not sure that—"

"You may wish to go there *now*." The keeper's voice is a growl and his eyes change shape, turning reptilian like the eyes of the black dragon he became in the forest.

Lucian's lips press together. "Okay, but I'll be back to check on Veda first thing in the morning."

Diavolo scowls at my brother, who still doesn't budge from his current position, as if he's demanding the keeper's agreement.

"Fine," Diavolo snaps, at which Lucian proceeds to the edge of the porch.

My brother throws a concerned glance back at me before he checks the beach. Quickly descending the steps, he releases his wings, casting an aura of shadows as he takes to the air and speeds along above the white sand, rapidly disappearing in the direction the keeper pointed.

I'm alone with the keeper, but my senses are numb, my head spinning even more badly than before.

"My Veda, what do you need?" He turns me in his arms, moving me to face him again, an urgency in his question, but I'm already pushing myself out of his embrace.

What do I need?

I need the ground to stop falling away from beneath my feet.

I back away, my eyes burning hot with tears and my teeth slowly sharpening, even as I try to quell my body's reaction to the unwanted revelations I've faced today.

He doesn't let me go far, reaching out for me, cupping my cheek and peering into my eyes, his own widening. "My Veda… Where have you gone?"

In response, the corners of my mouth turn down.

I can't even shake my head.

I want my anger. I want my need for vengeance.

But I can't seem to find them right now.

Turning away from him, I descend carefully, deliberately, down the steps, stopping only to peel off my jeans and then my underpants.

Finally, my bra drops to the sand, leaving me completely naked as I walk toward the edge of the water.

Every step I take is steady because that's all I can fucking control right now.

One step in front of the other.

My feet *crunch* in the sand, not a new sound or a new sensation since I've walked on sand before, but both punctuate the way my foundations are no longer solid, so many grains shifting beneath me.

The scent of my own blood is strong. My earlier efforts to remove it from my hair didn't do much good and, now that I'm naked, I can also see the slivers of dried blood across my chest and legs.

The blood didn't bother me so much before, but it does now.

I don't stop walking, even when the cold water shocks my toes, rushing and pulling at my calves and then my thighs as I wade deeper into the waves.

I don't know how to swim, which makes it easy to sink beneath the surface and let the thrashing water toss me back and forth, tumbling me around until my chest is burning because I'm holding on to a breath I can't seem to exhale.

Suddenly, within my mind, I once again see a blue butterfly in the forest, its wings whipping back and forth before it lands on that little girl's nose.

I remember the way her mother breathed in and out, as if anger were as easy to control as exhaling and inhaling.

Well, maybe it is.

I exhale.

Scream into the water.

A roar that rips through my heart and mind and into the waves. A sound that shreds my memories into bloody pieces.

I was loved?

Fucking. Lies.

CHAPTER NINETEEN

I rise from the water, digging my feet into the sand, letting the water stream off me. Ribbons of darkness fall within it, my blood washing away.

The keeper is standing much closer to the water's edge than I expected, right where the waves lap at the beach and rush across his now-bare feet.

Black light glows around his fingers, his shoulders are tense, and his weight is on his front foot, as if he were about to dive in after me. He's wearing his angry face. The blue-eyed one with the beautiful cheekbones and fucking perfect lips.

I'm not concerned about where he might be drawing his energy from now. If this is an island, it's a vast one. A wash of thick greenery stretches out far into the distance. The keeper said there's a jungle at the center of this island, and I don't doubt it for a second.

I splash toward him, not caring that I'm still naked, picking up speed until I'm running, my strong legs carrying me forward in a matter of seconds.

He braces when I don't slow down, his fingers flexed and the light around the crown on his forefinger gleaming brighter.

I ram into him so fast that I knock him off his feet, forcing us into a tumble. White sand glistens around us, kicking up into the air and sticking to our skin when we end up in a near-heap.

But somehow, I'm on top, my legs on either side of his hips, my palms resting near his shoulders, and my claws digging into the sand beside his neck.

My voice is nothing more than a guttural snarl, but I can't temper it. "Why are you still at my side?"

In the face of my rage, he dares to grin up at me, his eyes alight with energy. "There you are, my Veda."

"Answer my question!" I snap. "Why are you still here when your vow to me means nothing anymore?"

A faint crease appears in his forehead. "What are you talking about?"

I glare down at him. "I asked you to help me kill the man who murdered my father, imprisoned my mother, and stole the empire that should have been mine."

Still, his brow remains furrowed. "Yes?"

My fingers curl around his shoulders, my claws dragging through the sand and stopping dangerously close to cutting his skin. "Well. My father's alive. It's highly likely that my biological mother wasn't imprisoned, after all. And the Nostra Empire isn't mine to claim while my father lives."

"Ah." He doesn't look away, his dark eyes gleaming up at me as the furrow in his brow vanishes. "But that wasn't what I promised you."

I'm surprised. And wary.

My whisper is filled with skepticism. "What?"

He certainly doesn't seem remotely alarmed by the proximity of my claws. His dark gaze passes across my face while the tension releases from his shoulders, as if whatever he sees in my expression now reassures him.

"I promised you that in return for the power in your heart, I would give you the vengeance you seek," he says. "I vowed that whatever you need to achieve your revenge, I would do it."

His hands have come to rest low on my hips and now his thumbs stroke down toward my thighs. "When you asked me to help you kill the man who murdered your father and stole your empire, that was only the *how*. Not the *what*."

His fingers stop their downward descent to trace my curves upward while a challenging light enters his eyes, as if he's testing how much he can soothe me with his touch. "The *how* can change in the blink of an eye. But the *what* remains the same."

It isn't the response I expected.

I've spent every minute since learning that my father's alive with anxiety hovering at the back of my mind that I couldn't shake. All the while wondering why the keeper hadn't left my side already. And now it seems I needn't have worried at all.

His eyes flare with amber light and his voice hardens. "I promised you vengeance, my Veda. Brutal, bloody vengeance. And I plan to deliver it."

"Then… you're still bound to me."

"I am." He rears up beneath me, his hands stroking around my neck, sending shivers through me before he strokes my back, down and then up again. "And I will remain bound to you, until *you* decide your revenge is complete."

For the first time since I woke up in my father's lair, I feel like my foundations aren't quite so fragile.

I retract my claws, my hands finding the collar of his shirt. There's a gap between our chests, but my pelvis is pressed up against his core and the hardness of his body between my legs is undeniable despite his clothed state.

"My Veda," he says, his voice soft as his fingers reach my hair and trail through the strands. "You're cold. Will you let me warm you?"

"I... uh..." I consider the soft curve of his lips, the way he's drinking in my form.

A trickle of warmth slides down my spine from his look alone.

Softly, I ask, "How warm?"

"As warm as you like." His fingertips stroke down the side of my neck, my shoulder, then the outside of my arm, a light touch. "A little warm..."

Black light flares once more around his fingers and a sensation like flowing water passes from his fingertips across my breasts, making my nipples harden.

I gasp and he smiles.

"Or very warm," he says. "It's your choice."

I give a low moan. After all the pain I've experienced today, both physical and emotional, I need this balance.

I need the pleasure he's offering me.

"Very warm," I say, my anticipation growing before I remind myself that giving away control could hurt me as much as a fist. "But—"

"I know," he says quietly. "There are boundaries." His gaze becomes distant for a moment. "How did you put it? No *full-on cock and vagina* sex."

My cheeks heat a little, but not because of the way he repeated my description. I thought he'd been asleep when I said that to him. It was a moment of vulnerability I wouldn't normally indulge in.

At my nod, his smile returns.

"There's a whole world of pleasure to be experienced without that," he murmurs.

His fingertips resume tracing a circle on my upper arm, a swirling sensation that repeats itself around both of my breasts.

When the keeper's dark light flickers across my torso, pleasure spikes down to my core and my thighs clench around his waist.

Before I can lean forward to close the gap between his mouth and mine, he says, "My Veda, you're in control. Tell me more about your boundaries and I'll respect them."

Well, now I have to think.

Damn him for making it hard to concentrate.

But oh, he's waiting so patiently for me to respond, even though his power brushes down across my stomach to the tops of my thighs in tantalizing sweeps.

"Your mouth is welcome," I say, focusing on his lips, those lips that can look so fierce. Lips I want to capture mine. "So are your hands."

My forehead creases as I force myself to focus past the pleasure he's eliciting. "But don't go near my butt if you plan to go near my clit next. Not without washing your hands in between."

The woman in the cell may have kept secrets from me, but I don't doubt for a second what she taught me about staying healthy during and after sex—including all the ways to avoid getting a painful infection. Of course, my healing power defies many illnesses, but it's not something I want to risk.

His lazy smile immediately banishes my concerns. "It's a good thing there's a whole body of water nearby, then." He slowly closes the distance between us to brush his lips across mine, a tingling caress. "What a shame we might need to immerse in it at some point."

His hands glide from my thighs up to my neck, making me gasp when he brushes my nipples along the way, a quick touch that leaves me wanting more.

I'm just about to lean down to him and close the gap between his chest and mine when he wraps his arms around me and swiftly reverses our position, placing me on my back in the sand.

I'm completely naked while he's fully clothed. But not for long. His power flares, his shirt and long pants disappearing with the wash of magic across his body, although his underpants remain—a boundary of cloth that further confirms for me that he takes my wishes seriously.

He lowers his lips to mine, but he doesn't kiss me. Not a proper kiss. Only the slightest brush.

The one time we kissed deeply, he was half-asleep, and he wore a very different face and body to the one he's wearing now. A body with a golden sheen across it and a face I haven't seen since.

His mouth follows a path across my jaw, to my earlobe, down my neck, and across my collarbone, where he purses his lips and blows gently, dislodging the grains of sand that were stuck to me there.

The flowing air makes me shiver, my hands pressing to the sides of his bare chest. A harder press when his mouth closes over my left breast and his hand kneads my other.

Heat pools between my legs, a physical need that pulls me away from any shred of lingering anger and hurt.

I dig my fingers into the sand as he moves downward, his mouth taking a slow path to my core, making me shiver in anticipation.

Finally, his tongue flicks across the sensitive nub, a quick caress, followed by a longer one. Then he groans against my clit.

"Fuck me, you taste like beautiful darkness."

With a swift movement, he lifts my hips off the sand, hooking my legs over his shoulders, tilting my body to gain better access to my core. His hands play across my lower back, gripping my hips, then my backside as his tongue strokes become more demanding.

My body responds with a rush of need, moans leaving my lips as I give in to the instinct to press against his mouth.

But control is everything to me and within the haze of desire, I'm aware that *he* seems to be losing none of it.

His gaze darkens as he watches me from between my legs

and I reach for my own breasts, stroking them slowly, taking in his reaction.

"Touch yourself," I command him. "I want you to come when I do."

I sense him smile against me before he defies my wishes. "No."

My voice is ragged with need, sounds amid moans. "Why would you deny what I want?"

"Because you deserve all of my attention."

Well, damn. How can I argue with that?

I'm trying to think of a way when his dark light curls around his fingertips where they're stroking my lower back and travels along my sides, up to my shoulders, and then down across the sand.

"You deserve all the pleasure," he rumbles against me. "Will you take it or deny it?"

The sand swirls at my sides before sections of it transform into thick, glistening liquid.

I imagine this is what honey looks like—a food I definitely need to try.

The honeyed sand is soft and silken against my skin as it flows in strands up across my sides. It snakes across my stomach and to my breasts, where my fingertips rest. Two strands wrap around my wrists and solidify, still silken-feeling but now firm as they pull my hands away from my chest.

Within moments, my arms are pressed into the sand at my sides, ribbons of honey pinning them to the spot.

I don't struggle against the ropes, simply meet the keeper's dark eyes as his tongue continues to stroke me.

My body tells me to take the pleasure he's offering, even if he's now pushing my boundaries and we both know it.

"Take," I whisper.

His dark light lifts more sand, sending it stroking across my chest, up and around my neck, flowing across my lips, leaving sweetness on the tip of my tongue.

Within seconds, the honeyed strands are warming my skin like his fingertips, warm ribbons flowing across me, tightening and releasing, finding every pleasure point in my body until I'm no longer able to tell what's up and down, only that every aching muscle is relaxing. And tightening again. And relaxing again.

And tightening.

The keeper buries his head between my legs, his tongue pushing my senses to breaking point. And then further than I thought possible.

I try to steady my ragged breathing and delay the crash that's coming, but it's impossible.

The orgasm sweeps over me in a rush of heat, lifting me and crashing me down in hot waves that extend for long moments.

It feels like it could last forever, but I come back to myself far too soon, my mind and body flooding with awareness.

An awareness that's fueled by a basic but overwhelming, need.

I wrench against the honeyed strands that have slowed their flow across me. They crumble back into grit the moment I push against them, a wash of sand rushing off my torso.

I wrench my legs off the keeper's shoulders, twist, and come up in a crouch.

He remains kneeling, watching me warily now. "My Veda?"

"It wasn't enough," I snarl. "I need more."

CHAPTER TWENTY

There's a storm inside me and at its heart is a desperate, physical need. Far more intense than it was before.

Across from me, the keeper breaks into a dark smile.

Then he moves at a flash.

I gasp as his arms close around me and he pulls me up against him, wrapping my legs around his hips. The press of his hard length within his underpants meets my core, and I want more of it.

Now.

Before I know it, he's striding in the direction of the water.

"First, we're washing the sand off," he says.

I seek his neck, pressing my lips to the soft skin beneath his earlobe, my tongue hungrily meeting the tiny granules of sand that rest there. "You could do that with your magic."

"True," he rumbles, "but it would be much less fun."

He wades into the water, as far as I went before. "Take a deep breath, my Veda."

I lean back a little so he can see my face, take a deep breath, and then close my lips.

His smile broadens before he immerses us both into the waves.

I'm aware of his dark light streaming around us and the way the water doesn't tumble us around, leaving us in a sort of calm cocoon.

My hair billows softly around my head as he runs his hands through it, then across my shoulders and down my sides, his touch soothing within the weightlessness of the water.

Not soothing enough.

I press closer to him, crushing my breasts against his chest, hooking my ankles at his back, trying to ease this need deep within me. Trying to find its source.

It's deeper than my core. More than the physical parts of me.

And so fucking elusive.

Even more so because the keeper's face and body are changing, his shape shifting.

His body is like a dark shadow within the waves. Or maybe, more accurately, like the wraith he was when I first met him. The moonlight filters through the surface of the water above us and seems to stream through his form, stopping only when it reaches the ring on his finger.

For a moment, I experience a strange fear because it's as if...

He doesn't exist at all.

As if the ring could slip off his finger and nothing else would remain.

I grip him even harder, pressing forward, finding his lips, needing the crush of them, even if it means I lose my breath.

Air bubbles around our mouths as he kisses me back, a hungry kiss, his tongue flicking over mine, one arm closing across my upper back while his other hand wraps around the back of my head.

It's a desperate kiss, filled with all the heat and desire and longing that I need.

He is, once again, solid and strong within my arms.

I groan against his mouth, a sense of relief filling me, but it's a mere taste.

With a rush of movement, he lifts us up toward the sky.

Our heads break the surface and our kiss breaks at the same time, snatched away from me.

Dragon wings burst from his shoulders, black scales rippling across his skin as we burst upward, sending water spraying around us. He beats his wings, suspending us in the air above the water, moonlight streaming across us while his eyes transform. Fierce and reptilian and uncompromising. A dark beast with primal intentions.

My wet hair drips down my back and sides, water sloughing off my legs where they're wrapped around him, my sudden shiver so violent that I shake in his arms.

I don't know if it's anticipation or a strange sort of terror or even a deep relief after my moment of fear in the water.

"My Veda." He growls, a deep rumble that feeds my shiver. "My Veda, who gave me her heart."

Warmth rushes over me and with a flicker of his magic, every droplet of water evaporates from my body, my skin instantly dry and my unruly hair wafting around me.

I don't second-guess it. The air is awash with dark light and the reflections off his dragon scales—reflections that don't hurt my eyes.

He beats his wings and soars toward the building, landing lightly at the bottom of the steps before he carries me across the porch and through the doorway surrounded by softly billowing white curtains.

We enter a rectangular room that's large enough to be some sort of meeting room. The soft scent of grass wafts up from the floor, which is confusing because there isn't any grass in sight.

The floor is covered in very large, square-like mats of some sort of woven, beige-colored ribbons. Each mat has a dark edge, and they're all fitted neatly together so there are no gaps between them.

There's another doorway toward the far-right corner, but I'm not sure where it leads because the keeper turns in the other direction.

It's a little hard to tell in the dark, even with my sharp eyesight, but it looks like the walls are similarly beige-colored and made of large, but smooth, plaster panels, all meticulously put together.

With a flick of the keeper's fingers and a flash of emerald light—his warlock power rather than dark magic this time—he sends four little glowing balls of energy into each corner of the ceiling, giving off the merest hint of golden light through the room.

At the far left side of the room is a low-lying table—a large one with a top surface that looks wide and deep enough for eight people to sit around it. Assuming they were sitting on the floor, since it's so low to the ground.

He carries me toward the table, stopping directly in front of it, where he extricates my legs from around his hips, firmly placing me back on my feet.

His wings retract fully, but his dragon scales remain and his eyes are dark and beastly.

He wraps a hand in my hair again. "Take or deny?" he asks me, searching my eyes once more as if he's looking for me and uncertain if he'll find me.

The water did nothing to lessen the need within me. *How could it?*

I reach up on my tiptoes, wanting his mouth again, but he stops me with a firm grip on my head.

My lips rest an inch from his.

"Take," I say.

"Then turn around."

It's a command, but oh, how he's restraining his power.

I sense his immense self-control in the tension within his glistening shoulders, the flex of his fingers at the back of my head, and the way his lips press together in an unforgiving line.

Lips I want to kiss.

I hold his gaze until the very last moment as I do what he asks, turning in the circle of his arms while his hands fall away from me.

For a heartbeat, he isn't touching me, and the distance between us suddenly feels like falling into an abyss; a shockingly cold sensation that nearly makes me scream.

Before any sound can leave my lips, he pulls me against him, my back to his front.

I groan with relief at the contact, my breathing resuming, even though it's ragged.

One of his hands strokes my lower stomach while his other cups my breast. Slow, swirling strokes that increase the wetness between my upper thighs.

"I'm going to lay you across the edge of that table and I'm going to finger-fuck you now," he growls into my ear, tugging on my earlobe softly with his teeth. "If you want this, say so. If you don't, I won't."

Oh, I do.

But retaining control means making him wait three long seconds for my response.

Not that he seems to mind.

His fingers slip from my stomach toward the top of my clit, stroking across the edge of the folds. His lips graze my neck, his tongue licking at the water droplets that I'm surprised defied his power and still cling to the nape of my neck.

"Veda?" His mouth nudges at my skin.

The finger he continues to rest at the top of my clit—the *unmoving* finger—is driving me crazy with need.

My voice is hoarse. "Yes."

"Yes, what?"

"I want you to lay me across the edge of this table."

"And then what?"

I groan.

I nearly say, *"Fuck me,"* but I manage to make the distinction. "Fingers," I say. "But not more than two."

"I only need one," he whispers at my ear before he pulls me down to my knees and bends me forward.

I stretch my arms out across the table, relaxing into his hands as they sweep my hair to one side and stroke down my back, across my backside, and the backs of my thighs, easing all my muscles. Firm strokes that travel back up to my neck as his hips press into the back of mine, the material of his underpants a constant boundary between us.

He strokes my back and hips and thighs for so long that I'm rocking against him with need by the time he slips a finger inside me.

With just one finger, it feels as if he fills me completely.

I moan with relief as he pulls me back against his hip, his finger sliding deep within me while I brace my upper body by planting my hands on the table.

His other hand reaches around, his touch finding my clit and moving against it, and then I'm rocking against him, an impulse to move that sweeps me up into a storm of sensations.

I push against the table and into him as dark light flares around us and his power strikes through me, a flood of heat reaching my heart and my mind.

It feels like a closing loop, a completion that I desperately need.

Abandoning every other thought, I take the pleasure he's giving me, accepting the stroke of his hand against my clit and the push of his finger within me and the wild ache that's building to a crash that brings a scream to my lips.

It's a wild, needy cry. Because the crashing sensation only grows stronger, building until I'm ramming myself against him, pushing so hard against the table that it grinds across the floor.

The tiles beneath it tear apart, but I don't care that I'm ripping them up. Or the table, for that matter, when my claws extend and I ram them into the wooden surface to anchor myself as hard as I can.

Through my pleasure, the tension in the keeper's body strikes me, even though he's behind me and I can't see his face.

His soft curse reaches me beneath my moans.

"Fuck."

I can barely form intelligible sound as I rock wildly against him. "Come with me."

He doesn't argue. His hand leaves my clit. I'm aware of the sudden nakedness of his skin pressing against the back of my thigh, the absence of that material boundary, but he doesn't take his finger from within me, and I know he won't step over the line I've put in place.

He pulls my thighs together, his hard length grinding between them, matching every thrust with his finger.

Finally, I let go.

A release that drags me into beautiful, screaming darkness.

Wave after wave, it's like pure, endless night. A peace I didn't think I could feel.

Somewhere in the middle of it, I'm aware of the keeper's groan, his deep shudder, and the increasing slickness between my legs.

I ride the night within my mind, the darkness within my body, until it fades, little by little, the beautiful completion slipping away from me.

I'm not afraid to leave it behind.

What's waiting for me is worth coming back to.

I return to myself with a satisfied groan on my lips.

Oh, what a glorious mess we've made.

The table has torn through the mats. My claws cut and

scratched the wooden surface. And there's a wet patch on the floor between my knees.

But it's the keeper I need to see right now.

I'm turning even as he's pulling me around to face him. I catch the flash of his dark-blue eyes before he clasps me up against his chest.

At some point, he must have shifted back into his darkest persona. The angry one. Maybe it was when he cursed. Maybe earlier or later. It doesn't matter as he lays us down on the floor —the undamaged section behind him.

Whatever grassy-scented material the mats are made of, they're soft. Lying on them feels faintly prickly but oddly comfortable.

Resting my head against the keeper's shoulder and nestling into his side, I quietly hook one leg across his hips, a possessive move.

But as I settle against him, he rubs his chest, and I lift my head to reach across and press my palm to his heart. "Hurting?"

I'm uncertain why he would be feeling pain since I'm certainly not hurting right now.

He shakes his head, his dark hair splaying across the floor.

"We're bonded. You and I," he says, his blue eyes shadowed. "A bond of fire and betrayal."

My chest suddenly squeezes and my breath stills. I'm reminded that we are both dark creatures, born to lie and cheat and betray each other.

Born to be alone.

But I will defy that.

Take or deny—that's what he asked me—and by fuck, I'll take everything and deny the risks.

I breathe through the tightness in my chest and softly arch an eyebrow at him. "That sounds mildly ominous."

The shadows clear from his expression. His chest moves

beneath me, a sudden rumbling sensation as he gives a light chuckle. "It does."

"Although I'll agree with the fire part," I say, attempting to press kisses to his chest while he laughs. Difficult while his torso is bumping up and down.

His smile slowly fades as his fingers trace the curve of my hips, a hint of desire darkening his eyes again. His lips press to the top of my head, then to my neck as he pushes me onto my back, his mouth traveling languidly down to my breasts, nudging against my nipples.

I'm surprised when my body responds and a needy ache builds between my legs.

"I can't possibly go again," I say with a soft laugh.

He arches an eyebrow at me. "If you're certain?"

I narrow my eyes in thought. *Am I?*

While I give it some serious consideration, he presses a kiss to my jaw, his lips whispering a path up to my ear, then across to my jaw, then briefly to my lips.

His voice is hushed as he speaks, and I become very still to listen.

"When I saw you... broken and bloody... I felt something I didn't expect to feel."

I meet his eyes, my heated thoughts banished by his solemn tone. "What was that?"

"Fear," he says.

A little confused, I tilt my head, my hair fanning out against the floor. "But you had nothing to fear in that situation. There was no threat to your life." I rethink what I just said. "Well, not until I asked you to rescue Lucian."

"Nothing to fear?" he asks, moving swiftly, his arms sliding around my back as he pulls me up into a sitting position, my legs around his hips.

His hands cup my cheeks, run through my hair, and slide

down my back. He grips my hips and pulls me closer to him, grinding my core against the top of his length.

His voice is rough, his breathing rougher. "You think I had nothing to fear when I saw you so broken, I thought I might not be able to save you?"

My eyes widen. "You were afraid... for *me*."

"Why did that not occur to you?" he asks.

His cock is hard beneath me, the press of my core against him creating the intense temptation to defy my own boundaries and slide back enough to take him inside me.

My response is ragged. "Because love is a lie."

I run my hands across his shoulders and upward, pressing one palm against the back of his head and wrapping the other around the back of his neck. "Dark creatures can bond, form alliances—even have family. But we can't love. Or be loved in return."

His hands tighten on my hips, a rough pull toward him, as if he disagrees.

I wait for him to say so.

The glare in my eyes *dares* him to tell me I'm wrong.

Control. Power. Pleasure. It's all a dark storm inside my mind, but pleasure is my dominant need once more.

His pleasure as well as mine. Dragging me toward a peak that I want more than anything.

His hands are tangled in my hair, his forehead against mine as he continues to grind me against him, my wetness making the movement slick.

"One day, you will allow yourself to lose control," he snarls.

Maybe.

Maybe.

I throw my head back and let the release take me, hot and chaotic, clashing sensations of hard and wet driving me to an edge I want to step over but won't.

CHAPTER TWENTY-ONE

The morning sunlight hurts my eyes.

It blazes beyond my eyelids, making it impossible for me to open them.

With a groan, I reach across the floor, hoping to find something I can use as a blindfold. In the next moment, the keeper's voice sounds and soft material is pressed against my arm. "Use this. It's a strip of material from the curtains."

I crack my eyes open to take a quick look at the cloth before wrapping it around my eyes. It has a gauzy weave, but it's wide enough for me to fold it over a few times, and then it's the perfect thickness to protect me from the sun's glare.

Sitting up, I find the keeper kneeling beside me, holding out a little, black cup. It doesn't have a handle and the rim is a dark, glossy, green color.

It's steaming and its contents smell like grass, similar to the floor.

I consider the liquid with wariness. "What is that?"

"Green tea."

I take the cup and sip at the liquid, expecting to dislike it because of its smell. It's unexpectedly refreshing and, by the time I swallow the last drop, I'm no longer feeling sleepy. "Why do I feel more alert?"

"It contains something called caffeine." He shrugs. "Or so I recall from a dark creature's memories."

He rises to his feet, his gaze passing from my tangled hair to my bare toes before he gestures to the side of the room. "As much as I like you naked, there's plenty of clothing this way."

We remained in this large room for the rest of the night before we fell asleep here.

Other than the light, not much has changed. The curtains continue to billow in the windows and beside the door, although one of the curtains is visibly shorter than the others and I guess that's the one from which my blindfold came.

The air brings with it the intensely salty tang of the sea and feels filled with moisture, probably the cause of my clumped hair and sticky skin.

Well, maybe I can't blame the salty air for all of it.

I side-eye the keeper with a satisfied smile as I rise to my feet, and sashay past him with the cup in hand.

My stomach growls on the way.

"I don't suppose there's food in here, too?"

"Unfortunately not. There's a little kitchen to the side of the back room, along with a small bathroom, but the kitchen contains only tea-making facilities."

At my groan of disappointment, he continues.

"But your brother was true to his promise and arrived at the crack of dawn, asking how you were. I told him to come back with food."

"At the crack of dawn, huh?" My question is a careful one. "I take it you didn't sleep much?"

The keeper feels the pain of my dreams and he once explained to me that they can keep him awake.

"Your nightmares were worse last night," he says.

I suppose I hoped they might not be. I try to shake off the

dream of a home that never existed and a mother who is somehow always out of my reach.

"I'm sorry," I say, but he wraps his hand around my shoulder.

"Don't apologize for your pain. You have a right to feel it."

The intensity of his anger surprises me.

"I don't have the right to hurt you with it." I lean in to him, conscious of my nakedness and the warmth of his body. Even fully-clothed, his heat is a comfort. "I would rather put my pain to good use than waste it on nightmares."

How I'm going to put my pain to use is the question, and I don't have an answer for that yet.

Pushing myself up on to my tiptoes, I plant a little kiss on the edge of his jaw.

Then I step out of his hold and into the very large dressing room at the side of the front room.

Three walls are lined with shelves containing what appear to be items of folded clothing. Every item is white or black.

To the left is the bathroom the keeper mentioned. After using it and returning the cup to the little shelf in the small kitchen, I return to rifle through the shelves of clothing.

I discover that it's mostly tunics and long pants, all made from a light material. Soft to touch. And in all sizes, with the smaller items on the bottom shelves and the largest items at the top.

I choose a black tunic and hold it up to my frame, testing its size. Too big. The one on the next shelf down seems perfect.

"Why are there so many different sizes here?"

"This building was some sort of training hall," he says. "The clothing was for the students."

I purse my lips. "What kind of training?"

"Combat."

Well, that makes sense. "What kind of students?"

He shrugs. "Dark creatures."

I scowl at his evasive answer, but I let it go. "There's no underwear here."

"Over on this side." He heads to a shelf on the other side of the room that holds a row of baskets. "I investigated the options while you were sleeping."

After tipping a basket toward me so I can see inside it, he pulls out what looks like a bra, although it's a little less structured than the ones I've seen before.

"What about this?" he asks.

"Okay, yes." I take it, find that it's too big, and test another, which is perfect.

The next basket contains a style of underpants that extend down to the tops of my thighs and then a little farther. They're a far cry from the stringy pieces of material that were in the witch's apartment.

I return to the shelves containing tunics and pants, adjusting my blindfold, which got a little out of place when I pulled on the bra. "Do you think I'll ever get used to the light?"

"I wish I could help with that." The keeper holds up his hand to wave dark light through the air before closing his fist and snuffing it out. "But it would require making your eyes less sensitive to light."

"Yes," I say wryly. "That would be the point."

"Which could have unwanted side effects in dark situations," he continues. "As it currently stands, your eyesight is extremely powerful. I don't think it's a good idea to take that away."

"Fair point," I grumble before I shrug. "My eyes *are* slowly adjusting to the light in the outside world. I can tolerate full moonlight now. So I guess I just need to be patient."

I pull on a pair of black pants, followed by the tunic I chose before. Then I attempt to straighten the strands of my hair so I can braid it. It's a thankless task.

"Let me," the keeper says, emerald light glimmering around his fingertips.

I remain still as his magic curls around the clumped strands, separating them. He's careful. Never tugs. Finally, my hair falls softly down my back once more.

I'm quiet when he finishes, and he looks to me with a question. "My Veda?"

"She called me *Daughter*."

His hands close around my shoulders before he slides his arms around me, pulling me close to his chest.

I swallow past the lump in my throat. "She called me *Daughter* and I called her *Mother*."

And now I don't know what I'm supposed to feel.

I sense his nod, his cheek lowering to brush mine. "Names have power."

They do. Which is why it hasn't escaped me that, ever since the keeper found me in my father's lair, he has called me, 'my Veda'.

My Conqueror.

Our fates are bound, just like he said.

He promised me that *I* will decide when my vengeance is achieved, and after that…

Well, I'm not really sure what will happen once the keeper's no longer bound to me.

Assuming we survive, he will have choices and so will I.

It's all a huge unknown, but I tell myself to focus on the present, not the *what ifs*.

I let myself rest for a moment in his arms, listening to the silence outside the building. Well, not silence, exactly. The waves on the beach make a constant *whooshing* sound. The soft breeze filters through the far doors. In the far distance, I can hear the creaking of tree branches, even the furtive scurrying of little creatures.

Closer to us, I make out the crunch of footfalls on the sand.

Lucian must be coming back.

Judging by the number of footfalls, he isn't alone.

I picture Anarchy, whose two-legged steps are lighter than Lucian's heavier gait, along with the three male panthers, whose padding paws sound a little heavier than they did last night.

They must have had a good meal.

The deliciousness of the scents wafting ahead of them indicates that they're bringing the food the keeper asked for.

My stomach growls again, but I pause a moment longer.

"How long do you think we can stay here?" I ask the keeper.

"In this training hall or on this island?"

I tip my head back. "Why do you make that distinction?"

He breaks into a grin. "Because there's a lot more to this island than this training hall."

I'm sure my eyes have lit up. "I want to see everything."

Back in my father's lair, I had regrets.

I'd barely lived when I thought I was about die.

I won't make that mistake now. I won't waste the time I have.

I lean inward, seeking his lips. "I want to fill my chest with fresh air, swim in the ocean, run through the jungle, eat until my stomach feels like it's going to burst, and experience everything else this island has to offer."

His fingertips feather my jaw as his lips nudge mine. "You can have it all, my Veda." His gaze heats me all the way to my pointed toes. "I want you to have it all."

CHAPTER TWENTY-TWO

The crunching footfalls outside the training hall are rapidly drawing nearer.

I step out of the keeper's arms and head out to meet them—my family. My pack. Because that's what they are to me now. I may not believe in love, but I believe in connection and loyalty.

Hurrying through the training room, I reach the edge of the porch just as they arrive at the bottom of it.

Lucian and Anarchy are both dressed in the same style of clothing that I'm wearing—both in black. They're also each carrying a large, covered bowl, from which the delicious smells are drifting.

The panthers race up the steps before I can descend to them, their silver eyes bright. They greet me with purrs, their big bodies pushing me this way and that until I'm forced to kneel so they don't knock me over.

I greet them each in turn, nudging my head against theirs. "Riot, Rumble, Strife."

Anarchy hurries up to the porch, deposits the bowl off to the side, and pushes through the panthers to drop to her knees and give me a hug.

Oh. I was not expecting this.

The strength in her slender arms is surprising, but it's the way she presses her cheek to mine that gives me an incredible sense of comfort.

She draws back, her hands resting on my shoulders, her pale-blue eyes solemn, and her lips pressed in a worried line. "How are you?"

She's searching the location of my eyes, even though the blindfold will conceal them from her.

I take a quick breath and exhale it slowly.

"I'm okay," I say.

She gently arches an eyebrow at me. "Really?"

I grimace, knowing that she'll be listening to the tone of my voice for clues as to my actual state of wellbeing. "Well… Not really… but I'm working through it. I'll feel better once I figure out what I'm supposed to do."

She gives an emphatic nod. "We're here for you when you make that decision. All of us."

Lucian has hung back, only now reaching the top of the steps, but he wears a significantly more concerned look on his face than Anarchy. "Veda, did you hurt your eyes?"

Oh, that's right. He's never seen me wear a blindfold. When I met him on the train, I was wearing sunglasses. And then, in my father's lair, it was so dark, I didn't need anything to protect my eyes.

"My eyes don't tolerate bright light yet," I explain as Anarchy shifts to the side, giving me a direct line of sight to Lucian. "All those years in a dark cell took their toll."

"Oh." He seems to take a breath. "Of course." His focus shifts to the keeper, who is a glowering presence in the porch doorway.

Lucian instantly scowls back, the aura of shadows around his form darkening. "We brought food."

Before the keeper can respond, I give a groan of appreciation. "*Food.*" Then, "Where can we eat it?"

There aren't any tables or chairs within the training area or dressing room.

"This way." The keeper is already moving past me with a gleam in his eyes. "It isn't far, I promise. Just around the back."

Anarchy scoops up her bowl and then we follow the keeper down the steps and to the right, heading around the back of the training hall. Along the way, I scoop up my dropped clothing from last night—the blood-stained jeans, bra, and underpants—and chuck them onto the porch.

When we reach the back of the building, I'm pleased to find a shaded clearing with a large, paved courtyard surrounded by trees. Their inner branches stretch across the air above us all the way toward the middle, where the boughs seem to have knitted together. The canopy they form allows only the softest sunlight to filter through, reducing the glare and making it possible for me to lift the edge of the blindfold.

Hmm. A gentle stab of pain tells me I'm not quite ready for this level of light yet. But hopefully soon.

Stone tables and stools are situated around the clearing, forming a neat, circular pattern. Moss extends from the base of the trees around the edge and meanders toward the tables, along with a few vines.

The entire area is simple, but everything is in balance. It seems to have been meticulously designed. Even a dark creature like me can appreciate the sense of peace it invokes.

It's also nowhere near overgrown. Which makes me wonder if whatever beings lived here might have died not so long ago.

I'm not sure if I should be worried about that, but my hunger is too demanding right now to focus on much else.

Anarchy and Lucian deposit the bowls onto the nearest stone table and I'm quick to lift off the lids.

Each bowl is filled with noodles immersed in cloudy-looking broth and I'm instantly salivating.

"We ate already," Anarchy explains when she and Lucian sit down but don't touch either of the bowls.

The panthers position themselves like guards around the perimeter of the clearing, but the keeper sits closest to me on my left, wraps his fingertips around the edge of the other bowl, and watches me carefully as he pulls it toward himself.

Well, I guess I did imagine myself devouring both of them, but I can share. Especially given that he must be as hungry as I am.

But... "How do I eat this?"

"Oh!" Anarchy reaches into the deep pocket at the front of her tunic. She produces two ivory-colored sticks with gently tapered ends and hands them to me, then another two to the keeper. "Here."

I grip them in my fist. "Huh?"

"Chopsticks," she says.

Have I seen these in a book? While I rack my memory, Lucian rounds the table.

"Let me show you."

I hand over the sticks and he gives a demonstration, deftly holding the sticks in one hand and using them to lift several noodles at once.

"Don't be afraid to slurp," he says with a grin.

The keeper is studying the demonstration too but scowls back at Lucian when my brother notices.

Lucian hands the chopsticks back to me. "Try it."

I mimic the finger position and before I know it, I'm slurping noodles like I've been eating them my whole life.

Every mouthful brings a groan of happiness to my lips. "This is delicious."

Different to hamburgers and pizza, but so incredibly tasty despite how simple it looks.

Lucian's smile broadens and it makes me wonder if he was the one who did the cooking. As if he reads my mind, he murmurs, "A small atonement."

I give him a nod, acknowledging his effort.

Within minutes, I'm halfway through the bowl and about to start on the other half when, opposite me, Anarchy and Lucian start exchanging glances.

It makes me nervous.

I pause with a noodle half out of my mouth, biting it off to ask, "What's going on?"

"I have something to show you," Anarchy says. "Something unexpected."

I put down my bowl, instantly tense. "Good or bad?"

Before Anarchy can answer me, Rumble gives a snarl from the side of the clearing, drawing our attention. At the exact same moment, the hairs on the back of my neck stand on end, and the keeper rises hurriedly from his seat.

"Something's coming," he says, studying the trees around us with a deepening furrow in his brow. "Multiple somethings. But I can't tell which direction they're coming from."

The panthers, too, are circling the clearing with increasingly agitated steps, their ears pricked up, but the way their heads are turning from side to side indicates they're equally confused about the location of the threat.

I've suddenly lost my appetite. I can't sense any sort of approaching physical presence. It's more like a very distant energy that's coming closer with every passing second.

The hairs on the back of my neck are now prickling so badly that it's as intense as the crawling sensation I experience before my wings burst from my back.

Whatever's coming through the trees, it's triggering my survival instincts beyond what I might be able to control.

No! I don't want my wings to reveal themselves. I need to control when that happens.

Revealing them needs to be on my terms.

But, dark saints, they're pushing at my skin, threatening to tear through, and the sensation is only getting worse.

I jump up from my seat, positioning my back away from my family, trying to focus on something other than my panic. "Could the creatures who lived here before have come back?"

"Not a chance." The keeper shakes his head firmly. His form doesn't change—remaining blue-eyed—but a myriad of magic is building around his hands. Black light, sapphire light, emerald light—even pink light, which I can't recall seeing him use before.

Despite the tension in his shoulders and the intense concentration on his face, he suddenly throws me a dark grin.

"The shark shifters who lived here before were annihilated," he says. "I promise you."

Wait... what? *Shark shifters?*

My eyebrows shoot up, and I stop backing away.

There's no such thing.

My panic is momentarily dampened by my skepticism, and I latch on to that new emotion because it's a damn sight more welcome to me right now than the fear that was pushing at my body.

A glance at Anarchy and Lucian tells me they're also thrown by the mention of shark shifters. They exchange quick glances with each other, their eyebrows raised.

My interpretation of their response is confirmed when Lucian mutters, "No such thing."

I spin back to the keeper. I'm not sure why he'd make up shark shifters right now, but I scowl at him as I echo what Lucian said. "There's no such thing as a shark shifter."

The keeper looks affronted. "How do you know?"

"Because the woman who raised me never mentioned them."

Now, it's the keeper who's arching an eyebrow at me. "Spent a lot of time in the ocean, did she?"

"Well. Maybe." I plant my hands on my hips. "I don't know. She might have."

His small smile becomes a wide grin. "If you insist, my Veda."

I meet his eyes.

He tips his head a little before he taps his chest, all the power around his hand splashing like a rainbow across his torso.

It's the gesture he makes when he's telling me he feels my emotions.

Oh.

He must have sensed my panic. A panic that wasn't doing me any favors.

He may not be able to discern *why* I felt it, but he pulled me away from it. The sensation in my back has settled. It's still there—a dangerous sensation that's being triggered for reasons I can't explain. But it's under control again.

"Well," I say softly, "if we aren't dealing with shark shifters, what could be coming for us?"

His grin fades. "Like I said last night, I placed protections around this island from the moment we arrived. We shouldn't be dealing with anything."

"Creatures strong enough to break through your protections, then?"

He gives a single nod. "I'm not sure *how* they could break through, but yes."

With a shiver, I whisper, "I asked the wrong question before, didn't I?"

Again, he nods.

"It doesn't matter what kind of creatures lived here before," I say. "It matters what killed them."

CHAPTER TWENTY-THREE

At that moment, a high-pitched shriek breaks the air. It isn't like a scream. More like the sound of something approaching so fast that it's causing the air pressure to change.

Pain stabs through my head and I slap my hands over my ears. *"Fuck."*

I'm suddenly pulled back to the moment when the spell around my cell broke open.

I'd felt a *pop* in my ears as strong as this.

The male panthers have also flinched, jolting to the side with their eyes squeezed closed, hisses leaving their lips. Anarchy is grimacing, but it seems more in empathy for her brothers than on her own behalf, since her focus is on them.

Lucian has jumped out of his seat, tipping his head back as he gives a warning cry. "They're in the sky!"

Except that we can't see the sky because of the canopy.

Damn. If they're in the air, it could explain why my wings were pushing at my back. Some sort of inbuilt instinct telling me I might need them.

Indeed, Lucian releases his own wings at that moment, as if in response to the threat. The dark shadows of his aura gather around his body and I see once again the face of a cold killer that he wore when I first met him.

Anarchy, too, is now poised on her front foot, her focus on the pathway back to the beach.

But I take a breath.

"We have a choice," I say. "Diavolo can transport us out of here in the blink of an eye. We don't have to meet these creatures head on—whoever or whatever they are. We could escape and go… somewhere else."

Even though I need this place.

It's given me the first peace I've experienced since I escaped from the prison and I haven't yet done a single thing that I told the keeper I wanted to do.

Anarchy, Lucian, and the panthers are all angling toward the path, as if they're about to break into a run, but I'm not sure if they plan to veer toward the keeper or head out toward the beach, where we'll be able to see the threat.

"Run or fight?" I ask, casting my question at all of them.

The panthers snarl at me, their noses wrinkled. I'm attuned enough to their emotions to understand that they're insulted.

Anarchy and Lucian answer me by veering wide of the keeper and heading in the direction of the beach. Lucian seems to have barely registered my question, but Anarchy arches an eyebrow at me.

"Oh, my Veda," the keeper says, grinning at me by the time I reach him. "You already know the answer."

Fight.

I don't hesitate another moment, breaking into a run.

Anarchy and Lucian see me coming and increase their speed, racing along the side of the building with the panthers close behind them.

The keeper is a wash of dark energy bringing up the rear, a soothing presence in the face of the unknown we're facing.

We burst onto the wide, white beach.

The air above us is clear for another second before it fills with streaks of energy.

Fifteen figures shoot through the air, seven of them from the east and the other eight from the west, approaching so fast that their bodies are mere streaks of energy.

Each streak halts so abruptly that multiple cracks sound, each one as sharp as a whip snapping across the sky.

All fifteen figures—eight men and seven women—now hover in the air above us, positioned in a very strategic-looking oval in the air that will allow them to cut us off from every direction.

My strong eyesight allows me to see the details of their features through the gauzy blindfold. They're wearing clothing similar to ours, but in a variety of colors from blood red to sky blue. Their pants are long, but their short sleeves and V-necks reveal skin that's dusted in brilliant scales, also of different colors, from cream to sapphire to bronze.

These supernaturals may not have auras, but their dragon scales and wings are unmistakable.

I'm looking at the first dragon shifters I've come across since escaping my cell. Well, the first I've known about.

We gather in a circle, back to back, facing the threat in the sky.

One of the women tucks her wings and soars a little closer. She has pale-teal scales and wings that are a dark teal at the top merging into glistening ivory at the tips.

Her hair is inky black—in fact, they all have dark hair—but hers has bright-teal streaks running through it.

"We are the Dragon Masters," she says, as if we should bow down immediately and grovel at her feet. "You're trespassing on land that rightfully belongs to us and—"

"Don't tell me," I interrupt her. "The penalty for trespassing is death."

She narrows her eyes at me. "Well, you're a clever one."

"Used to dealing with stupid supernaturals, are you?"

She shrugs. "In my experience, dark creatures aren't the smartest." She gives me a sweet smile. "So to avoid misunderstandings, I'll spell it out for you: We're here to kill you."

I know she's trying to goad me into reacting recklessly. I tell myself not to fall for it. But, by fuck, her patronizing tone is making me mad. And besides, like she said, they're here to kill us, so it won't matter what I say.

We may as well get this fight started.

I allow my claws to descend and my teeth to sharpen, picturing my two sharp, black canines as they reveal themselves.

Directly to my left, Anarchy draws back her lips, showing off her fangs while Lucian, who is on *her* left, rolls his shoulders and extends his wings, shadows gathering around his form despite the early morning sunlight.

I'm even more grateful for my blindfold now. I'd be struggling in this light without it.

As for the keeper, who is directly to my right, I'm startled to see that, in the seconds since we reached the beach, his form has changed and he's now wearing a face I've never seen before.

Although he's still humanoid, his skin has become a dark blue, the hair on his head has disappeared, and his body has increased in size—apparently so fast that his clothing is torn across his chest and thighs.

It's the smell of death around him that really hits me. I don't love sunlight, but the scent of darkness clinging to his body seems to make the light disappear, banishing all happiness with it.

I may not have recognized what he was the first time he turned into a demon of smoke and ash, but I recognize the creature he's become now.

It scares the fuck out of me.

I'm gratified to see the teal-haired dragon master's eyes have widened while her comrades all edge back from us in the air.

"A draugr outside its den," the teal-haired one whispers. "*Impossible.*"

Draugr are undead warriors. They usually exist in the place where they died, remaining there to protect whatever treasure they had been seeking. They can change their sizes at whim and can only be killed by decapitation. Which I'm sure the dragons will try. I imagine the keeper will then employ his smoke-demon form to evade their every effort to cleave him into pieces.

He smiles at me. It's a hideously ugly grin that reveals blue teeth, all of which have sharp tips.

Hmm. Draugr don't usually have sharp teeth like that. An embellishment, no doubt. *Hell, why not?*

Above us, the teal-haired dragon is now scowling. I'm sure she won't be happy that she revealed a hint of concern at the keeper's appearance.

I tip my chin at her and widen my smile—mostly because with my lips drawn wide, she can get a good look at my own dangerous teeth.

Then I call up to her. "Come on down here, Dragon Master, and let's see who's stupid."

"Gladly." She doesn't hesitate a moment longer, tucking her wings and swooping straight for me.

At the same time, the other dragons attack, shooting down from the sky toward us.

I plant my feet and ready my claws for the teal-haired woman's first strike, but just as she would reach me—just as the air shifts with the force of her approach—Riot appears from behind me.

His panther body is a vicious blur, his front claws slashing the air in silver streaks and his snarls making the hairs on my arms stand on end.

He crashes into the teal-haired dragon from the side, knocking her so hard across the sand that she spins in midair, her wings tucking inward a split second before she tumbles across the beach, splashing up white grit. Riot leaps after her, his athletic body and legs stretching and giving him incredible speed.

I don't have time to see what happens next between them.

Another dragon is upon me, this one a man with fists that crash through the air at speeds that take my breath away.

My reflexes fire as I evade each blow, darting backward and to the side, watching for the opportunity to ram my claws through any part of his body.

Damn, he's fast.

For now, all I can do is avoid his rapid kicks and punches, each one coming at me fast enough to make my head spin.

Around me, the fight has already extended across the beach and the air is filled with sparkling sand and the sounds of thrashing wings and battling bodies.

The keeper leaps high enough to pluck two dragons from the air simultaneously, a move that propels him farther down the beach before he throws one of them into the sand with a bone-breaking *thud* and the other out across the ocean—right before another four soar after him.

Lucian has taken to the air on my left and is grappling with a male dragon shifter, their fight taking them over the top of the training hall. He lands a punch to the man's face that sends him straight down into the sand at the side of the hall. The man hits the ground with a massive *thump*. If he'd fallen a little to the left, he would have crashed through the roof.

Fuck, my brother can hit.

It brings home to me just how strong our father must be that the whack Lucian gave him over the head did no damage at all.

Like the keeper, Lucian barely has time to take a breath

before another two dragons charge at him, one male and one female.

Spread out on the sand behind me, Anarchy and her remaining two brothers are fighting in coordination with each other, well and truly holding their own against the final four shifters.

I can't see Riot now. He could be much farther along the beach with the teal-haired dragon, or his fight with her could have taken him into the trees.

I take in everything around me in a flash, a mere blink of an eye, but I suppose the dragon coming at me thinks I'm distracted because he makes a reckless move.

His hand reaches for my throat.

At the same time, he sweeps his wings, as if he intends to wrap his fist around my neck, lift me off the ground, and break my neck. But it was smarter for him to keep employing quick hits and moving fast. As soon as I allow his hand to close around my throat, his outstretched arm becomes a stationary target for my claws.

My feet have barely left the sand, the force of his attack lifting me from the ground, when I slash at his wrist, slicing through his scales.

The pain in his arm must register fast enough that it saves him.

His eyes fly wide and he retracts his hand so quickly that the air shrieks around him, the same screeching sound as when the dragons first arrived.

My claws scrape across the top of his fingers as he darts backward, and I imagine I've removed scales but not much else before he backpedals in a rush of wind.

A moment later, Rumble appears in a blur, leaping past me on my right, crashing into the retreating dragon. Rumble leaps, catches the edge of the man's wing in his powerful jaws, and snatches him from the air.

I spin to the dragons behind me, ready to help Anarchy and Strife, only to pull up short.

While Strife has pinned one of the dragons to the ground about ten paces away—a dragon who appears to be on the verge of unconsciousness—Anarchy is fighting the remaining three.

She moves like a graceful reed, using every part of her body to block and then retaliate against every strike they throw her way.

It's like watching her dance.

She's barely breaking a sweat. Her pale-lilac hair flies about her head as she moves fluidly from one spot to the next, spinning and ducking, only to land hard hits to her opponents' lower backs, necks, ribs, one after the other, as if she controls the very air around her.

It's fucking mesmerizing.

And then, to my surprise, she leaps, her body transforming midair into the shape of a panther once more.

A cry of surprise leaves my lips.

She can shift!

This must be the unexpected thing she was about to tell me about when the dragons arrived.

Her teeth sink into her opponent's shoulder before she shifts back into her dark elf form, leaping away from his unconscious body before he's even hit the sand.

She spins and catches the next man around his neck, forcing him to bend backward at the waist and, before he can right himself, she once again sinks her teeth into his neck—this time while she's in her elf form. Like the first man, it's the quickest graze, but he plummets to the sand, his eyes closed and his legs folded awkwardly beneath him.

Within seconds, she's bitten the remaining dragon, laying his unconscious body neatly down onto the white sand.

"Goodnight, sweet dragon," she whispers before she lifts her gaze to mine and gives me a smile. "Out like a light."

I wonder if she's making a joke. Dragon shifters are powerful creatures of light magic. In fact, they're on par with angels.

She gestures to the men lying on the ground around her. "I've left them alive for you to interrogate them when they wake up. But they'll sleep for a few hours first."

"Oh, my fucking dark saints." I can't seem to do anything but stare at her. She's barely broken a sweat. "You *have* to teach me how to fight like that."

I'm not too proud to admit that I need her skills. The woman who raised me taught me how to fight dirty. Basic survival moves that rely heavily on my claws. She didn't teach me how to fight in a way that could result in complete domination of my opponents.

I need that.

I *needed* that when I was fighting my father.

Anarchy slaps the sand off her hands and arms and steps over the unconscious man lying between us. "Anytime, Darkness."

Her focus quickly turns to Lucian, then flickers to the keeper. Both are holding their own, but a little help can't hurt.

"Strife and I will help Lucian," she says, indicating the panther who has returned to her side.

"I'll get the keeper." I'm preparing to break into a sprint toward him when Anarchy's eyes widen.

"Darkness!" she shouts. "Look out!"

She dives toward me, a desperate expression flooding her face at the same time a shadow descends over me.

The shadow is accompanied by a shriek of sound so piercing that it cuts through my hearing and for a terrible moment, everything goes black as I pass out from the pain. It's only for a second, but it's long enough for my legs to buckle.

I sense Anarchy's fingertips brush my arm before a male body collides with me and I'm whisked into the air.

CHAPTER TWENTY-FOUR

*A*narchy's scream is snatched away in the wind.

The speed of the attack knocks the air from my lungs and crushes my ribs. Oh, wait, no, that's the guy's arms, wrapped around me like bands of iron from which I can't escape.

Unlike the first group of dragons, this assailant doesn't come to a quick stop.

Within heartbeats, we've left the beach far behind and ocean waves crash beneath me. *Enormous* waves that would drag me down and drown me within moments if I were to fall into them.

My attacker finally pulls to a halt, but it's so abrupt that he nearly flings me wide. Suddenly, I'm holding on to him as hard as I can, my legs wrapped around his hips and my hands gripping his sides for dear life.

On instinct, I've retracted my claws, because hell, if I cut him to shreds, I'll only fall, and I'm not ready to deal with that yet.

"Wolf," he snarls. "You don't belong here."

I don't waste time screaming. My goals right now are simple: stay airborne while snatching enough air that I can breathe again.

"Who says I don't?" I gasp.

"Me." He growls.

I risk a look at his face. So far, I've ascertained that he's solidly built, a slender body with a lot of muscle, but by fuck, his face should belong to an angel. Certainly not to a man threatening to kill me.

Jagged, black hair whips around his head. It's hard to tell in the wind, but it's probably shoulder length. His eyes are dark brown and fierce-looking beneath black eyebrows. In contrast, his skin is dusted with silver scales and his wings reflect the sunlight so brightly that I'm struggling to keep my eyes open. The gauze in the blindfold isn't helping.

I'm lucky he's once again busy pinning my arms to my sides or he'd be able to rip off the material and then I'd be in even more trouble.

"Well, who are *you*?" I ask.

"My name is Ryuji. I'm the alpha of the Kaito Dragon Family. It's my sworn duty to destroy any dark creature who dares to step into my territory."

I guess I didn't really need to ask. I thought the teal-haired woman was in charge, but this guy, well, there's no doubt in my mind he's telling the truth about being the alpha.

"Oh, dear," I say. "Your family started the party without you. That must be annoying."

His response is a snarl. "Give me one good reason why I shouldn't snap your spine right now, dark one."

I have no doubt he really could break me that easily. His biceps are pressing so tightly against my arms, I'm surprised my bones haven't shattered under the pressure already. My spine would simply be another twig for him to crack in two.

He may be fucking strong, but I've experienced enough broken bones in recent days to last me a lifetime. Not to mention I'd like to avoid the death that would follow. The keeper may have managed to bring Anarchy back from the dead, but I'm not sure he could do the same for me.

I fight to remain calm, an increasingly difficult task, as I try a different approach.

"Why be enemies when we can be allies?" I ask hopefully.

Ryuji's glower deepens. "There is no alliance to be made between the light and the dark."

"Oh, I'm sorry." I narrow my eyes at him, even though he won't be able to see it through the blindfold. "Have I insulted you? Maybe you expected me to beg for my life." My anger is quickly rising now and the sarcastic plea on my lips tastes like poison. "Please, please, dragon alpha, won't you spare my pitiful life?"

His lips twist. "You joke about your own death."

"No," I say, my lips twisting. "I'm making fun of your arrogance. What are you going to do about it?"

He doesn't immediately respond, his brow furrowing, but his hesitation gives *me* time to think.

My fingertips are pressed to his ribs.

I'm not sure if he saw me fight on the beach, but he called me a "wolf," so he must know I've got claws. Maybe he doesn't realize that I only have to extend them and they'll pierce his lungs. He'll lose the ability to breathe right before I rip open his torso.

I suppose he must think that my claws won't be able to pierce his scales. Regular wolf claws wouldn't be able to.

Still, I wait and allow him to think. A moment for him to decide what he's going to do. Because it would be so much easier if he decided to call a truce. For one thing, I could go back to my breakfast.

"I'm going to kill you," he says.

Sigh.

What a waste.

I ram my fingertips even harder against his ribs and release my claws. I sense them slide through his scales and into the flesh beneath—

"Fuck!" he shouts.

Well, it seems the angelic-looking dragon can curse.

His arms fly wide, releasing me while his wings beat up a storm of wind around us, as if his first instinct is to get as far away from me as he can.

I catch a glint of light reflecting off golden bands he's wearing around his forearms that weren't visible to me before.

Then he grabs my hands and wrenches my claws away from his chest. Blood soaks through his shirt from the cuts, but he reacted so quickly that the tips of my claws didn't descend deep enough to do any significant damage. Just nasty flesh wounds.

What's more, his wings are thrashing so wildly that I can barely keep my balance. It's only because my legs are still wrapped around his hips that I don't tumble away through the air.

I grip as hard as I can with my thighs, using my stomach muscles to push back toward him, attempting to free my hands from his hold so I can slash my claws across his chest.

I come within an inch of slicing up his shirt when he gives his wings a single, powerful beat and I anticipate that he intends to shove me away from himself this time. He'll push at my hands first, then wrench my legs off him and rid himself of me.

I'm shocked when, instead of shoving at me, he pulls my hands inward and upward. At the same time, the golden bands around his forearms unfurl, wrapping around my wrists in a flash and binding them together.

What the—?

An instant later, my hands are wrenched high above my head. Not physically by him, but seemingly by the gold he wrapped around them. I'm sure he's controlling it, although it feels like the metal has a mind of its own.

It happens so fast that my hands are high above my head before I can take a breath. But they don't stop there. I'm jolted forward, my hands descending again—what I'd think was a reckless move on his part, except that he ducks under the triangle my arms have formed so that they land on top of his shoulders.

My hands—and my claws with them—are now trapped behind his head. My claws are pointing outward, away from his body, where I can't do any damage with them.

I fight back, attempting to push against the force keeping my arms on his shoulder. I struggle with my legs, but moving them only increases my body weight and presses my arms more tightly down onto his shoulders.

I try closing my fists and angling my claws backward, hoping I can cut through the metal. Assuming I don't cut through my own wrists first.

That's when I sense the gold sliding across my arms. Not releasing them. I'm not sure what's happening until golden bands appear at his sides and wrap around the front of his torso.

I can only imagine that the bands binding my wrists have stretched out into these long ribbons.

The two ends seal together across his upper chest and now I'm bound to him, unable to fight against whatever power lives in this gold.

Not that I'm about to give up.

I struggle even harder, snarling at him. "What the fuck is this?"

"Dragon's gold," he says. "Don't try to fight it. It's mine and will obey only me."

Somehow, we've progressed farther to the far left of the beach, which was already alarmingly distant. I'd like to believe that shark shifters really do exist and somehow infest these waters, because if I fall in, I might be able to ask them for help.

At least I might have a chance of reasoning with them, one dark creature to another.

It's impossible to reason with a creature of light.

"Who are you?" he demands to know.

"Oh, so *now* you want to know who I am." I narrow my eyes at him, although again, he won't see it. "Before you were all: *I'm going to kill you, you pathetic wolf.* Now you're wondering how the fuck I cut through your scales. Am I right?"

He makes a snarling sound that doesn't sit well with his beautiful face, followed by a sharper demand for an answer. "Who are you?"

I shoot back. "Who are *you?*"

Oh, that's right, he already told me.

It takes a little of the wind out of me, but it seems he's more than happy to give me his full title.

"I'm Kaito Ryuji, son of Rin and Yuma, alpha of the Kaito Dragon Family."

I snarl back at him. "Well, I'm Veda Nostra, Daughter of Assholes. Also, you interrupted my breakfast and I'm beyond hungry now, so you could simply call me *Angry.*"

"Why are you here, Veda Nostra, Daughter of Assholes?"

"I came for a little peace and quiet. Which you've disrupted, so again, call me *Angry.*"

"Dark creatures don't seek peace," he snaps, his brown eyes flashing with apparent fury. "They seek destruction and death. They hunger for blood and pain. You cannot defy your nature."

Oh, if I could only slap him right now.

He sounds too much like my father, justifying his violence as if it were for the greater good.

"Don't give me that predetermination bullshit!" I snarl, baring my teeth at him. "I'll defy whatever the hell I want."

Come to think of it, since he's keeping me close to him, I could simply defy *him* by leaning in and tearing out his throat.

Not something I've done before, despite my efforts to bite my father's neck, but I'm willing to give it another try.

I smoosh my chest against Ryuji's torso, attempting to get as close to him as I can, darting in and aiming my teeth for the side of his neck—

Only to be met by a hot patch of gold.

It hits my face so fast that I'm left replaying within my mind the heartbeat of time before it reached me: a flash of light in his eyes, a chunk of gold ripping off the band around his chest, the stretching of that chunk into a shape like a muzzle before it smacked me across the mouth.

"Tell me why you're really here," he grinds out.

As if I can tell him anything now that he's covered my mouth.

I roll my eyes at him and manage to make the sound of a *fuck you*, but that's all.

His hands lower to my legs.

The gold bands suddenly separate at the front of his chest, whipping backward, and then they're wrenching my hands back up into the air. My claws are now pointing skyward.

The force of the gold's changing position is so great that my head is wrenched back too. No chance of biting him now.

"Maybe I'll simply let you fall to your death," he says.

With another flash of energy within his eyes, the patch of gold over my mouth peels away. But now the gold around my wrists is pulling me farther backward. So much farther that my legs are beginning to slip away from his waist.

What is he doing?

I cling with all my might, attempting to lock my ankles together as I take a quick glance at the water far below us.

I try to keep my tone nonchalant but fail badly. "That water doesn't look so bad to me."

His voice lowers. "But the rocks beneath the surface are very bad, indeed."

The gold around my wrists begins to slide slowly against my skin, a gradual unfurling motion that I'm certain is designed to make me afraid.

Fear certainly pushes at me as I glance down again.

Are there dark shadows beneath the waves? Are those rocks?

Dammit, I think they might be.

He pushes at my legs and that's all it takes for them to slide away from his sides, and now I'm dangling in the air by the force of the gold alone.

I try to grab hold of it, trying desperately to cling even as my shoulders wrench with my own body weight and the gold continues to slide effortlessly through my fingertips.

Oh. Fuck.

There's only a short portion of the bands left before I'll fall.

I only have one option now.

With a sense of burgeoning despair, I focus on the intense, crawling sensation that tingles all the way from my lower back up to the base of my skull.

The sensation surges, an unyielding energy, scarily easy to call since it's been pushing at me ever since the dragons first appeared.

I swallow my scream as my jagged, black wings tear from my back with a painful *thump*.

They're so sharp that they slice right through my tunic—rips I can't see but can easily feel when the material flaps in the wind and the cold sea air rushes across my skin.

The force of my wings bursting from me wrenches me away from the gold bands.

Opposite me, Ryuji's eyes shoot wide as my wings stretch to either side of me.

"There." I give him a broad grin. "Have fun trying to drop me now."

It's a moment of triumph that quickly fades.

My body tips to the right and I desperately try to make sense of the sensations in my shoulder blades and spine, the burn in my upper back and the searing heat of overstretched muscles all the way around my ribs.

I know I need to beat my wings, but I don't know how. I don't even know if they *can* be beaten. For all I know, I needed to develop the muscles to use them throughout childhood, to grow with my wings.

Fuck.

I'm like a butterfly in a book.

My wings are stiff, remaining outstretched and unmoving while my feathers ruffle uselessly in the wind.

I'm airborne for a mere heartbeat longer.

The breath leaves my chest as I plummet toward the water, the rocks beneath the surface rearing up at me, clearly visible now.

I wrench my arms inward and push them outward, trying to throw myself to the side, trying to glide away from the darkest, rockiest section of ocean below, trying to control my descent in any way I can.

It doesn't work.

The wind simply whistles through the gaps between my feathers.

Well, damn. I was right all along: My wings are fucking useless.

I brace for impact as the rocks rush up at me.

CHAPTER TWENTY-FIVE

The air *pops*.

Wind rushes around me and a pair of arms close across my chest.

I'm snatched away from danger right before I would have hit the rocks. Water splashes up and around me as silver wings cut through the waves and droplets kick into the air like hateful diamonds.

I recognize Ryuji's wings beating at the edge of my vision as he soars so fast with me that the air once again leaves my chest and my ears fill with pain.

I barely have time to process the fact that he scooped me out of harm's way—despite being the one who dropped me—before we reach the large, rocky outcrop at the left-hand end of the beach.

He slows down only marginally before dropping to the rocks and letting go of me.

I wobble on the spot, crouching low to regain my balance, conscious of the battle still raging farther down the beach.

I'm also acutely aware that the keeper is running toward me and will reach me within seconds.

There's no hiding these wings from anyone now.

"Veda!" His roar breaks across the distance as he leaps from the ground, punches a dragon in the face on his way past, and transforms midair.

Black scales rush across his body, which remains humanoid in shape, while inky wings burst from his back and his features become furiously reptilian.

His appearance is now that of a dragon shifter far bigger than any of the others, including Ryuji.

My focus quickly returns to the Dragon Master, who has taken up a battle stance only five paces opposite me, his feet planted right at the edge of the rocky outcrop and his hands lifted and ready to defend himself.

His focus is divided between me and the keeper, but it's me he should be worried about.

My wings are wet. The top of a wave literally ran through my feathers right before Ryuji scooped me away from the water.

I'm bedraggled. Exposed. And anger is seething within my chest.

"You dropped me just to catch me?" I launch myself across the distance between Ryuji and me, retracting my claws in time for my fist to collide with his face. "Fucking asshole!"

His arms are up, but I'm surprised when he doesn't try to block the blow or even retaliate against it.

I take advantage of his sudden reluctance to hit me and aim another punch at his face, the force of which should push him off the rock.

This time, he catches my fist. Or attempts to. It turns out that without the advantage of flight, he's no stronger than I am.

I punch through his hold and clip him on the chin.

If my claws had been extended, I could have sliced his face apart.

The only reason they aren't is because he didn't let me fall and I need to know why. Once I have my answer, well, then I'll decide if my claws should come back out.

"What sort of game are you playing?" I snarl as he steps to the side where he can retreat a few steps while still facing me.

He rubs his jaw, his fingertips grazing across the cracked scales, and sucks in a sharp breath. "You broke my skin."

"More than once," I remind him since I rammed my claws into his sides before. "Maybe I would have survived the rocks too."

I'm surprised when he nods. "Maybe."

That's when the keeper lands ten paces to my right, folding his wings away and watching me warily.

His voice is thick with fury, but I hate that there's a hint of uncertainty in his tone that I'm sure is caused by my wings. "My Veda?"

Behind him, Lucian is streaking across the air toward me while Anarchy and two of the panthers are running across the beach below him. They reach me within heartbeats and, even though five dragon shifters are on their tail, they all pull to a stop in the middle of the outcrop, their focus entirely on me.

My breathing is ragged, and my cheeks are burning.

My awful wings are on display and there's a storm of humiliation within me. I try to retract them, but I can't seem to make them do anything I want.

I wanted to choose when I revealed them.

I needed to control that moment.

Now that choice has been taken away from me.

With every passing second, the damned things grow heavier across my back, a weight on my soul.

"Darkness?" Anarchy asks, surging forward until she collides with the keeper's suddenly outstretched arm, snarling at him when he holds her back.

Only Lucian doesn't look surprised since he's seen my wings before. His lips are pursed and he glances at Anarchy and the keeper as if he doesn't quite understand their reactions. He probably thought they knew about my wings already.

Growls rise to my lips and my claws finally snap out.

"Keep the other dragons away from me," I say, unable to meet their eyes. "Ryuji and I have some things to sort out. One alpha to another."

Three of the dragon shifters from the beach have reached us, but both the keeper and Lucian shoot up into the air while Anarchy, Rumble, and Strife take up position like a wall, all of them blocking the way.

"Hold your positions!" Ryuji shouts to them and I don't miss their raised eyebrows and pursed lips. "Do not approach."

Despite their visible concern, they obey him without question, retreating to land on the rocks closer to the beach, where they watch us with angry eyes.

It isn't lost on me that Ryuji could take flight at any time, gather up his fallen family members, and leave. He'd have to move fast, but that seems to be a particular skill he and his pack possess.

Yet he doesn't show any signs of doing that. No spreading wings. No bent knees as if he's about to take off.

The only question in my mind is whether or not I'll attempt to take the choice of flight away from him.

"I could shred your wings," I say.

"You could try," he replies.

I haven't forgotten the golden bands he used to subdue me, both of which are back on his wrists and once again masquerading as pieces of jewelry.

"I could pierce your heart," I say.

Again, he replies, "You could try."

"Why did you catch me when you said you'd kill me?"

"I changed my mind."

I huff. "You *changed your mind*?" I pace back and forth, feeling like a caged animal. Every instinct in my dark soul is telling me to strike, but I'm sure he has something up his sleeve and I'm not reckless enough to abandon all caution. "Why?"

"Because I need answers."

"Why did you suddenly need answers?" I ask, although I suspect I know the answer.

"Because a wolf with wings is unheard of. And trust me when I tell you, we've heard of everything."

"So you're still going to kill me. You just want to satisfy your curiosity first."

He inclines his head. "It depends. Why are you here?"

"I told you," I grind out. "I came for peace and quiet."

"I don't believe you."

"Well, I don't know how to prove it to you." My brow furrows as I steady my balance, ready for a fight, all the while resisting the temptation to plant my hands on my hips in exasperation. "Except maybe for the fact that your people attacked us and not the other way around. We were doing nothing more heinous than eating breakfast when your family arrived and picked a fight."

His forehead creases at that. "There are dead boars on the other side of the island. Their bones were gnawed clean. Your version of 'eating' isn't so peaceful."

I don't know anything about dead boars, although the hisses Rumble and Strife are aiming at Ryuji tells me they're probably the culprits.

"The panthers are carnivores," I say. "They kill out of necessity."

"Or for the fun of it," Ryuji snarls.

I snap back. "Why would you assume that?"

"Because that's what dark creatures do."

It's not like I can deny it.

I shake my head and take a step back. We're getting nowhere. There's no reasoning with him.

But the alternative is a lot of dead dragon shifters and he's made it clear he's from a powerful family—or at least he wants me to believe so—which means there will be more of them. If we kill these ones, others will come for us.

The keeper's gaze burns me, and I feel the slightest twinge within my chest, as if he's trying to silently pour his own feelings into me.

His restraint in this situation reminds of what happened when I first escaped from my cell. I fought a warrior angel—the Serene Commander of the Philadelphia Order. The keeper had stayed out of that fight and at the time, his choice had confused me, since he could have easily killed her.

His explanation afterward echoes back to me now.

"You saw an enemy, but I saw more. She only fought us because she was frightened by our presence."

So must Ryuji be.

My chest deflates before I say to him, "If I tell you all of the reasons why I'm here, and you find them satisfactory, will you leave us in peace?"

He lowers his hands, his voice faltering. A hint of surprise. "Maybe."

I stare at him. "Maybe?"

His only response is a narrowing of his eyes, as if he could tear through my thoughts with his gaze alone.

Carefully, I say, "I'm here because my father wants me dead and my biological mother abandoned me."

He scoffs. "That's hardly news. Dark creatures always hate their children."

"Well, it was news to me!" I snap, my anger rising. "Experiencing near-murder at the hands of the father I loved wasn't exactly something I'd prepared for."

His expression doesn't change. Not even a hint of softening.

My lips draw back in a snarl. "I thought creatures of the light were supposed to have empathy."

"A trait you thought to use against me?" he asks.

I catch my tongue. Well, I suppose I did think to appeal to his compassion. But it seems he has none.

Dammit. I'm still getting nowhere.

I shake my head, wondering how I can answer his question in a way that will defuse this situation.

Why am I here?

Well, if I go right back to the moment when freedom presented itself...

"I'm here because I escaped my cage," I say, suddenly drawn back to that mysterious moment when the magical seal across the bricked walls had *popped* and I could finally cut through the stone to reach the other side.

"I'm here because something or someone broke the magical seal that had kept me imprisoned for twenty-three long years, but I've never known who or what—"

I take a sharp breath.

Wait a minute.

I've been sensing that same magic ever since the dragon shifters arrived: The *pop* in the air when they fly.

The change in air pressure around my cell had the same impact on my ears.

I've never known what happened on the other side of that bricked wall because I couldn't see through it. I heard a male voice and a female voice and then there was a burning heat across the bricks that I could feel all the way through to my side.

The panthers were on the other side of the wall at the time.

They saw what happened.

They couldn't tell me before, simply because they couldn't speak to me in anything other than snarls and hisses and purrs, but now Anarchy can tell me.

I take a chance to spin to her, only to find her already focused on me.

"Yes," she says, her pale-blue eyes bright. "It was a dragon shifter." She hurries on. "Actually, an angel and a dragon shifter.

Two creatures of powerful light magic fighting each other. The dragon's fire burned across the chains that shackled us and at the same time, the flames cut through the wall that imprisoned you."

How ironic.

I spin back to the dragon master. "I'm here because light magic set me free."

I dare to close the gap between Ryuji and me, watching the way his scales glisten as I approach, a defensive mechanism.

"A dragon shifter set me free," I say. "And now you, another dragon shifter, have the power to decide what happens next."

CHAPTER TWENTY-SIX

I have to convince Ryuji to leave us in peace.

I need this time—just a little bit of time—to plan a way forward that will keep my new family safe.

Drawing myself upright and taking advantage of Ryuji's intense silence, I issue a challenge in the form of a question. "You have sworn to destroy dark creatures, but I ask you this: How do you know that's what I am?"

"A dark creature?" He falters a little. Not much. But his sudden uncertainty is undeniable. After all, he said himself that a wolf with wings is unheard of. It has to be making him question his assumptions about us.

"Well, only a dark creature associates with other dark creatures." He points to each member of my family in turn, starting with Lucian. "Dark angel, dark elf, shadow panthers, and…" His eyes narrow at the keeper. "Something else. But most certainly of dark magic."

I'm not surprised that he accurately identified the shadow panthers since he claimed he's heard of everything, but I'm gratified that he can't seem to label the keeper.

"And me?" I persist. "What of me?"

Ryuji scowls. "I will concede you are a mystery."

Another 'something else'.

"And I will concede there is darkness within me," I say, knowing that subterfuge will get me nowhere. "But I challenge you to deny that there's darkness in you, too."

He huffs but doesn't refute it.

"If you can't precisely identify what I am, then you can't risk killing me." I lift my hands to emphasize that I'm putting away my claws. "If you kill me and afterward discover that I was not wholly of the dark, then you, yourself, could be said to have succumbed to evil."

He visibly grits his teeth, but I believe I've hit on the reason why he couldn't let me fall once he saw my wings.

There's a question in his mind about what I am.

As much as I'm certain of my own nature, I'm not about to squander this chance for a truce.

"I've told you why I'm here," I say softly, taking the chance to continue. "Now I'm asking for amnesty."

He's already shaking his head, but I plow on.

"A month on this island," I say. "If you object to the death of wild boars, I'll convince the panthers to eat fish. You can post guards around the perimeter if you like, whatever it takes for you to convince your family that you're in charge. All I ask is that you otherwise leave us alone. When it's time for us to go, I'll let you know, and you'll never see us again."

He folds his arms across his chest. "You propose that I make peace with the devil."

Well, what a shame the keeper isn't wearing his devil face right now or I may well be proposing literally that.

"Or we can fight," I say with a heavy sigh to emphasize my point. "Your people will die. A war will begin. And we will never know the end of it."

At the back of my mind is a possibility I can't shake: that this could be the start of the bloodshed my father was so certain I'd bring about.

Of course, my father said I would start a war among dark creatures, not between the light and the dark, but it's impossible to know what spark might light that fire.

How can I know what choices will define me?

My wings are starting to drag at my back now. Actually, they've been dragging at my back the whole time, but the weight is making my shoulders ache very badly.

Ryuji unfolds his arms and I try not to hold my breath.

"Why be enemies when we can be allies?" he asks, repeating what I said to him earlier. "An old god said that very same thing to me—right before he cheated me out of my favorite sword."

"Oh." I grimace. "So you've met James Vanguard?"

"Met and disliked."

"If it helps, he seems to love that sword."

"As did I."

My mind whirls with a new possibility. Probably a false promise, but I'll do anything to bring about this truce. "Perhaps I could get it back for you."

Ryuji's eyes light up, an eagerness in his expression that he quickly shuts down.

His expression once more blank, he lowers his hands and announces loudly, "We need tea. We will discuss terms."

Terms. It's a far sight better than discussing death.

As if I don't pose any sort of threat, he steps right up to me before indicating the training hall in the distance. "We will sit together and discuss this with civility." He gives me a challenging smile. "Assuming it's possible for dark creatures to behave courteously."

I fight the urge to scowl. "We will join you there."

No doubt, he'll place his soldiers all around the building, but the panthers can prowl around it to even up the numbers.

I'll be glad to get off this rock and back to the beach.

With a brief, polite nod to me, Ryuji heads toward the narrow gap between Anarchy and Rumble, sliding on through it as if he barely notices them or their sharp teeth.

I glance at my family. "Uh… Looks like we're drinking tea."

Before I can follow Ryuji, the keeper tucks his wings into his sides and drops to the rocks beside me, his firm hand wrapping around my arm.

His voice is incredibly hushed, barely audible. "You're in pain."

My shoulders hunch. "I didn't want you to see these… *things* on my back…"

He catches my chin in his hand, urging me to look up at him. "My Veda, I've known about your wings since you first gave me the power in your heart. They're a part of you. As strong as your mind and your need for vengeance. If you have trouble embracing them, I will help you."

His gaze passes from my face to my feathers, his lips parting, his eyes soft. "They are as beautifully dangerous as you are."

My eyes are slowly widening. "But they're useless."

A smile lifts his lips and a gleam enters his eyes. "Far from it."

His hands lower to the sides of my neck and then my shoulders, kneading the muscles, releasing the tense knots. His voice whispers in my ear as he leans in close. "But right now, you need to retract them—"

"I can't—"

"You *can*." His lips brush mine, a heated distraction as his fingertips curl around the back of my shoulders and a glimmer of dark light flickers at the edge of my vision.

My muscles relax under his power and my wings finally pull inward, folding back against my spine before fully retracting.

I smother my groan of relief against his lips.

Anarchy and the two panthers are waiting for us nearby while Lucian has dropped to the sand closer to the dragons. It's clear he doesn't trust them an inch, as he retains his battle stance.

In the distance, Ryuji is now speaking with the other dragons, none of whom look terribly happy.

I pick up Ryuji's order for them to "tend to the wounded" before half of them lift into the air and head toward their fallen comrades. The other half fly toward the training hall and take up position around it, just like I expected.

Anarchy edges toward me at that moment and the keeper moves aside for her.

"We have a problem," she whispers.

"My wings—"

"No, nothing to do with you. Your wings are fucking beautiful." She places her hand on my arm, a reassuring touch followed by a grimace. "It's Riot."

But of course… Only Rumble and Strife are here with us. The last time I saw Riot, he was tumbling across the beach with that teal-haired dragon.

The air *whooshes* out of my chest. "Dark saints, what's happened?"

My imagination is suddenly going wild. None of the other dragon shifters were killed in the fight, but if that woman is hurt or dead, I'm certain it will break our fragile truce.

"You need to come and see."

I hurry after Anarchy, the keeper on our heels, and we collect the panthers and Lucian on our way.

Farther along the beach, Ryuji watches us carefully, becoming visibly tense when Anarchy veers toward the trees to our left—a good hundred paces before we would have reached the training hall.

The keeper, Lucian, and the panthers break off and stop like guards on the beach, which is good because they'll be fully visible to Ryuji, so at least he won't assume we're all angling for some kind of surprise attack.

Anarchy pulls me along a narrow path into the trees and my throat is tight as we step into a little, circular clearing with stone benches around its edges.

In the middle of the mossy space, lying on her back with her wings spread out on either side of her, is the teal-haired dragon.

Stretched out on top of her as if she's a comfortable lounge chair is Riot.

He's licking one of his front paws and paying particular attention to his very sharp, silver claws.

The woman's dark eyes are wide, her cheeks are pale, and she appears frozen where she lies.

Well, at least she's alive.

Her gaze swivels to us and she squeaks, "A little help?"

CHAPTER TWENTY-SEVEN

I lean in close to Anarchy, keeping my voice at a whisper, even though it's likely both Riot and the woman can hear me. "If Riot was going to eat her, he would have done it already, right?"

Anarchy makes a non-committal sound. "Maybe."

I blow out a breath. "Time to step in, then."

Before the situation can escalate to dragon-eating, I pick a careful path toward Riot, my footfalls soft on the moss. "Okay, Riot. Time to let her go."

He stops licking his paw and hunches down on her chest, his snarls so sudden and vicious that I pull up short.

"Whoa." My hands fly into the air as he continues to hiss and snarl until I begin backing away. "Oh-kay. She's all yours."

To the teal-haired woman, I call, "Sorry, lady. You're on your own."

"What?" she cries. "You *cannot* leave me like this!"

She's right. I can't. The fact that she even asked for help tells me she sensed that the fight between our people is over. I'm betting she has the same sensitive hearing I do and can hear

Ryuji's voice farther down the beach, ordering his people to stand down.

I count the steps it takes for Riot to stop snarling at me: It's a good five paces before his hissing stops and his attention returns fully to the woman.

He grins at her in his panther way before he leans down very close to her face, his gaze honed in on her very wide eyes.

She remains frozen beneath him, her arms and hands flat against the ground, her wings not even fluttering as she whispers, "Please don't kill me."

He retracts his claws and she exhales audibly, her face regaining a little color.

But she tenses again when he turns his head to the side—until the tips of his whiskers brush her cheek.

Then she blinks rapidly.

He doesn't bite her. Doesn't extend his claws again or show his teeth. Just narrows his eyes at her as his whiskers slide across her skin. At the same time, a deep, rumbling sound resonates from his chest. A purr like some kind of thrumming machine.

She continues to blink at him as his whiskers brush her cheek and his eyes become relaxed slits.

"That tickles," she whispers.

He draws his head back, his nose wrinkling in another ferocious snarl before he surprises me by leaping deftly off her chest and onto the moss beside her, landing clear of her wings.

Now free of his weight, she launches herself to her feet, glittering, white sand drifting off her back and wings. No doubt it had gathered there during their tumble across the beach.

Without taking her eyes off Riot, she gives herself a little shake, sending grit through the air before she fully retracts her wings and watches him warily.

Riot rests down on his haunches, positioned between her and us, and begins nonchalantly licking his paws again.

"Okay. That was… interesting." The woman squares her shoulders, lifts her head, and attempts to step past Riot in the direction of the path.

Immediately, he leaps to his feet and snarls at her, forcing her to backpedal.

Her gaze darts to the other side of the clearing. Carefully moving toward it, she tries again to get past him, only for him to leap into her path, snarling viciously at her.

She stops dead center, and he settles down again.

I almost feel sorry for her. She can't fly out of here because, like the clearing where we ate breakfast, this one also has a ceiling of tree branches. She could try vaulting over the stone bench behind her and making a break for it through the jungle at the back of the clearing, but it's far denser on that side, so the chances of escape on foot are much slimmer than via the path I'm standing on.

With an edge of panic in her voice, she looks to us, as if we have answers. "What is happening right now?"

I look to Anarchy, who has pursed her lips.

"Huh," she says, folding her arms across her chest as she studies her brother.

"Hmm?" I prompt, hoping she'll explain.

"Not sure." She shrugs. "Time will tell."

The woman calls across the distance, the panic growing in her voice. "Tell what? What will time tell?"

Anarchy opens her mouth. And closes it again.

Then a mischievous smile plays with her lips. "Whether or not he plans to eat you."

"Fuck," the dragon shifter whispers, backing away from him —which only prompts him to snarl at her until she stops.

I roll my eyes at Anarchy. "Stop scaring her."

"Why?" Anarchy widens her eyes at me. "She deserves it."

I acquiesce. "She does. A little."

We both turn back to the woman, who stares at us, beads of sweat forming on her brow.

Then she gives us a fierce scowl.

And then she does something I don't expect.

She takes a step toward Riot and rests down on her knees in the moss so that she's nearly eye to eye with him.

He immediately stops licking his paws and hisses at her.

She flinches. Her chest stills, as if she's holding her breath. But then she lets the air out again. "You're not going to hurt me, are you?"

His snarls only grow louder.

"You're not going to hurt me," she says again.

He rises to his feet and paces to the side and then circles around behind her. Once again, she stiffens and this time, her eyes close, but she doesn't twist toward him or move in any other way.

He pads around to her front, continuing to circle her, each turn becoming smaller and smaller as he veers inward toward her.

"I respect that you could," she says, her eyes still closed. "I'm grateful that you haven't."

Her breath catches when he brushes up against her arm on his way around the back of her. This time, his body nudges up against her so heavily that she's pushed forward over her knees into what must be an infuriatingly submissive pose.

"I know that you won't," she says, finally opening her eyes as he rounds her front again.

His head and neck and upper body push against her side, rumbling purrs pouring out of him as he rubs the side of his face against her arm and stomach.

"Oh." Her cheeks regain their full color. Very slowly, she lifts her other hand off her lap and reaches for him.

Her fingertips are just about to brush the top of his head

when he swings away from her and prowls all the way back to us.

Still on her knees, she curls her hand closed in the air and her head tips to the side, as if she's deep in thought.

Riot barely pauses at my side before he stalks away toward the beach, but Anarchy snatches that moment to sigh down at him.

"Oh, brother," she murmurs, shaking her head. "Your heart is doomed to break."

When he disappears along the path, the woman rises to her feet.

"My name is Kaito Miku," she says. "I'm Ryuji's sister. I would appreciate if you'd keep your distance."

I don't deny her request, stepping back from the path so she can pass us by without any hint of interference.

But then she pauses, peers in the direction Riot disappeared, and asks, "Who was that?"

Anarchy makes a sequence of sounds I can't follow and I can only guess it's Riot's dark elf name. When she finishes speaking, she grins at me and speaks in a barely disguised whisper. "Let's see if she caught that."

"Nihi...kah... sun..." Miku's attempt doesn't come close to matching even half of the quick sounds Anarchy made, but she tries.

"Riot," I say, firmly. "His name is Riot."

In the distance, I can hear voices coming closer.

It's time to get out of here before all hell breaks loose again.

I hurry with Anarchy into the open, keeping my distance from Miku, who plows across the beach toward Ryuji.

"Everything okay?" Lucian asks when we reach him.

"Fine," I say, taking a deep breath. "For now."

Anarchy sidles up to Lucian with a soft, "Are *you* okay?" She looks him over while catching her bottom lip between her teeth. "Any wounds I need to tend to?"

Yesterday, he would have frozen as surely as Miku froze when Riot snarled at her. Today, Lucian gives Anarchy a lazy smile. "Sadly, no."

With a little smile, I return my attention to the dragons farther down the beach and the discussion I'm about to have.

We may have knocked out as many as ten of the original fifteen dragon shifters, but it appears that more have arrived, many of them now standing outside the training hall as I predicted while others take care of their wounded.

However, only Ryuji—and now Miku—stand on the porch, so it looks like only the two of them will be heading inside.

I make a quick decision. "It looks like I can only take one of you inside the hall with me and it's better if I don't look menacing. I'll take one of the panthers and that's all." I quickly bend to Strife. "Will you come with me?"

He hisses up at me, as if he's insulted.

"Of course you look menacing," I croon, nudging my face against his. "But they're more likely to underestimate you. Especially if you behave yourself, yes?"

At that, his hissing stops and he returns my nudge.

When I rise, the others have wrinkled brows, especially the keeper.

"I need you all outside, watching the other dragons and ensuring they don't encroach on my discussion with Ryuji," I say firmly, despite the fact that I'd prefer my family to be standing directly at my back. "An ambush is the last thing I need."

The keeper doesn't nod. Nothing I could say would make him happy. But he doesn't protest, either.

I take a deep breath. "Time to drink tea."

CHAPTER TWENTY-EIGHT

*I*t's unsettlingly quiet around the training hall, where the dragons keep guard, and even quieter within it.

While Miku disappears into the kitchen, presumably to boil water, Ryuji kneels on the mat flooring, his focus briefly flickering to the damaged floor at the far end of the room.

He doesn't immediately comment on it, seating himself with his back to that side while I drop to the floor opposite him, both of us now sitting side-on to the wide door. Equally free to leave. Assuming the supernaturals outside don't stop us.

He clears his throat pointedly when I cross my legs, pointing to the way he's neatly furled his own legs beneath him.

I stare at him for a moment before I pull my legs under my butt, prepared to honor his customs and take up the same kneeling position.

I expect him to say something about my blindfold. I'm very surprised he hasn't tried to remove it or ask me about it already.

Strife prowls around and between us before he settles down on his haunches on my right, his claws nowhere in sight.

"I can provide new *tatami* mats for the damaged portion of the floor, if you wish it to be repaired," Ryuji says.

I don't pretend to recognize the word "*tatami*," but it's clear he's talking about the woven matting. "I would appreciate that."

"Good," he replies. "The new mats should last you a month. I don't expect you will enjoy them longer than that."

Somehow, I don't think we're talking about mats any longer. Is he trying to tell me he agrees to us staying?

I carefully phrase my response. "A month is as long as they would be needed."

"Good."

Miku returns with a black tray on which there are two black tea cups along with a teapot that's painted with an intricate mountain design that continues all around its surface.

She pours the tea and then takes up a kneeling position behind Ryuji and to his left, where I can see her.

He sips from the steaming liquid, somehow without appearing to burn his tongue, and then sets down his cup, all deliberate movements before he exhales heavily, his chest deflating.

"Your presence here will raise questions for my family," he says, meeting my eyes. "Questions that might cause conflict."

I chew my lip. "I understand the difficulty of your choice." I reach for my cup and then veer to the teapot instead, my fingertips brushing its surface. Since we seem to be talking in metaphors...

"This is beautiful artwork," I say, my fingertip following a path through the air around the pot. "A thing of beauty created with care. But if I were to break it, I could use the pieces as weapons." I pull my hands back to my lap, keeping my tone even. "This thing of beauty could become a weapon with which I could take life."

When he tilts his head, the dark strands of his hair fall across his eyes. "Are you a broken thing, Veda Nostra?"

"Daughter of Assholes," I finish for him. "My father believes, strongly enough to try to kill me, that I will fill the streets with the blood of dark magic creatures."

His eyebrows rise. "Then you are the hand that holds the broken thing."

"A broken heart," I say, even though I can't feel the full force of my heart's feelings since the keeper took the power in it.

If he hadn't… I wonder if I'd be sitting here now, drinking tea with a creature of the light and trying to forge a peace agreement. I wonder if the full force of my broken heart wouldn't have driven me to bloodshed already.

"Will you?" Ryuji asks. "Fill the streets with blood?"

He gives no indication of his feelings about his question. His face is so blank, I can only assume he is a master of masking his thoughts when he wants to be.

"In my father's words: I will incite a war among dark creatures that even the forces of light would never wish for." I lean forward a little. "So I suppose *my* question to you is this: If that were true, and dark creatures were to die, will you care?"

He breaks my gaze to consider the steam rising from his tea. His forefinger taps his thigh, the lightest motion, as he appears to consider his response.

He raises his eyes to mine once more. "I will not."

"Then I ask that you don't disturb the broken pieces or stop the hand that uses them."

He's quiet for a long moment. "What of the pieces that can be mended?"

I start to shake my head but he leans forward to run his finger lightly over the pot. "With a steady hand and the right mix of lacquer and gold, even the smallest shards may once again form a thing of beauty."

"Not today," I whisper. "Not yet."

"Perhaps in time." He inclines his head. And then, "One month. Not a day longer. Your panthers will eat fish. You will not set foot on the mainland. Miku will visit you daily to ensure you're honoring these terms."

"Agreed."

"What?" Miku's soft protest sounds a second after my agreement.

Ryuji's jaw clenches. He doesn't reply to her and she quickly resumes her obedient kneeling pose, her expression closing off.

"You have promised me that only dark creatures will die," Ryuji says to me, and for a moment, his dragon scales shimmer across his skin, as if to emphasize the importance of this part of my promise. "That is our agreement."

I give him a firm nod. "That is our agreement."

"Then it is settled."

The tension releases from my body, and I finally reach for the cup of tea, grateful for how calming it is.

With a soft exhalation that carries the heat of the liquid off my tongue, I ask, "Would you mind if I ask you a question?"

"Go ahead."

"How did you know we were here?" I keep my voice light, but it's a loaded question. I need to know where our vulnerabilities are, especially since the keeper was adamant he'd cast a protection spell around the island and I would have thought it would conceal us completely.

Ryuji looks a little smug before his face falls blank again. "Our mermaid allies reported your presence."

My forehead creases as I consider the possibility that we were being watched the whole time. I purse my lips at my tea, nursing the cup in my hands. "We didn't see any mermaids."

"No. And they didn't see you. But they heard you."

"They… what?" My cheeks flush.

How much noise did I make last night?

"Dark saints, they should mind their own business," I snap.

I expect Ryuji to laugh at my discomfort, but his expression remains sober. "Pain can't be ignored."

Pain...?

Now I'm even more confused. Until I remember.

I screamed under the waves. I expelled all of my fury and betrayal into that scream. I guess the keeper's protection spell hadn't been cast so far as to suppress it.

Damn. It's my fault these dragons attacked us.

I wipe the regret from my face and whisper, "Well, they *should* have ignored it."

Clearing my throat, I quickly move on before he makes further uncomfortable observations—assuming he would. "I'm curious about how you fly so fast."

And a little envious, given that I can't fly at all.

"We're air dragons."

I wrinkle my nose. "Aren't all dragons air dragons?"

"You mean because we have wings?"

"Well, yes."

Now, he laughs, his eyes lighting up. "I appreciate your reasoning, but no. Most dragon shifters may have wings and the ability to fly, but only air dragons can master the energy in the sky. Just as only a fire dragon can breathe fire and a water dragon can control liquid."

I tip my head, curious. "You said, '*most* dragon shifters.' Surely, all dragon shifters have wings?"

A shadow passes across his expression. "Not necessarily."

Before I can respond, he gives me a gentle smile. "You ask a lot of questions."

"I need to learn about my world."

He arches an eyebrow at me "*Your* world?"

I flush. "The world around me."

"Hmm."

I roll my eyes at him. "No, I'm not going to turn into a raging megalomaniac, trying to take over the world."

Ryuji's tone is far sterner than I was expecting. "Your own father seems to believe otherwise."

I take a breath. And then two more. "My father may create the very thing he fears."

Ryuji folds his hands in his lap. We've sat like this for long enough that my legs are going numb, but he doesn't seem even slightly uncomfortable.

"That is the nature of fear," he says. "It can be self-fulfilling."

I can only nod, the tension returning to my voice. "Then I have no hope. Only revenge."

Ryuji suddenly looks baffled and bemused, an expression he doesn't seem to try to hide as he shakes his head at me. "A dark creature who speaks of hope. I never thought I would behold such a thing."

With that, he rises to his feet. The moment I try to follow, my numb legs get the better of me. I'd rather stay put than wobble in front of him, so I remain where I am.

Somehow, he doesn't loom over me. His presence now is as peaceful as the ocean air gently cooling my frayed emotions.

I wonder if this is the true power of an air dragon, to slip between breaths as easily as a breeze and create a sense of safety. Safety that could be false or true.

"We will leave now," he says. "Miku will return tomorrow. I will visit from time to time and we will have tea, Veda Nostra, Daughter of Assholes. We can talk more then."

So it's to be a daily guard and random check-ins from the boss himself.

It's to be expected. I'm more surprised by the fact that he isn't leaving a guard with us at all times.

"I look forward to your visits." I finally rise to my feet, managing to ease upward without embarrassing myself.

Strife also rises from his haunches, having remained resolutely quiet the whole time, just as I asked. The back of my hand nudges his head, brushing behind his ear, a gesture of gratitude.

Ryuji gives me a shallow bow and then crosses to the door,

calling to his dragons. Miku follows close on his heels and within moments, they're airborne.

The entire horde of dragons takes off into the air in a rush of wind and wings, disappearing across the bright sky.

I stand in the shadow of the porch, considering what Ryuji said about the nature of fear while my family gathers around me.

"Fuck," Lucian whispers. "That is not how I thought that fight would go."

Anarchy gives him a sultry smile. "With Darkness, anything is possible."

The keeper's attention is on me, his dragon eyes dark and full of shadows. "What now, my Veda?"

My mind is churning. There are so many things I want.

I want the panthers to have the chance to be elves again.

I want to learn how to fight like Anarchy, so that the next time a supernatural like Ryuji or my father comes after me, I'll have all the skills I need.

I want to keep my family safe.

But as for vengeance?

"What now?" I whisper. "Well, that depends on my brother."

CHAPTER TWENTY-NINE

Lucian stiffens. "Me?" His golden eyes consider me warily. "How does it depend on me?"

"Will you come inside?" I ask, gesturing to the interior of the training hall where I sat with Ryuji only minutes ago. "I have questions and you have information I need—"

"I told you, Dad never shared anything important with me."

I squint at him. "I don't think that's entirely true."

He withdraws a little but doesn't look away. A guilty person would look away, but again, dark creatures rarely feel guilt.

But, no. There isn't guilt in him.

There's… pain.

I see it in the downturn of the corners of his lips, the tightening of his shoulders, his defensive body language. The same body language he exhibited when he told me that affection comes with strings attached or worse, it's followed by a fist.

Anarchy steps quickly to his side, the lavender scent of her skin wafting across the air. She doesn't slip her arms around him, but she leans in close. "Whatever it is, you can tell us."

As I wait for Lucian to respond, I'm fully aware that the keeper could make my brother speak. The keeper could try to use his compulsion power—he's used it on angels before—but it's unlikely to work on an angel of Lucian's power. It would only break any trust I've built with my brother.

I give the keeper a small shake of my head and the oily, black magic slithering around his fingertips disappears.

"You can tell us," Anarchy whispers again, this time with a smile as she brushes her hand down his arm. "We're dark creatures. We won't judge."

He reaches for her, his fingers feathering her jawline, the expression in his eyes changing. A pinch in his forehead. A hurried press of his lips.

He's worried. But for the life of me, I won't know why until he tells me what he knows. Whatever it is, it can't be good.

"Okay," he murmurs, his focus on Anarchy. "But will you sit with me?"

He suddenly looks far more vulnerable than I ever expected to see him, another hurried press of his lips, the pucker in his forehead deepening.

Her eyes widen, her lips parting, a mirror to his worry. "Of course. I won't leave your side."

He gives a nod. Swallows. Turns to me. "Lead the way, Veda."

After moving back inside with the three male panthers milling around me, I gesture for Lucian to sit opposite me.

True to her word, Anarchy stays close to him, gliding into a sitting position, her knee touching his when she crosses her legs.

The keeper remains standing like a dark shadow at my back, somehow blocking out the sunlight on my left.

"Ask your questions," Lucian says, his shoulders and torso tense, his hands curled into fists and resting on his thighs.

I start quietly. "My father told me I was too dangerous for this world. He told me I'm destined to start a war. I don't want to believe him, but his conviction was intense. It was absolute. I need to know why. I'm hoping you can shed light on that."

More than anything, I want to know why Lucian reacted with relief at the sight of my wings. Why he said that my wings had changed everything, but it's the *everything* I need to know about first.

Lucian gives a short shake of his head, so jolting, it's like a twitch more than a voluntary movement. He has so much of our father's appearance with his pale skin and black hair and the same golden eyes. But he wears nothing of our father's arrogance. Not anymore.

"I want to tell you." He winces and his cheeks become even paler. "But I can't…" He gasps for breath, pressing his hands to his temples, squeezing his eyes closed. "What I saw was dangerous. Opening my mind to it again is…"

What he saw?

Anarchy has leaned toward him, reacting as soon as he winced. "Lucian?"

His face is now turning gray, as if the life is bleaching out of him and his fingers are going white with the pressure he's applying to his skull. "I can't… I can't…"

He shudders violently and rocks forward.

I don't know what's causing him so much pain, but I'm alarmed by it. Worried enough that I'm about to retract my question—despite how badly I need the answer.

That's when Anarchy catches hold of him.

Slipping her slender arms around his broad chest in a firm hug, she nudges her cheek against his before she nips the backs of his fingers where they rest against his temple, her teeth sinking briefly into them.

His eyes fly wide, his focus suddenly on her, his indrawn breath parting his lips.

Without missing a beat, she changes direction, nipping his bottom lip, leaving two pinpricks of blood when she leans back.

"How about now?" she whispers.

The tension releases from his shoulders as he pulls his bottom lip between his teeth, sucking on the bite.

"Better," he says, although his eyes are slightly glazed.

Yesterday, Anarchy explained that her teeth secrete a healing solution. When she mended Lucian's wounds then, she didn't bite him, but she must have felt it necessary to do so now.

It makes me concerned about the level of pain she must have sensed he was feeling.

I know I need to proceed carefully. "Lucian? Can you speak about it? Please tell me if you can't."

Even as I speak, Lucian is already talking. "Dad forced me to see what I saw," he says. "He knew it could drive my mind into oblivion, but he didn't care."

Anarchy's arms tighten around him, her lilac hair falling across his chest and arms.

"It was right after I brought you to him, Veda," Lucian continues. "You were still unconscious. He strung me up and forced me to watch." Lucian's hands lower from his temple to his neck, as if he's remembering the rope that his father must have put around it—the burn marks from which I saw when I woke up. "He needed me to confirm what he saw."

My stomach swirls with fear, but I try to bring moisture to my lips to ask as gently as I can, "What did he make you see?"

"Read, actually," Lucian says, in a low murmur. "He made me read *The Book of Dark Magic*."

Anarchy jolts, her gasp sounding a moment before the keeper looms dark and ominous over me.

"Your father has *The Book of Dark Magic*?" the keeper snarls, his features becoming more dragon-like, black scales flushing across his skin and his shoulders tensing as if he's about to release his wings.

There are four books, one for each type of magic. Only a week ago, I held a page from *The Book of Dark Magic* in my hands. The woman who raised me told me where to find that piece of paper. At the time, I didn't know that it had been torn from *The Book of Dark Magic*. I thought it was merely a picture on a piece of black paper.

It was only when the keeper caught a glimpse of it that I found out what it really was.

He reacted with the same alarm that's written all over his face right now. His entire body was stiff with tension and the corners of his lips were turned down in a savage expression, just as they are now.

He told me not to let anyone else touch that piece of paper.

Not even himself.

He told me it could destroy me.

"My father has the book, and he lives by it!" Lucian snaps back, a fire in his eyes, a furious, hurt gleam. "He's had it for decades, and it guides his every fucking move. He's fucking obsessed with it."

The keeper begins pacing back and forth behind me, and as he does, his outward appearance changes once again. Even though he keeps his black scales, any hint of wings vanishes and a black cape forms around his shoulders, floating down to the floor. Its hem scrapes across the *tatami* matting with every step he takes, reminding me of the swishing of his cloak within his realm the first time I saw him.

"*The Book of Dark Magic* only serves itself," he says. "If your father's following it, and has been for years, then he's well and truly set on a path of destruction."

Around me, the panthers are hissing and beside Lucian, Anarchy is nodding rapidly.

"We heard about each of the books," she says. "They were created when the keepers were created. They were intended to record history as it happened, to show the past to all who sought wisdom so that the same mistakes wouldn't be repeated."

The keeper stops pacing and holds up the hand on which he wears his crown-shaped ring. "*The Book of Dark Magic* is not like the others. I saw this in the dying memories of those who held it in their hands and were betrayed by it."

Again, Anarchy nods, her cheek brushing Lucian's. "That book goes beyond the nature of dark magic," she says. "It's insidious. Bloodthirsty. Even among dark creatures, it's considered a dangerous, unreliable object."

Lucian gives a harsh laugh. "That's why Dad needed me to read it at the same time as him. He told me that *The Book of Dark Magic* can show different things to different people, even if they're looking at the same page. He made me describe to him what I saw, as I saw it. When he finally closed the book, he told me that I'd confirmed what the book had shown him, too."

I try to calm my racing heart. "Can you tell me what it was?"

Lucian's golden eyes are haunted and full of shadows. "First, I saw bodies," he says. "More than even a dark creature wants to see. They were piled in basements, scattered along hidden passages, choking the sewers. All manner of supernaturals— shifters, witches, mages, vampires, and others—but all were of dark magic. I could tell by their dying auras.

"Their bodies filled every shadow, every place that dark creatures like to hide: dens, and caverns, and concealed rooms. The blood splatter was so bright... Claw marks were scratched across the walls of every place where they lay."

His focus is suddenly on my hands and I fight the need to tuck them away from sight.

"Claw marks were gouged deep into concrete and through thick metal," he says. "Surfaces that other creatures' claws can't cut, but yours can—"

He suddenly winces again, his fingers rising to his temples. Anarchy leans in, her teeth bared, but Lucian nudges his face to hers before she can bite him. "I'm okay. For now."

She gives him a little nod but doesn't retreat far, her head resting on his shoulder.

"The claw marks..." I swallow and try to gather my thoughts.

"Surely, there must be other creatures with powerful claws." My suggestion sounds hollow in my own ears, but I rally. "How could you be sure they were mine?"

"Because I saw you," Lucian says. "Just as you are. Right down to the color of your hair." He shakes his head at my locks. "Black with silver streaks at the front and tipped with blonde. You were standing at the end of a trail of bodies, cutting down yet another being. Don't ask me who they were. All I saw was blood."

My chest is constricting. My heart is thumping.

"You were so quiet about it," Lucian continues. "Intent on your task. The screaming was theirs. And then it stopped."

I try to breathe, clinging to what the keeper said—that the book only serves itself—along with the reason why I started this conversation in the first place.

My source of hope.

"When you saw my wings for the first time, you said they changed everything." My throat squeezes as I ask, "Why?"

A little of the darkness leaves Lucian's expression. "Because when it all went quiet, when you stepped over that final body, there was another shadow. A new being. I couldn't see their face. I don't know who they were. The image was blurred and fuzzy and all I know is that they had wings. Maybe red ones, but I can't be sure."

He pauses, slowly blowing out a breath, his face becoming pale again.

I know I can't expect him to keep remembering. I know there will be a limit to what he can tell me and we might be nearing it.

But Anarchy darts in and nibbles his earlobe, bringing a sigh of relief to his lips.

"Can you go on?" she asks softly.

He nods and raises his eyes to mine. They're glazed again,

but also bloodshot now, and I'm certain we'll only have moments before he needs to stop.

"You fought this supernatural," Lucian says, his voice slurring. "And unlike every other creature before it, it defeated you."

My heart jumps. It feels like everything within the room stops. An intense silence falling. "It kills me?"

The keeper is a looming shadow at my side, breaking the motionlessness when his hand flies to his heart.

But for once, I'm not entirely sure if it's due to *my* emotions because... I feel nothing.

The initial shock has vanished and an emptiness fills me.

It's like a cold breeze wafting through me, taking my fear and turmoil with it.

"That being lifted your body into the air, bleeding and broken, and dropped you from a great height. You were alive before you hit the ground. I'm certain of it because your mouth moved. You said something. I don't know what. But it was the fall that killed you. After that, you lay still." Lucian sways against Anarchy, his breathing labored now, a rapid deterioration.

He needs to stop and there's a part of me that wants him to, but he persists. "You never spread your wings. If it had really been you, you would have spread your wings..." His voice is a bare whisper now, a forced and strangled sound. "You could have saved yourself. The version of you in the book didn't have wings. The book is wrong... It wasn't you... It won't happen..."

He closes his eyes and leans into Anarchy.

"Stop now," she whispers to him. "You don't have to remember anymore."

He nods against her as he drags air into his chest in the growing silence.

The emptiness within me becomes colder, expanding through my chest and spreading through my arms and legs until my whole body is numb.

"It changes nothing," I whisper. Just as my father said.

Lucian's eyes fly open. "But—"

"I can't fly."

Lucian's forehead creases. I keep my focus on him because I'm not ready to face the others.

"What do you mean?" he asks.

I guess he didn't see me fall when Ryuji dropped me. After all, Lucian arrived at the rocky outcrop to see me with my wings spread and safely standing on solid ground. He probably thought I flew there.

"You saw my wings and assumed I could fly." My voice is wooden. "You would be forgiven for believing that someone with wings would spread them to save themselves from a fall."

"But..."

"My wings don't work, Lucian." A horrible, awful, terrible laugh pushes at my throat. "Which means everything in that book could be true."

CHAPTER THIRTY

"No!" Anarchy's cry cuts through the tension. "That book is full of lies. Your life is your own, Darkness."

Her voice continues to rise as she slips away from Lucian and closes in on me, her beautiful features marred with anger. "Your life and death will not be decided by a fucking book!"

The intensity of her anger breaks through the icy cocoon that was forming around me.

A sob rises to my throat as fear threatens to choke me. It's a full rush of hot fear, like a wave crashing onto me.

Will I be the source of so much death?

Will I die, broken from a fall because of these stupid, fucking wings?

As Anarchy practically launches herself across the space toward me, the male panthers also crowd around me, bumping into me so forcefully that I fall forward over my knees before they round me, slip their heads under my chest, and lift me back up. Just in time for Anarchy's arms to close around me.

Over her shoulder, I can see Lucian shuffling toward me in an uncoordinated manner, all feet and legs, clearly a consequence of reliving the dark visions while being imbued with Anarchy's venom.

He presses in beside Anarchy, his hand closing over my shoulder. His gaze is unsteady, but he holds my eyes.

"You can't be the killer I saw," he says with a conviction I wasn't expecting. "You asked about the wings, so I told you about them. But that's not the only reason I know it isn't true: Your eyes aren't dead like hers." He arches an eyebrow at me. "Besides, you have an internal moral code all your own, remember?"

I soak up the warmth I find in his words. Take in the strength of Anarchy's embrace. Fill my ears with the panthers' purring and snarls, forceful, alternating sounds, as if they can't decide which will soothe me most.

I focus on the defiance of those around me since I'm struggling to find my own.

"What do I do now?" I ask, my voice small. "What am I supposed to do?"

"What did you want to do?" Anarchy asks, her arms remaining around me. "Before you heard about the book."

"Well..." I blink away the tears in my eyes. "Simple vengeance lies in taking down my father." I draw back a little. "Him alone. Nobody else has to get hurt. No other dark creature has to die."

I might have spoken with Ryuji about broken teapots, but that was in the context of convincing him that I wouldn't hurt his people. And as for the dark beings that follow my father, my vengeance has never lain in punishing them for belonging to the Nostra Empire or following orders. The empire is my family and that makes all of them family, too.

Anarchy's eyes gleam. "You will become the head of the Nostra family, just as you originally wanted when you thought your father was dead."

"Nobody else has to die," Lucian says, nodding his head, his dark hair falling across his eyes, which are brighter than before. "Only our father."

"And what of you, Lucian?" I ask softly.

His forehead creases at my question. "What do you mean?"

"Well, until I turned up, you were the heir—"

He makes a soft, scoffing sound. "I was never the heir. In fact, I'm certain my father intended to have me killed and blame it on a rival."

I wish I were shocked at Lucian's theory, but oh, that does sound like something our father would do.

"What better use for me?" Lucian's bloodshot eyes leak a little and he squeezes them closed, blinking hard. "He could orchestrate my death at a time that suited him and create justification to take someone out as 'revenge' for my death." He grimaces. "No, sister, you will never have to watch your back with me. If I help you end our father's reign, all I will ask for is my freedom."

I believe him.

When I was seeking answers from him back in the apartment, I sensed that he was keeping something from me. Now, there is nothing but openness in his eyes, as if he's peeled away the secrets and the burdens.

"You'll have your freedom," I say.

He's pressed in beside Anarchy and at my declaration, she casts him a little smile, side-eyeing him from beneath her lashes. He swipes at the liquid dripping down his cheeks with his free hand, the corners of his mouth lifting a little at her.

But his smile quickly fades as his focus returns to me. "How do we take him down? He's the Ultima Nostra. Other supernaturals have tried again and again. Even the Assassin's Legion has failed to end him."

"Because they would have tried to kill him, I'm sure," I say.

"Well... yes."

My jaw clenches and my teeth grit as a little of my fire begins to build again.

"We won't take his life until we've taken everything else from him," I say. "We'll tear him apart, piece by piece. Slice by slice. *Then* we will finish him."

Lucian's eyes have widened, but the panthers are grinning at me, as if they're already imagining the little pieces into which I'll cut my father.

"Back in his lair, you said it yourself, brother," I continue. "Our father is vulnerable now. James Vanguard, the old god, no longer stands at his side. The protection our father enjoyed from that alliance is gone."

There was a time when both James and his sister, Halle, used to protect my father. From the little that Vanguard told me, I've surmised that Halle ended her alliance with my father at the same time she had the disagreement with her brother. Now Vanguard has ended his alliance with Taiven, too.

"You weakened Dad," Lucian says, exhaling slowly as a little light returns to his eyes. "When you helped Elijah escape. Dad's leverage over Vanguard is gone."

"I'm assuming Jonah's left our father's side now, too?"

Jonah, the fire jotunn, behaved like a beta toward Vanguard. His loyalty to Vanguard and his protectiveness of Elijah was clear. He would have laid down his life for that boy.

"Jonah helped me deliver you to Dad, and then he left." Lucian shifts a little, his lips pursing again.

"Lucian?"

"On our way back to Dad, while you were unconscious, Jonah asked me if I really wanted to hand you over. I think he was giving me a choice, but I didn't see it at the time. I'm sorry I went through with it."

My eyes widen. "It's okay. It's what I wanted. I needed to meet the man I thought killed my father. And I guess… in a way… I did."

"Where do we hit him next?" Lucian asks.

I take a deep breath, feeling a sense of calm returning. "If our father believes so strongly in what *The Book of Dark Magic* shows him… if he's had it for years and followed it for that long… then he'll be lost without it."

Lucian jolts. "We're stealing *The Book of Dark Magic*?"

I smile. "We are."

CHAPTER THIRTY-ONE

My brother blows out an exhale, caution filling his eyes. "Veda, no. You saw what even *thinking* about that book did to me. You can't look at it, let alone touch it—"

"But I can."

Lucian stares at me. As does Anarchy.

"I have already," I say.

Anarchy glances at Lucian before she focuses back on me. "Darkness?"

"The woman who raised me left me a page from it. I wasn't hurt when I held that page or looked at it."

All the time we've been talking, I've been conscious of the keeper. Of the way he has remained silent and hunched in his cloak. At some point, he stopped pacing and now he's like a pillar, his head a little bowed as if by a weight, his hair falling forward over his face, his features in shadow.

He finally speaks and his voice is hollow, so much so that a cold chill settles at the base of my spine. "My Veda is one of the few beings who can hold a page from *The Book of Dark Magic* and resist its power."

Why does that sound like a bad thing all of a sudden?

At the time, he seemed to marvel at my ability to resist the power in that piece of paper, but now...

I shake off my misgivings. This is the first real step I can take to truly weaken my father's hold over the Nostra Empire. It's my best next step.

"Once I have the book, our father will make mistakes," I say, refocusing on Anarchy and Lucian. "I just need to know where the book is kept so we can figure out how to steal it."

Lucian leans back a little, shaking his head. "I'm sorry, Veda. This falls into the category of important information that I wasn't told."

Damn. My shoulders sink as I try not to deflate.

"But James Vanguard could tell you," Lucian says.

My lips part in surprise. "Vanguard?"

"He let it slip once that he knew how to find it."

"Okay, then. I'll make Vanguard tell us." Maybe I'll get Ryuji's sword back for him in the process. "That is... assuming we can find Vanguard."

Ugh. I don't want to get stuck in a loop, looking for one thing to find another.

"I can help you there," Lucian says. "Before he left, Jonah gave me a way to contact him if I was ever in trouble."

That does sound like Jonah.

I may have been at odds with the fire jotunn, but once we had a truce, he was far more thoughtful than I'd expected him to be, even giving the panthers water when they needed it.

"If we find Jonah, we'll find Vanguard," Lucian says.

"There's one more thing," I say, peering at my brother and hoping he has answers. "What do you know about the way our father controls light magic?"

"That was a surprise to me, too," Lucian replies. "I don't know how he's doing it. It shouldn't even be possible. All I can tell you is that it's a recent development. Even two weeks ago, he didn't have that power. I'm certain of it."

I was hoping for more, but for now, that will have to be enough.

"Okay, then. We have a month to prepare," I say. "Anarchy, I need you to teach me your combat skills, and Lucian..." I swallow my pride. "Can you show me how to fly?"

I could ask the keeper—and I will if Lucian can't help me—but it seems like a good chance to spend more time getting to know my brother.

"Gladly," Lucian says.

"Thank you." I give him a nod. "In the meantime, the keeper can turn the panthers back into elves." I turn to the keeper, a little more hesitant now. "Yes?"

"Tomorrow," he says with a low snarl before he turns and strides from the hall. His cloak swishes across the *tatami* flooring until he reaches the porch, where it retracts as his countenance changes yet again, his clothing becoming simple blue jeans and a gray T-shirt.

As he crosses the porch and disappears down the stairs, I catch sight of the face he showed me when he was healing me back in the forest.

Seeing him like this fills me with shivers. Of fear or anticipation, I'm not sure.

His eyes are the gentlest green, his jaw cut and chiseled, his shoulders broad, his arm muscles defined, and his hair catches the sunlight. The silver strands gleam so brightly, I'm forced to look away even with my blindfold on.

When I open my eyes again, he's gone, his quick footfalls down the beach fading from my hearing.

The rest of my family has remained around me and now Anarchy's arms tighten again.

"The keeper disagrees with your plan," she murmurs.

"It seems so," I whisper.

"He's right to be concerned." Lucian tilts his head. "You remember what Dad said about loving you and Galeia before his 'eyes were opened'. Well, one guess as to what might have opened his eyes."

"The book," I say.

"It turns love to hate," Anarchy whispers, tears sparkling on her eyelashes.

I freeze at the sight of them.

"It's rare for dark creatures to find love," she whispers, holding my gaze. "To lose that love is a tragedy. But to *choose* to destroy it is truly monstrous. Even the vilest dark creature can recognize that."

I lift my arms around her, trying to reach for Lucian at the same time, wishing I had more arms to pull the panthers closer too.

"It won't change me." I hold on to them tightly. "Do you hear me? That book won't change me."

I fight the possibility that I'm speaking a lie.

For a few horrible moments, when Lucian was recounting what he saw and I thought the book might be telling the truth, it turned me cold. It washed through me and took all my warmth and left me empty. Even a few days ago, I would have told myself it didn't matter how many empty pits opened up within me on my path to revenge, but that, too, has become a lie.

It does matter. These dark pits matter.

I remind myself that I've touched the book's darkness before. On that torn-out page, I saw the image of a family that never existed: my father standing beside Galeia, his black wings curving around her, both of them smiling down at the baby in her arms. It was the dream of a family that was never true. That moment never happened.

And now, that knowledge only strengthens the fact that everything in the book is a lie.

And maybe, that's what the woman in the cell wanted me to know.

Everything was a lie.

"My destiny will not be determined by images on parchment." I snarl. "My destiny will be my own."

"Yes," Anarchy says, a determined light in her eyes. "And we will help you reach it."

Half an hour later, I follow the path through the jungle, tracking the way the keeper went.

He left my side abruptly—a first for him—which probably means he wants to be alone, but I'm not about to avoid what could be a very difficult conversation.

I left Anarchy, Lucian, and the panthers back at the training hut with a single task: Figure out how the fuck to catch fish now that wild boars are off the menu.

I can't hear the keeper, or sense him in any way I can quantify, but when he told me he would be able to find me anywhere, I didn't imagine that it might work both ways.

He may be out of my sight, but I find myself aware of a tug within my chest, a feeling that draws me inexplicably in his direction.

I don't stop to marvel at the strangeness of the flowers hanging from the branches, some so large and heavy-looking that the boughs are weighed almost to the ground where the blooms form a carpet lining the path.

In the distance, I can hear falling water, and I track the sound as the path gently turns and finally lets out into a new clearing, this one open to the sky.

Every part of the clearing appears carefully sculpted, a sharp contrast to the wildness of the jungle around it.

A pond surrounded by stones sits in the middle of the

clearing with two large rocks rising up from within it, both flat and mossy across the top.

On the far left side, a third smooth-faced rock rises up higher than the others at the side of the pond. It's surrounded by foliage while water cascades over it and into the pond, forming a little waterfall. I can only assume there's some sort of stream behind it from which the water comes.

Beautiful fish with ivory scales interspersed with bright-orange patches glide through the water, the amber splashes of color on their backs appearing like flowers glimmering beneath the surface.

These fish look like they'd be easy to catch, but somehow, I don't think I should feed them to the panthers.

On the far right is another hut made of polished wood, which is open on three sides and closed in at the back, almost like a porch without a building attached to it.

The keeper stands near the hut, his focus on the pool of water, although I'm sure he senses my presence.

He's wearing the same face he was when he left the training hall and it gives me pause, but I forge ahead, prowling toward him. Waves of emotion rise off him like a physical force pushing at me—all of them volatile. Frustration. Anger. Worry. Flickers of dark energy play around both of his hands but more intensely around his crown.

He looks up at my approach, watching me with gentle, green eyes that shouldn't belong to a dark thing like him. Far too gentle for the emotions that seem to be radiating out from him.

I've seen his angry face. His blue-eyed fury. I've seen him take the form of a devil with blood-red horns and a scaled tail. I've watched him turn into a blue-skinned draugr that reeked of death and into a white-eyed demon of smoke and ash.

And yet *this* face...

This beautiful face scares the fuck out of me.

And it's like he knows it. Or maybe wants me to feel that way, because with every step I take, it's as if he's pushing at me, telling me to walk away, but I can't for a second understand why.

And I won't, even for a second, choose to back off.

CHAPTER THIRTY-TWO

 I can hardly breathe as I stop a few paces away from him at the edge of the pond. "Diavolo?"

He shakes his head, his silver hair brushing his jaw. "Is that still my name?"

I suggested he call himself "Diavolo" because I thought he might like it, but it occurs to me now that ever since he healed me in the forest, he has stopped being *Diavolo* to me and has simply become *the keeper*.

"Keeper," I say, more quietly.

He nods. "That's who I am." The corners of his mouth turn down. "You can give me any name you like, but I'll never be anything else."

Names have too much fucking power.

But then... so do intentions.

"You're angry with me," I say, refusing to look away from this face that scares me for reasons I can't define.

His only reply is the sudden burst of dark light around his fingertips, flickering around and around his ring—the source of his power. When I first met him, I imagined taking his crown from his head, but I haven't thought about taking it since.

"You disagree with the path I've chosen," I persist, more quietly, still refusing to release his gaze.

"I do."

"You think it's dangerous."

"It is." His growl is deep and dark. "It's fucking dangerous. It's reckless and impulsive—"

"But you can't be surprised that I chose it," I say, standing firm in the face of his objections.

He's slower to respond this time. "I am not. You are who you are."

"Then… will you help me achieve my goal?"

His features harden. "Do I have a choice?"

My lips part as I draw a quick breath. *Of course he does.* But my tongue stills before I can utter those words because maybe… that's a lie.

"We made a deal," he says, his voice becoming cold. "You have the power to choose *how* we complete it. So do I have a choice?"

He doesn't. He's bound to my vengeance, living and breathing by the power of my heart, and I have all the power right now.

"No," I whisper. "You don't."

His features wipe clean of emotion, the dark light around his hands fades, and all of the anger and turmoil that was roiling around him seems to vanish into nothing.

"You chose not to lie," he tells me, his voice flat.

"I don't want to lie to you. Not ever."

Maybe there was a time when I wouldn't have hesitated to lie. I would have told myself it was merely my nature as a dark creature to tell untruths, but it would be a flimsy attitude after everything we've experienced together.

His response is silence. A long silence as he stands still, like he feels nothing at all.

I search his eyes, desperate to know his thoughts because the absence of feeling is even more shocking to me than the barrage of fury I sensed in him before.

"What are you thinking?" I ask at a whisper.

He turns away, stepping back, but I grab his arm, making him pause.

"What are you thinking?" I ask, more forcefully.

He tugs on my arm, a warning light in his eyes, as if my touch will make him snap.

I'm not about to back down. I reach for his face with my free hand. "Tell me!"

He is rapidly furious once more, his expression so savage that dark light breaks across his body, flickering around his lips and eyes and jaw like shadows trying to claim him.

He snarls back at me, "I'm thinking I don't want to see you break."

My eyes widen, my hand slipping from his arm.

"You won't." I swallow past the lump in my throat. "I won't."

Needing him to hear me, I dart forward again, reaching up to wrap both hands around his shoulders, needing to follow my instinct to kiss him and wipe away his fears. Despite understanding the unspoken rule that somehow, kisses are rarities between us.

My fingertips brush his neck and I'm unsettled by how cold his skin suddenly feels, so startlingly icy that I gasp as I run my fingertips to his jaw.

He wrests free of my hands, leaving them raised in the air so I'm holding on to nothing.

"You shouldn't make impossible promises," he says, his eyes empty now.

I can't keep the hurt from my voice. "My promises are only impossible if you're not by my side." I reach for him again, prepared for the chill in his skin. "Stay with me. Stand with me. And nothing is impossible."

His beautiful lips part, his green eyes flooding with pain, and he presses his hand to his chest. "You truly believe that."

"I know it," I say, every part of my body thrumming with the need to close the gap between us and make him see that together, we can defy the impossible.

Before I can make contact, he drops to his knees, his arms hanging loosely at his sides.

His face turns up to mine and he whispers, "No matter how badly you want to believe you'll remain unaffected by that book, it will destroy you, my Veda." His voice is hollow as he repeats himself. "It will destroy you."

Looking down at him, drowning in his gentle eyes, trying to see past the dark light flickering around him and the strands of his silver hair that act like a mirror to all that darkness, that's when I realize…

This is his broken face.

All his anguish, all his fear is bared for me to see. He has no shields and, despite my convictions, that realization brings me sudden dread.

I sway toward him, uncertain if he'll push me away again, only for his arms to wrap around my hips, tugging me closer.

He buries his head against my stomach, kissing me through the material of my shirt. "Don't break, my Veda," he says, his voice muffled as he tugs at the base of the shirt. "Never break. No matter what."

My voice sticks in my throat as he pushes my tunic up, his mouth working across my bare skin to the base of each breast, his tongue swirling against my skin, his needy groan rumbling through me.

I run my fingers into his hair, closing my eyes with a moan when he pushes my bra up and out of the way to access my breasts, his hands and mouth stroking away all shreds of worry.

He travels a path to the top of my pants, tugging them down

a little and kissing along the edge of the waistband, tasting every inch of skin that he reveals and my sigh mingles with his groan.

Sweeping his arms across my back, he rises up and takes me with him into the trees, where the foliage wraps around us and the flowers bend at my back. I can't tell what's bough or branch or trunk, only that there's a solid surface now behind me, and the keeper's mouth and hands are feeding the ache within my chest.

An ache that ascends into my mind and floods my awareness.

A need that's all-consuming.

I reach for the waistband of his pants, but he's already dropping to his knees again, dragging my underwear down, his mouth closing hungrily over my core.

I grip his shoulders, sensing the wetness between my legs— from his mouth or my body, probably both—before his finger slips inside me, easing the ache while his mouth flicks across my clit.

My hands find his neck, his hair, gripping his shoulders again, needing to touch him wherever I can reach, wanting to connect more fully than this.

Needy gasps leave my lips, becoming moans as the pleasure builds, a force between us.

"Let go, my Veda," he says against my core, his tongue pressing and releasing, a desperation in his voice that I wasn't expecting. "I need you to let go."

I give in to my body's needs, rocking against his hand and mouth, dragging his free hand back to my breast, letting the heat build within me, taking everything from it until the crash breaks across me.

When I open my eyes, his broken face is gone. His eyes are the darkest blue, his hair is as black as the panthers' fur, his body sleek and deadly as he should be, his smile even darker. And yet his angry face brings me peace, not fear.

I catch my breath, leaning forward to kiss his upturned lips, conscious of the glistening moisture on them, which he licks away before I can reach him.

Wrapping one arm around me, he pushes aside the foliage around us and we sink together onto the carpet of leaves and flowers, still cocooned within the trees.

I leave my pants off and quickly slip off my bra and shirt before we meet the ground.

As I settle in beside him, my fingertips glide beneath his shirt, following a path across his chest, stroking his warm skin, pushing at his clothing. I lower my mouth to his chest, tasting his body as he watches me from beneath his lashes.

Today, he tastes salty like seawater, but also somehow sweet.

I reach for the waistband of his pants, tugging them down before I slip my left leg across his hips so that I'm straddling him while my wet core rests right up against his length. I don't take my eyes off his face as I wrap my fingers around him, stroking across his silky skin.

As his breath hitches, his lips part and then settle into a soft line that I'd kiss if I could reach his face, but for now, my focus remains on his length.

His eyelids lower with every stroke of my hands, the tension releasing from his stomach and shoulders until he appears more peaceful than I've ever seen him—despite the way his breathing increases and his thigh muscles tighten.

Sensing he's close to the crash, I lean forward, laying myself close to his chest, my breasts brushing his skin as I reach for his lips.

His hand closes around the back of my head, drawing me down to his mouth, his lips crashing against mine, a hunger that devours me, mouth and tongue and heart and soul.

Suddenly, I'm the one moaning, needing this kiss like I need the darkness of night.

I sense the tightening of his stomach muscles before he shudders beneath me, his groan mingling with my gasps.

I inhale the sound of his pleasure like it's air and I need it.

Our kiss softens, slower, lighter by the second until it breaks.

He opens his eyes and within them is the slightest hint of soft green, seemingly a trick of the light, before they're strongly blue again.

With a satisfied sigh, I draw back into an upright position, still straddling him while he sweeps his hand across his stomach, his emerald-green warlock power glimmering and taking his cum with it.

I sink down against him, letting the silence settle around us, tracing the contours of his muscles, pressing kisses where I can reach him.

Too soon, reality presses in on me again. I need to pee, to stay healthy, and after that, I have so many questions for him. I eye the nearby bushes unhappily, only to find him smiling at me.

"There's a bathroom at the back of the little hut," he says.

"Oh?" I didn't see any doors, but then, this place seems to be made of camouflaged spaces.

"Here." His emerald magic glimmers again and my clothing rises from the ground while he scoops me up into his arms.

I nod, pressing my face, blindfold and all, to his shoulder as he carries me from within the trees to the little hut at the side of the pond.

Once there, I make out the very faint lines at the edge of panels that slide open to reveal a small area at the back with a toilet, sink, and what appears to be a little dressing area.

Once I've finished up, I return to the outer area of the hut to find the keeper sitting calmly there.

After pulling on my clothing, I slide down beside him, slipping my arms around him.

"Why are you so reluctant to help the panthers?" I ask softly, propping my chin on his shoulder. "I understood your reticence when we were in that little apartment, given the explosion, but why now?"

"Because curse magic is never purely dark magic," he replies, shifting a little to stroke my hair down my back. "It also carries something of its maker. The magic that gargoyle would have used is what he would have called 'deep magic,' but now we call it 'old magic.'"

"Of course," I muse. "It wasn't exactly 'old' at the time."

The keeper chuckles. "Precisely." He sobers. "But breaking a curse like that carries a risk that I wasn't fully aware of when I did it."

"What kind of risk?"

"The release of old magic could harm anyone it touches."

I remember the billowing smoke, which I thought was a byproduct of the explosion, but now I remember just how forcefully the keeper reacted... "Is that why you inhaled the smoke?"

He nods. "I had to do everything in my power to contain it."

I narrow my eyes at him. "But you're dark magic, not old magic, so then..."

How did he break the curse, let alone contain it?

His jaw clenches. He shifts a little. Hunches his shoulders a little. Squints at me. "Yes."

"Yes... what?" But then my eyes widen with a realization. "Oh, but of course... The magic that created you was old magic, wasn't it?"

His lips thin and then turn down at the corners. "It was the oldest of creation magic. Extinct now, like so many of the old beings."

I consider the solemnity of his statement. For all he knows, he could once have been one of those beings that doesn't exist anymore.

I once asked him if, despite not knowing who he was, he would have become the keeper by choice. He answered me with a question: *Is there truly a choice when the world you know will be consumed if you don't act?*

Whoever he was when he became one of the four keepers, he stopped the world from being destroyed.

And now, here he is with me... and I am a dark creature who, according to *The Book of Dark Magic*, will tear the world apart again.

CHAPTER THIRTY-THREE

I squeeze my eyes shut, trying to block out the dark thoughts invading my mind so I can focus back on the panthers' curse.

"Are you concerned that when you broke the curse, you somehow accessed that old magic?"

"The magic at the fabric of my being." He nods. "It shouldn't be possible, but it would be incredibly dangerous. I can't quantify the risks if I were to accidentally trigger it again."

My voice is a bare whisper. "Are we fucking lucky to be alive?"

"Probably."

Damn. "I'm glad I didn't know that at the time."

"Now you do."

My forehead puckers, my hand flexing against his chest. "But we can't leave them as panthers."

He scoops a finger under my chin. "I will try to help them, my Veda. I'll do everything I can to break the curse using only dark magic. But I won't risk anyone's life in the process."

"I understand." At that moment, the sun comes out from behind the clouds. I turn my face against his chest and squeeze my eyes closed, my voice becoming muffled. "The sunlight's too bright."

He wraps his upper arm around me. "We should return to a nocturnal existence. Sleep in the day—"

"Train at night," I murmur.

"I'm sorry I can't turn day to night," he says. "But I can give you a comfortable place to sleep during the day."

I'm aware of the dark light flickering around his fingertips before screens form across the hut's open sides, each appearing to be made of black paper stretched between pieces of wood.

I breathe out a sigh of relief and my muscles relax as the screens drop us into a lovely, murky darkness.

Dark light flares again and, in the next moment, a pillow and blanket appear, both in just the right place as he lays me down onto the floor and settles in beside me. I prefer a hard surface for sleeping, but I won't deny how luxurious it feels to have a nice pillow beneath my head.

"Better," I mumble, nestling into his side before I fall asleep.

I wake to low voices outside the hut and immediately recognize the keeper's voice and Anarchy's melodic tones. Or perhaps... not so melodic since there's a tension in her words I wasn't expecting.

It must be nighttime now because the sun no longer glares behind the black screens. Fresh clothing sits in a neat pile next to me, but I don't reach for it yet.

I don't want them to sense that I'm awake because their heightened tension is giving me pause.

Of course, if Anarchy were in her panther form, she would certainly notice the change in my breathing, and I can't be sure what form the keeper is currently in, but it seems they're too absorbed in their conversation to notice my alert state.

"You asked me what I knew of your creation, and I answered truthfully," Anarchy says in a quiet snarl. "I don't know who you were, Keeper. But that's the thing... nobody did."

The keeper's response is terse. "Your point?"

"There were whispers about the other keepers," Anarchy says. "Rumors about who they were *and* who they weren't. But as for your identity, there was only silence."

The sound of soft footfalls reaches me, bare feet on stone, and I picture one of them stepping toward the other. Most likely Anarchy moving toward the keeper, given the lightness of the sound.

"It was a terrible silence, Keeper," she whispers in a near hiss. "For all this time, I've wondered why." She pauses, her voice strained. "Why was there such silence around you?"

The friction in the air increases and now I wish the sun were still shining because then I might be able to see their silhouettes.

"What are you hiding, Keeper?" she asks, a hint of desperation in her voice now.

"We're all hiding something," he replies, so coldly that I picture him in his tall, blue-eyed, black-haired form. "We are dark creatures, are we not?"

She lets out another hiss, but this time, it sounds like an expression of frustration before her voice hardens. "Whatever it is, know this: Do *not* hurt Darkness. Don't shatter the heart she gave you. And whatever you do, don't try to circumvent her path."

Again, there's a soft footfall and now I picture her stepping right up into his space. "The creatures of the dark have waited a long time for someone with the power to unite us. Don't stand in the way of her destiny."

"And what of your destiny, Anna-ve-shaleia?" he asks, his low growl making it sound like he's morphing into his dragon form now.

There's another silence and then she whispers, "My destiny is my own."

"On that, we are agreed."

Anarchy's response is clipped and polite, but now it seems she's moving away. "When Darkness wakes up, let her know that Lucian and I will be on the beach. It's best if she works on her wings before I tire her out with combat training."

With that, her footfalls recede and I'm left to wonder at their conversation and how much friction the coming month could bring.

When I'm ready for my first session with Lucian on the beach, Anarchy and the panthers seem to sense my unwillingness to spread my wings in front of them and they quickly disappear into the jungle.

The keeper, too, makes himself scarce, telling me he's going to meditate on how to break the panthers' curse. Meditation seems like an uncharacteristically peaceful thing for him to do, but I don't question it. Whatever it takes.

My brother appears far more relaxed than I was expecting, his golden eyes bright, and I wonder if he, too, is finally well-rested—assuming he also slept the afternoon away.

"Learning how to fly isn't about beating your wings," he says, standing opposite me on the sand. "You need to learn about your wings as a part of your body and how every other part of your body relates to them. Can you release them for me?"

I brace for the pain as I allow the crawling sensation, the tingling in my back, to dominate my senses. Gritting my teeth in anticipation of the tearing sensation, I force my wings to burst forth.

Lucian winces. "That looked painful."

"It always is."

He clears his throat. "Okay, well, first you're going to sit down and let your wings flop to the sand. I want to check your feathers and then your back muscles. If that's okay with you?"

"Sure."

It's a relief to kneel on the sand and curl forward, letting my wings' weight rest down on either side of me—even if I'll be shaking off the grit later.

Lucian starts with my feathers, just as he said he would.

"These are heavily metallic," he says, and when I look up he's wearing an incredulous expression.

He carefully splays one of my largest feathers across his palm. "See how the core shines? And if you touch it, it's cold like metal."

"Yeah." I grimace. "I sort of got that when our good old Dad rammed one of my feathers into my shoulder."

He grimaces but plows on. "Even the fronds are metallic... *ish*. Like some sort of impossible combination of organic material and..." His forehead puckers. "Titanium? Maybe? It looks like it's the same substance your claws are made of."

To examine my feathers, he was kneeling on the sand but now he rises to his feet, steps back, and releases his own wings before dropping to the ground again.

He curves his left wing toward me. "Do you see my upper feathers?"

"Yeah." I barely glance at them. "They're normal—"

"No," he says with a gentle smile. "They aren't."

I furrow my brow at him.

He leans forward a little. "Look closer."

I straighten as much as I can without having to lift my wings too much and reach for the outer edge of his feathers.

I'm surprised when my fingertips brush what feels like...

I close my eyes to sense it better...

"Stone?"

I can't keep the surprise from my voice. Opening my eyes, I find him nodding.

"My mother was a stone gargoyle. I must have inherited a little of her natural power. It makes the edges of my feathers hard and because the fronds are so fine, when I move quickly they can act like blades."

My lips purse with realization. "So that's how you fought Halle."

She had conjured deadly-sharp vines to spear the air, attempting to impale and capture us, but Lucian swept his wings through them, his feathers sparking as he made contact. He cut right through the vines with the tips of his wings.

"It's my belief that our father's dark angelic nature is so powerful that it forced combinations of physical traits on us that would never have otherwise happened," he says. "I think it was inevitable that you would be born with wings despite it never being the case for wolves." He flushes a little. "Just my theory."

I grin. "Or our biological mothers were so powerful that we took after them in a lot of ways instead of being purely angelic."

He mirrors my smile. "That, too." Rising to his feet, he heads to my side again. "I'll check your back now."

I hunch over my knees, relieved to let my wings flop to the sand once more.

Lucian presses each muscle, his touch clinical but gentle, as he explains to me why I would find it difficult to fly.

"These muscles here are too short, too contracted. They'll be stopping you from moving your wings. These muscles here are the opposite—too stretched out to have the elasticity you need. And then there are muscles that should have developed here and here but haven't. The good news is that there are exercises you can do to change all that."

I'm curious. "How do you know all this?"

"Jonah taught me."

"A jotunn without wings taught you about wings?"

"He taught me how to fly." Lucian shrugs it off. "Apparently, when he was a youngling, he spent a lot of time around the Valkyrie."

My eyebrows shoot up. "Seriously?"

"Seriously. That was before they were extinct, obviously." Lucian comes around to face me again, all business. "They had metallic wings, too. So hopefully everything Jonah told me will help you. We'll start with stretches and take it from there. It's a good thing we have a month."

For the next three hours, my body becomes what Lucian calls a "pretzel".

Apparently, they're yummy to eat. Not so great to fold myself into the shape of one.

After we break for food—or what I decide to call, "lunch at midnight"—Anarchy claims my time, taking me into the training hall where the floor is soft. Or maybe soft-*ish*, as Lucian might say.

It certainly hurts like hell every time she knocks me onto it.

"You rely heavily on your claws," she says, looming over me for the tenth time as I lie on my back and try to catch my breath. "Which is completely natural when they're your greatest weapon. But every part of your body can be just as deadly." She holds her hand out to help me up. "Don't worry. I'll show you how."

By the time dawn glimmers on the horizon and I reach for a blindfold again, I've got sore muscles everywhere.

But the night isn't over.

The keeper returns with the panthers, who mill about on the beach in seeming anticipation, and I can only guess that the keeper has decided to try breaking their curse.

Anarchy stays on the training hall's porch and Lucian joins her there, while I position myself at the bottom of the steps.

Based on what the keeper told me, I'm certain he won't try anything too dangerous to start.

Probably.

I reassess my assumption as I take him in. He's an imposing figure in his brown-eyed, dark-skinned persona, his feet planted in the sand and the look of concentration on his face intense.

He growls at the panthers, "Which of you is brave enough to go first?"

CHAPTER THIRTY-FOUR

Strife lurches forward, hissing and baring his silver teeth in the moonlight.

"Very well, but be warned: This might not work."

The keeper raises his hands, dark light splashing across his fingers before he draws his arm back and pitches the magic forward.

It arcs in the air, hitting Strife's shoulder and splattering across his side like liquid, the same way the keeper's magic hit Anarchy before he broke her curse.

I brace for the ripple of energy and the explosion that will indicate the curse is broken.

Instead, Strife lurches backward with a yelp, throwing himself into the sand, rolling side to side where the magic struck him.

The keeper's eyes widen and, with another shot of dark magic from the keeper's hands, Strife stops frantically rolling around and turns on the keeper with a savage hiss.

Now I can see that all of his fur is missing from the patch where the keeper's magic hit him.

Ouch.

At least it seems that the second blast of magic stopped the pain.

The keeper's brow is furrowed. He chews his lip before he seems to rally. "Who's next?"

Rumble and Riot cast glances at each other before Rumble prowls forward.

Meanwhile, the keeper is muttering to himself, "Maybe if I replicate the original sequence with an illusion first..."

Sapphire light shoots from his hand, taking on the appearance of the same illusion magic he used to turn Anarchy into a rabbit before he broke her curse.

The light is so bright, it breaks across the distance, lighting up the space around Rumble before it smacks into his body, which reacts instantly. His tail shortens, his teeth become rectangular, and his ears elongate.

A second later, the keeper sends another splash of dark light across the air, this one dark like ink.

Smoke explodes around Rumble's body, billowing out across the beach.

I hold my breath, filled with both hope and fear, needing to know that Rumble hasn't been hurt. Trusting that when the smoke clears, he'll be his elven self.

The keeper is acting quickly, his hands making a pulling motion in the air. The smoke rushes toward him, seeming to suck into his palms in streams, quickly leaving Rumble fully visible again.

Oh, dear.

Rumble chuffs and huffs with his rabbit mouth, his nose rapidly sniffing the air, his ears still big and his tail a cute ball of fluff while the rest of his body has returned to that of a panther.

He doesn't look impressed.

The keeper's mouth is downturned. "Next!" he shouts.

But Riot hisses and backs away. If he could speak, I'm sure he'd say, *No fucking way.*

The keeper glares at him and then his shoulders hunch. "That's fair," he grumbles, the corners of his mouth remaining downturned. He rubs his jaw. "I'll think on it some more and we'll try again tomorrow."

Riot rapidly shakes his head, as if trying again is never going to happen.

Rumble continues to chuff and huff, but the sounds he's making are more insistent as he prowls toward the keeper, his fuzzy tail fluffing up in the breeze.

The keeper shakes his head with a firm, "No. You'll have to wait for the partial illusion to wear off. I'm not removing it. I've already hit you with as much magic as your body can take tonight."

Rumble bares his rabbit teeth in apparent displeasure while Strife makes a chortling sound from a few paces away, sounding for all the world like he's laughing at his brother.

Rumble immediately leaps at him, the two panthers tumbling across the sand in a dark blur, Rumble proving that a cute little tail doesn't make him any less savage or agile.

Strife doesn't seem to care, chirping away as he leaps clear of his brother and then good-naturedly veering right back at him to bump his brother's shoulder.

Rumble chuffs sharply before turning his button tail and stalking away with as much dignity as I'm sure any bunny-panther could muster.

I grimace after him, feeling their disappointment deep in my chest.

In the realm of bad news, there's more to come since my ears suddenly *pop*.

"Incoming!" Lucian calls, he and Anarchy hurrying to join me at the bottom of the steps.

Five dragon shifters shoot across the sky and come to a sudden standstill above us.

I recognize Miku among them, her teal-and-black hair billowing about her face.

I guess it's a crack-of-dawn inspection, then.

I'm sure they thought they'd find us sleeping and must have intended to take us by surprise.

I haven't pulled on my blindfold, not needing it just yet, but I keep it ready, since the sun's rays will soon break across the horizon.

All five of them alight on the beach, the other four staying where they land while Miku strides toward us. She's holding two square pieces of matting that must be the replacements Ryuji promised for the floor.

In the distance, Strife and Rumble quickly vanish into the trees, but Riot stops and creeps quietly toward the teal-haired dragon.

He's as quiet as a shadow. If I couldn't see him, I wouldn't even know he was there.

The other dragons can see him, each of them eyeing him warily, their posture indicating that they'll step in if it looks like he's about to make a wrong move. As for Miku, she seems too intent on us to notice him for now.

As she approaches, she casts glances from me to Lucian, a crease forming in her forehead. "You have the same eyes."

"Good morning to you, too," I say.

I may have spent my life in a cage, but I'm certain that's how an early morning exchange of greetings is supposed to go.

"We have the same father," Lucian says to Miku, apparently finding her curiosity amusing—or so it seems by the predatory smile on his face.

"The Ultima Nostra of New York." Her distaste is clear in her tone. "Ryuji thinks you have a chance of beating him where others haven't succeeded." She gives me a hard onceover as she comes to a stop a few paces from me. "It's the only reason he let you live."

Well, probably not the only reason.

"If you say so." I retain my polite tone. "But please, don't let us keep you. Inspect away."

I sweep my arm toward the training hall, at which she pivots, tipping her chin at the other dragons. "Check the other—"

Her voice cuts off as she finally notices Riot, who crouches low to the ground right behind her.

He snarls up at her, every tense muscle in his body indicating he's deciding whether or not to leap at her.

She visibly gulps before she resumes speaking to her people without taking her eyes off him. "Check the other buildings," she calls. "I'll be fine here."

They look uncertain, but Riot hasn't made any significant moves yet, so I guess they're happy enough to split off, each heading in a different direction, although they all cast backward glances in Riot's direction.

Miku waits for her comrades to disappear, appearing to double-check that they're gone before she drops to her knees, resting the mats in the sand as the tension in her shoulders disappears. "Hello, Riot."

He slowly rises back to his full four-legged standing height, his head tilted, his snarls quieting.

She dares to lift her hand toward him, but he bares his teeth at her. Sharp, *sharp* teeth. He's torn apart an old god's weapons with those teeth, but she wouldn't know that.

His nose wrinkles as he hisses, a frightening, dangerous sight.

Within the trees at the side of the beach, there's a flicker of movement and I catch sight of Rumble and Strife poking their heads through the foliage to watch us. Rumble's rabbit ears catch in the greenery and he gives himself a shake, making a rustling noise, before he seems to realize that wasn't a good idea.

The turn of Miku's head tells me she's spotted them across the distance.

Her lips part and her forehead crinkles as she seems to zero in on Rumble's rabbit face. "Huh...?"

The two panthers quickly melt into the trees again, leaving her blinking. "Oh-kay."

Riot demands her attention with another snarl and she's wise to give it. Carefully scooping up the mats once more, she slowly rises to her feet.

"I'm going to fix the floor now," she says to him before slowly turning toward the steps up to the training hall.

Riot leaps across her path, getting underfoot, making it difficult for her to proceed, but she persists, managing to reach the training hall door and disappear inside it.

"Should we go with them?" I ask, deciding it's time to pull on my blindfold.

Anarchy shakes her head. "Leave them be. He isn't going to hurt her. And we could all do with some food and rest."

We ignore the dragons as we prepare a meal, which I dub, "dinner at daybreak," and then we head in our respective directions to get some sleep.

I have no fear that the dragons will cause problems—not only because Riot clearly intends to stay on Miku, but also since the keeper is watching them.

His skin is flushed with black scales, his full dragon form appearing to be seconds away if he needs it.

I know he'll watch over us until they leave.

CHAPTER THIRTY-FIVE

For the next three weeks, I spend the first half of my nights stretching and exercising, working on the muscles I need to strengthen so I can fly, and the second half of my nights learning everything I can from Anarchy.

Miku and her band of dragons visit us every morning. Each time, she tells the other dragons to check the rest of the island while she heads toward the training hall with Riot underfoot.

By the fifth day, she's stopped trying to go inside and instead sits on the top step, waiting for Riot to join her. She spends most of the time watching the waves while he prowls around her.

By the second week, he's sitting quietly beside her, studying the water with her, twitching whenever a fish flies up out of the waves, but he doesn't leave her side.

Then, at some point during the third week, he drapes himself across her lap, his head resting in the crook of her arm. She strokes his back as she speaks quietly. I catch mentions of mermaids and dragons and life in the Kaito family. Some stories sound like old myths. Others seem like recent happenings. She talks about how her training is going, and then random things like what she ate that morning, even the meaning of her name. Apparently, Miku means "beautiful sky". Until she falls silent again, her hand resting on his head.

She's always waiting back on the beach before the other dragons return. If they know she spends all of her time with Riot, they don't say anything. At least not within my earshot.

Ryuji is less predictable in his visits—the first at the end of the week, the next only a few days later. The second time, he arrives in the middle of the day when I'm sleeping and I hear afterward that the keeper fielded all of Ryuji's questions that day. After that, Ryuji only visits at the beginning and end of the night when I'm awake. We drink tea, but he doesn't ask me any difficult questions.

As for returning the panthers to their elven forms, the keeper seems to be tightly controlling his frustration. Neither Rumble nor Strife appear keen to let him try out his magic on them again, and Riot actively avoids all attempts, so the keeper takes to testing his magic on an old tree stump. He tries all sort of combinations of illusion and dark magic.

By the end of the third week, the tree stump has sprouted new leaves and starts to bear fruit in shapes oddly reminiscent of rabbits.

But I'm not sure if he's any closer to helping the panthers.

At the end of each night, I meet him at the hut by the pond, where he pulls down the dark screens that block out the growing daylight and eases my muscles in ways that send my senses into a spin, tempting me to step over the boundary I've placed between us.

Dark saints, I want to step over it.

In the space between choices, I nearly convince myself that I can remain in control. I may have been taught that sex is about power and manipulation, but I tell myself I'm strong enough to stay detached.

Oh, but then his hand slips between my legs or his tongue

strokes me or his power trickles through to my core and I know, without a doubt, that control would be an illusion.

Perhaps he'd lose control too, but I can't know that for sure.

So the boundary remains.

By the start of the final week, my back is much stronger, but I'm still nowhere near ready to fly and it's starting to scare me.

Lucian does his best to calm my fears. After all, I can't expect my body to adapt within a month, not after decades without using my wings.

As for combat training, that's where things are going well—and it also provides a way to take out some of my frustrations. I'm now putting Anarchy on her butt and she seems happy about it.

Even so, I sense a growing tension in her as we approach the end of the final week, and, after I perform a successful sequence of moves that forces her onto her back foot, I say, "Out with it."

She blinks her pale-blue eyes at me. "Out with what?"

"Whatever's bothering you."

She sighs, a soft exhale nearly drowned out by the rushing waves in the distance. "When you made your plan to take down your father, you didn't mention your biological mother."

I stiffen, but she arches an eyebrow at me.

"You started this conversation, Veda. I'll back off if you want me to, but you can't ignore the threat Galeia could pose to you."

"No, it's..." I shake my head as I reach for one of the little cloths lying on the floor nearby, using it to wipe the sweat from my forehead and neck. Taking a moment to gather my thoughts.

"My father told me the only reason he didn't kill me when I was unconscious is because he wants to know where she is. He thinks I know. When I couldn't tell him, it created confusion. I can use that confusion, that uncertainty. If I go looking for answers—if I go looking for her—I'll only be giving him answers too. I sure as hell don't want to do him any favors."

"But what if she comes for you?" Anarchy asks.

I look the dark elf straight in the eye. "Why do you think I'm training so hard?"

Some of the tension leaves her shoulders. "You'll be as strong as you can be to face whichever of them you have to."

I give a single nod. "If I thought I could have asked Ryuji for more time, I would have."

She chews her lips, picks up her cloth, and wipes it around the back of her neck. She's tied her hair up in a topknot—a style I've found useful too—but some of the strands have come down during training.

"What about the woman who was in the prison with you?" she asks softly. "Do you wonder who she was?"

"It's impossible not to wonder." I grit my teeth against all my uncertainty. "I don't know how to feel toward her. She can't have chosen her fate. Nobody would choose to be imprisoned and die in a place like that. So it follows that she never would have chosen to look after me there. She was cursed, for fuck's sake. Hell, even her facial expressions, her smiles, the way she spoke to me could have been part of the curse. I'm nearly certain that she would have been cursed to have my biological mother's memories. She probably even believed that she'd given birth to me."

I press the back of my hand to my forehead and Anarchy doesn't interrupt me.

"All I have are questions and theories, and right now, anything is possible," I say. "I mean, for all I know, she might have been part of the whole plot, effectively kidnapping me, and then she was betrayed and put in there with me. And if that were the case, then she was part of the cruelty, so am I still supposed to feel grateful toward her? Am I still supposed to believe that she cared about me? I trusted her, but she was a lie. I don't... I can't..."

I squeeze my eyes closed, grateful for Anarchy's quiet

presence. "All I know is that I need to focus on the battle ahead of me."

"If I may," Anarchy says quietly. "You need a name for her. A name that gives you permission to accept the care she gave you —whether or not it was willingly given—and allows you to move past the pain you feel when you think about her."

I ponder this for a long moment.

So long that Anarchy nudges my shoulder. "Be sure that the name you give her isn't about her. It's about you. The impact she had on you."

Finally, I say, "*Sosia.*"

Anarchy's lips part. "Of course. Someone who steps in for another."

"It carries no accusation," I say. "No judgment. She stepped in for my biological mother and kept me alive." I take a deep breath. "Maybe one day, when I have answers, I can give her another name. One that reflects who she really was and her true intentions. But for now, this is what I need to call her."

A little of my emotional turmoil fades.

I have no control over the choices my biological mother made—or makes in the future. I don't have answers about the woman who raised me—the woman I've now resolved to call *Sosia*. And I can't control what my father believes or how he acts.

I had no say over what was done to me.

But I *will* control my purpose.

At the beginning of our last night on the island, the keeper wakes me from my daylight sleep earlier than usual.

Also unexpected is the smile on his lips.

"I have the answer," he says, beaming at me in his brown-eyed, dark-skinned form.

"Answer to what?" I ask groggily, wiping the sleep from my eyes. I'm naked under the light blanket and the space where he would normally sleep feels empty now that he's kneeling opposite me.

"How to free the panthers from their curse."

I bolt upright. "Really?"

"Come with me."

I snatch up my clothes, stopping only to pull on the long, black pants and tunic and wrap my blindfold around my eyes before I hurry after him.

We meet the panthers on the beach, where they sit on their haunches, eyeing the keeper with narrowed eyes, their snouts near-crinkling with hisses. I don't blame them after what happened the first time the keeper tried to help them.

Lucian and Anarchy arrive a moment later, both at the same time and both from the direction of Lucian's hut, which seems to be where Anarchy sleeps these days.

I haven't pried. Simply noted the way the backs of their hands brush whenever they walk together, and the slight flush of color in Anarchy's pale cheeks when Lucian's around, and the way Lucian seems completely at ease with her.

The keeper plants his feet and his grin grows broader as he announces, "Gargoyle blood."

I eye him warily. "Huh?"

"Anarchy was biting Lucian when my magic hit her. It must have been the combination of gargoyle magic and dark magic that forced the curse to break. After all, the curse was imposed by a gargoyle."

Anarchy's lips are pursed. "That makes sense."

But Lucian is already backpedaling, all relaxation vanishing from his features. "No fucking way I'm letting them bite my fingers."

"Not necessary." The keeper chuckles, seeming darkly

entertained by Lucian's discomfort. "I just need a few drops of your blood."

Lucian glares. "Fine."

The keeper holds out his left hand, palm up.

I quickly extend my claws and give my brother a questioning glance.

He slides on over to me, lets me prick his finger, and then he squeezes a few drops onto the keeper's palm.

The keeper focuses back on the panthers, but I don't miss the tension around his eyes and lips that tells me there's worry beneath his confident façade.

If this doesn't work, I don't know when or if he'll be able to try again. He can't use his dark magic openly in any city environment—it involves taking life, and life-taking has the strong potential to draw attention we don't want.

I try to shake off my misgivings as glistening, dark light drips upward off the keeper's palm, concentrated around the droplets of blood, gathering them up and lifting them into what appears to be a ball of inky fluid.

The concentration on the keeper's face becomes intense while the sphere of dark magic floats above his palm, casting shadows that make his brown eyes appear black.

With a twitch of his fingers, the sphere splits into three smaller orbs, each one turning slowly in the air.

I back away, as do Anarchy and Lucian, our footsteps crunching softly in the sand while the panthers are now visibly shivering where they remain only a few paces from the keeper.

Above us, clouds gather in the sky, obscuring the remaining hue of sunset and casting us into sudden darkness. So dark that I pull off my blindfold.

The three spheres begin rotating around each other, each one also turning on its axis, now spinning faster and faster.

In the distance, the waves churn and lightning scatters across the sky. Goosebumps rise on my skin as the wind whips around us, and I find myself pressing my hand to my chest; the same gesture the keeper makes when my emotions are heightened.

Right now, it's his power that thrums through me, seeming to reach across the distance between us to tug at my body and mind.

A thrill of fear makes me shiver when, in the distance, a tree at the edge of the beach crumbles into dust—and then another —the debris swept up in the fierce wind.

The keeper raises his hands, at the same time releasing the spheres into the air at his eye level, and then silence falls, a deep, dark silence, even though the waves continue to churn, the wind plucks at my clothing and hair, and the force around us presses in on my chest.

"Trust me," the keeper whispers, his glittering eyes meeting mine, all black and full of magic, before the spheres shoot forward.

The dark magic takes on the form of spears a split second before they pierce the shivering panthers' hearts.

CHAPTER THIRTY-SIX

*a*cry of alarm rests on my tongue.

I'm leaping forward, only to be hit with the explosion of magic thrown backward in the rush of energy.

It ripples over me as my fall registers, the sand now a hard surface at my back while Anarchy and Lucian knock against the ground on my left and smoke billows across the air above us.

The keeper's form is changing in the distance, becoming the black dragon with furious golden eyes, dominating my vision.

He inhales deeply, so strongly that it tugs at my feet and then my thighs, pulling me a few inches across the sand toward him —along with the smoke.

Rolling onto my stomach, I make it up onto my hands and knees, clawing at the grit to stay in one place until the pull abruptly stops and the dragon's furious breathing fills the air.

I spin toward the panthers, feeling like I'm chewing on the heart I don't have anymore.

Please let them be okay.

My eyes widen.

I let my breath out again.

Three heartbreakingly beautiful men stand on the beach,

each one lean and as sleek as they looked when they were panthers.

All three have pointed ears, high cheekbones, and luminous, blue eyes the same shade as Anarchy's. Their hair is long, in varying shades of lilac, but that's where the major similarities stop.

One has a strong jaw and a look of easy confidence about him; the second has a pointed chin and a wickedly mischievous gleam in his pale-blue eyes that I can see all the way from here; and the third, well, he seems to be the serious one, his hair the palest lilac—so pale, it's nearly silver—and not a hint of a trickery to be seen.

I've become accustomed to telling them apart in their panther form, but now I'm not so certain who is who.

Anarchy gives a cry, scrambling to her feet, tears pouring down her cheeks as she races toward them. She's calling out, and I assume she's speaking their names or maybe a very long elven greeting, but I can't make out what she's saying.

She collides with them and they all sink to the sand on their knees, hugging each other at once.

"Damn," I whisper as Lucian draws to my side.

"Look at that," he says, a smile on his face.

Across the way, the keeper transforms back into his brown-eyed form. The lightning fades from the sky, the clouds part, and the evening moonlight shines softly down over us. No need for my blindfold now.

That's when the elves rise to their feet and approach me as a group, the male elves' footfalls a little wobbly and uncertain while they seem to be finding their feet.

One of them surges a step ahead of the others. He's the shortest of the three with the strong jaw and roguish smile.

I eye him carefully as he approaches. "Rumble?"

"That's me," he says, giving me a broad smile as he lumbers closer, his arms outstretched as if he's going to hug me.

I waggle my finger at his very naked form, backpedaling with a firm, "*Clothes.*"

He grins at me. "Who needs clothes?"

Then he tackle-hugs me, sweeping me off my feet and squeezing the breath out of me.

"You do!" I squawk, bursting into laughter a moment before he sets me onto the ground.

He tips his chin at me. "Okay, then. You're the boss." He spins to his brothers, barking at them. "Darkness has spoken: Clothes before hugs!"

"Oh, well… Maybe just one hug," I say when the other two veer toward me as if they weren't going to obey, anyway.

The first one hisses playfully at me and instantly, I recognize Strife's voice. He's the one with the pointed chin and mischievous gleam in his pale eyes.

"Strife."

He swaggers up to me, pulls me in, and drops a kiss on the corner of my lips before he scoops his arms around me in another breath-stopping embrace.

My eyes fly wide. "Uh—"

"Forgive me, Darkness," he croons into my ear. "But I had to steal just one kiss." He draws back a little. "You can punish me if you want."

He gives me such a lazy smile that I have to bite my tongue before I shake my head rapidly. "Not on your life."

"Suit yourself."

He releases me with a gleam in his eyes, and now I turn to Riot because that's who the third man must be.

Oh, but he's much harder to read.

Solemn in a way the other two aren't.

He takes a knee, reaches for my hand, and presses his cheek to the back of it. The silvery-lilac strands of his hair brush against my hand as he tilts his head. "Well met, Darkness."

"No hug?" I ask quietly, dropping to my knees so I'm eye level with him.

His expression softens a moment before he reaches forward and embraces me much more carefully than the others did.

"I'm glad you're… you again," I say.

"Thank you, Darkness."

When I rise to my feet, keeping my focus firmly on his face, he glides after his brothers.

Anarchy hovers at my side, swiping at the tears on her cheeks. At a clatter from inside the training hall, she grimaces. "I'd better help them."

I snag her arm before she can leave. "We can skip training tonight."

She pauses. "Are you sure? It's our last night."

We still have to get through the final visit from the dragons in the morning, and then my path to vengeance truly begins.

"I'm sure," I say. "You need to spend this time with your family. Besides, we've trained and planned as much as we can. The rest is a battle we'll fight when we get to it."

With a brief nod to me, she reaches for Lucian, who takes her hand and follows her inside the training hall.

I sense the keeper's presence as he steps up close behind me. "Our last night," he says quietly.

I turn to him, fighting the hint of finality in his voice.

We may have a fight ahead of us, but this won't be our final night together. Not by a long shot.

I'm determined about that.

I take his hand, drawing his fingertips to my lips, daring to press kisses along his finger close to his crown, stopping only when I get so near it that the energy within it sends a tingle down my spine.

He slips his free hand around my head, cupping my cheek, pulling me close and nudging my ear, little kisses trailing across my jaw to my lips.

I relax into his arms.

Over the last four weeks, I've done everything I promised myself I would. I've eaten noodles and exotic fruit until my stomach felt like it would burst. I've run through the jungle and sat for hours taking deep breaths of fresh air. I even swam again in the ocean, although my version of swimming was more like being tumbled around in the waves before they spat me back out onto the beach.

Planting my palms against the keeper's chest and tipping my head back to accept his feather-light touches, I whisper, "Let's enjoy the beautiful darkness."

Hours later, as the sun threatens to break across the horizon, I dress in a fresh tunic and pants, tuck my blindfold around my eyes, and wait on the beach with my family, anticipating the final visit from the dragons.

The keeper and I stand ahead of the others, while Riot, Rumble, and Strife stay back near the training hall's steps.

It doesn't escape me that Riot watches the sky more intently than his brothers, a quiet tension settling over him.

Miku's reaction to his new appearance can't be predicted.

She arrives alone for the first time, alighting on the sand and tucking her teal wings to her sides. Her focus is on the sand near my legs, her gaze darting around me, immediately searching where the panthers would ordinarily be.

"Ryuji's on his way," she says. "He gave me a few minutes on my own so I could say goodbye to..." A crease is rapidly forming in her forehead until she adjusts her line of sight, lifting it.

Her focus alights on the dark elves and she takes a step back, her dragon scales flushing across her skin and her wings shivering as if she's preparing for flight.

My hands have lifted reflexively and I'm on my front foot, ready to calm her. After all, Riot couldn't exactly tell her that he used to be a dark elf, and I'm regretting not throwing her some hints.

"Who are they?" she demands to know, the alarm in her voice making me grimace.

Funny how I didn't notice how trusting she became over the last four weeks until I see the faith in her expression rapidly draining away.

"Miku, it's okay—"

But Riot's hand lands on my arm and I fall silent, allowing him to step forward. Well, he doesn't so much *step* as *prowl*.

He draws his lips back and snarls at her, sounding so much like his panther voice that she must recognize it.

She stops backing away, her eyes wide as she takes him in, his silver-lilac hair, pale eyes, perfect lips, all the way down and back up his lean, dangerously-muscled body.

Her shocked whisper breaks the silence. "Riot?"

CHAPTER THIRTY-SEVEN

A predatory smile breaks across Riot's face, the smile that only a dark creature can make, but far from driving Miku backward, she steps forward.

Her shoulders rise with a deeply indrawn breath, her dragon scales glimmer across her visible skin, and her wings shiver, but this time, the motion takes her forward.

"Riot! You're a man!"

His eyes crinkle even as his smile remains scary as fuck.

She doesn't miss another beat, leaping at him so fast that I have to dart out of the way. She collides with him as thoroughly as if *she* were once the panther, knocking him off his feet so that they tumble through the sand.

It's so much like the first time he leaped at her that my jaw drops.

They come to a stop, her on top, sand settling around them and drifting off her wings. "You're a man!"

His chest vibrates with laughter that rumbles like purrs. "And you're a woman."

Color flushes through her cheeks. "Well, you always knew that."

"I very much did." He traces the curve of her chin and neck before his fingers tangle in her hair.

She closes her eyes and turns her face into his hand, but when she opens her eyes, they're downcast. "And now you have to leave."

He seems to hold his breath as he says, "You could come with us."

My lips part in surprise, but I bite my tongue. It's not as if I would have said *no* if he'd checked with me first. A quick glance at Anarchy and Lucian earns me a grimace and a shrug. Rumble and Strife don't look unhappy, but the keeper scowls.

He could be right to be concerned and I find myself reflecting on my first impulse. After all, Miku is a creature of the light.

How could I expect her to understand the things we need to do?

But it seems she is contemplating the same difficult realities.

Tears sparkle in her eyes and she bites her lips before she says, "A dragon shifter and a dark elf? We're creatures of the opposite magic. We're safe here on this island, but out there, both sides would target us."

His grip on her tightens. "Nobody will ever hurt you—"

"You would never let them." She slowly lowers her face to his, pressing her lips to the corner of his mouth. "And I would never let anyone hurt you, but they wouldn't stop coming. Even my own people—"

Her voice chokes and she closes her eyes, her words strained as she continues. "My own people don't understand."

Riot's arms slip around her back, wings and all, drawing her down over his chest, her head against his neck.

"I want to fight it," he says, his voice raw. "I'll fight the world and anyone who tries to keep us apart. All you need to do is ask, Miku, and I'll fight all of them."

"I won't," she whispers. "I won't risk your life like that."

She pulls away from him, her wings extending and catching

the air, undoubtedly making it difficult for him to hold on to her.

He launches himself after her as she makes it up to her feet, stumbling back from him.

"Miku—"

Her hands fly upward, her voice breaking. "Please know that I bonded with you, Riot. I won't ever take a mate." She's shaking her head, a sob on her lips. "Don't… Don't come after me."

She beats her wings, rising into the air in a rush.

Riot can't follow her into the sky, but for a moment, it looks like he's preparing to leap after her before she can ascend out of his reach. He has the reflexes and strength to do it. Especially if he shifts into his panther form.

Anarchy is already at his side, her hand snagging his arm before he can move, her knuckles turning white where she holds him tightly. "No, brother."

In that same moment, Miku's wings give a final sweep, her power bursts around her, and she's gone.

Riot turns on Anarchy with a hiss, but she doesn't back down.

"Accept the pain," she snaps, her voice savage. "We are dark creatures and we will never be anything but broken."

He drags in a ragged breath, his biceps bunching as if he would fight her.

"Our pain makes us stronger!" Her eyes bore into his. "Accept this pain. Let it feed your dark soul. This is who we are and will always be."

"It's rare for dark creatures to find love. To lose it is a tragedy."

That's what Anarchy said only weeks ago.

In the background, Rumble and Strife are like dark guards, their mouths turned down.

My chest hurts—my heart. An ache for which I have no balm.

Anarchy gives me a firm nod before she turns to her

brothers. "Darkness needs us to gather the final supplies before we leave. We should avoid the alpha dragon until he's gone."

Rumble and Strife give silent nods of acknowledgment, while Riot's expression remains hollow, but he doesn't fight her. Together, they prowl away down the beach and into the jungle. We've already packed extra clothing for our departure and just need food and water supplies, which I trust they'll gather now.

Meanwhile, Lucian and the keeper remain on the beach.

I try to shake off my tension and sadness as my ears *pop* and Ryuji appears in the sky above me. He alights on the beach, his silver scales reflecting the moonlight.

Miku must have well and truly avoided him on her path away from the island because he appears none the wiser about the friction he's stepping into. Or he's choosing not to address it.

I roll my shoulders, paste a pleasant smile on my face, and gesture to the training hall. "Tea?"

He shakes his head. His jagged, black hair is slicked back today, his dark-brown eyes no less ferocious despite his angelic features. His scales vanish from his skin as he fully retracts his wings. "How about we take a walk instead?"

I'm a little unsettled by the change of routine—maybe he sensed how upset Miku was?—but I don't object. "Sure."

I lift my hand, quietly indicating to the keeper and Lucian to stay put before I match Ryuji's slow stride across the sand.

"It's your final hours on this island, so I will speak clearly: You must never come back."

I can't be sure, but I read into his command that he did, indeed, sense Miku's pain. I take his order as a warning after what she said about her people not understanding her feelings.

"Understood," I say. "You won't see us again."

"Thank you." He gives a heavy exhale before he stops and contemplates the ocean. "Still, I feel compelled to ask: Are you ready to leave, Veda Nostra, Daughter of Assholes?"

"No," I say truthfully. "This is the safest and most peaceful I've felt in my entire life, so no… I'm not ready to leave." I close my eyes briefly, inhaling the salty air, letting the sound of the swooshing waves wash over me before I open them again.

"You talk of peace," he muses. "Constantly surprising me." He gives a shake of his head. "You're the Ultima Nostra's lost daughter, but nothing like what I would have expected."

I shrug. "Glad I'm not predictable."

He nods, turning away toward the ocean again, surprising me when he says, "I lost my daughter. She's six years old now, but I've never met her."

I tilt my head. "Why not?"

"Her mother is a powerful dragon shifter in Philadelphia. I first met her when she came here seeking refuge, and we…" He shakes himself. "She left when she was pregnant."

His whole demeanor changes while he's talking about her, a deep respect entering his tone, a warmth that started from the moment he mentioned his daughter.

I wait for him to go on and when he doesn't, I ask, "And?"

His forehead creases. "And what?"

"Well, you're both dragon shifters, no issues there, so did she tell you not to visit? Did you do something to hurt her?"

"Of course not." The crease in his brow deepens. "And, no, she didn't tell me not to visit."

"Then what the hell are you waiting for?" I snarl at him in disbelief. "Go see her already."

He hesitates and I fight the sudden rush of anger rising within me. "*My* father wants me dead," I say, managing to keep my voice low. "I've just watched someone I care about be rejected on the basis of other people's lack of acceptance. You clearly love this woman and your daughter. So for fuck's sake, go to them. Tell them that you love them and fucking act like you do."

"It's not that simple." He shakes his head and then continues quickly—probably because the tips of my claws are appearing. "I mean, it wouldn't be wise. The balance of power among dragon shifters in Philadelphia is precarious and my presence could easily put my daughter in danger."

I sigh. *Okay, so he's not just being obstinate.* "Then invite them here. It's neutral ground."

"Here?" He glances around. "You mean this island?"

"Why not? It's got places to sleep. Plenty of dried noodles. Excellent fish." *Even if I'm craving pizza and hamburgers now.*

"Well…"

I can't help but shake my head at him. "You're a creature of the light. You have every capacity to love someone with your whole heart, unlike us dark creatures who have to bite and claw for any good thing in our lives. So for fuck's sake, Ryuji, Son of Rin and Yuma, don't make me slap you."

He lets out a laugh, followed by a quiet, "Fuck it. Okay."

"Good."

I fold my arms, anticipating that this might be the end of our conversation, but he begins again, this time with a careful tone. "There's something I need to tell you."

CHAPTER THIRTY-EIGHT

"*D*o you remember our first conversation about the nature of dark and light?" Ryuji asks. "When you challenged me to determine if you were wholly born of darkness?"

"How could I forget?" I reply.

"Well, since you arrived on my island, I've searched for clues about your nature as a supernatural. As part of that, I accessed the ancient texts that have been protected by the dragon masters since the old times."

I fight the feeling of anticipation—or is it dread?—that he might have found out things about Galeia that I need to know. "What did you find?"

He continues to speak carefully. "First, I want you to know that this knowledge will stay with me. I haven't shared it."

Well, now I'm worried. "What is it?"

"In the history of our world, there have only been two other recorded cases of supernatural creatures who had claws exactly like yours."

I'm holding my breath as he continues.

"The first was the Vandawolf himself."

My eyes have flown wide. Sosia told me about the Vandawolf. Well, a little about him. He was a human who was captured and turned into a terrible beast by power-hungry beings whose magic nearly destroyed the world.

"The second was a woman who called herself 'Galeia.'" Ryuji's focus has been on me the whole time, but now his gaze is even more piercing. "Do you know what *Galeia* means in the old tongue, Veda?"

I shake my head. Sosia taught me many words in the old tongue, but not that one.

"You may be surprised to hear that it means 'new life.'" His eyebrows arch. "A confusing name for a dark creature, no?"

My lips part in surprise. I don't understand why she would have chosen that name—since it sounds like she did, indeed, choose it.

But my concern now goes beyond her name. I speak carefully. "My knowledge of ancient times may be tainted by the person who told me about them." In fact, everything Sosia told me could have been a lie. "But it was my understanding that the Vandawolf was *created*. He began as a human and was changed into a wolf. If Galeia had the same claws, what does this mean?"

Ryuji nods. "I had the same questions. Unfortunately, the texts are extremely vague about the arcane magic that created him. Most likely because this knowledge is dangerous."

My disappointment must show because he hurries on.

"But several things are clear. One is that this magic could be inflicted on any living creature—provided the wielder of the magic was powerful enough."

"So… Galeia wasn't really a hellhound?"

"I imagine it was her cover to explain away her unusual claws."

I shake my head. "Then she could have been anything." My eyes widen as another possibility occurs to me. "Was she related to the Vandawolf? A daughter or something like that?"

"Oh, no." He shakes his head rapidly. "There is no suggestion that they had any familial relationship. In fact, quite the opposite. They were entirely separate beings who were impacted by this magic at different times."

My shoulders slump. If she were related, then it would at least explain who or what she was.

"And the next thing?" I ask.

"Galeia had a mechanical heart."

I can only stare at Ryuji. "What?"

"It's clear from the texts that this arcane magic was always infused into metal. The metal that changed Galeia formed a significant part of her heart."

Ryuji reaches into his pocket and pulls out a piece of parchment. "This is a copy I drew from a page in one of the oldest books in my possession. Once you look upon this drawing, I will destroy it, for there should never be any copies."

He holds the parchment out to me, revealing a rough, hand-drawn image. It depicts the heart as an organ, the kind I saw in an illustration when my jailer saw fit to provide me with an encyclopedia that included human anatomy.

The upper portion of the heart looks like it's made of flesh, including the pipe-shaped parts extending up out of it, but it's clear that the rest of the heart is constructed of something metallic. There are cogs and pipes and plates and so many other interconnecting pieces that it's hard to distinguish them all.

"My drawing skills aren't up to capturing the detail," Ryuji says. "What you can see doesn't even come close to the complexity of interlocking pieces that are depicted in the original diagram. It must have been a feat of terrible genius to create a heart like that."

A mechanical heart.

My own heart is thudding harder in my chest. A sudden panic is rising within me. "If this heart turned her into a so-called hellhound, then what about me?"

Or Sosia, for that matter. Maybe it wasn't that a curse was placed on Sosia, but that this arcane magic was used instead.

Ryuji reaches out and catches hold of my hand, gripping firmly.

"No," he says, as if he can read my thoughts. "Unlike Galeia, you were *born* with your claws and teeth and feathers. Inherited directly from her."

"How can you be certain?"

"Because the ancient texts are very clear about this. The arcane magic was considered so dangerous—so full of darkness—that every piece of tainted metal was gathered up and destroyed. Even the metal that was used on the Vandawolf. All of it, Veda."

He pauses, his chest expanding with an indrawn breath before he says, "Except Galeia's heart."

His gaze bores into me as if he can see my fears—as if he can calm them—even with my blindfold on. And maybe he can, because the breeze picks up around me, a sudden wind that doesn't feel exactly natural but cools the sweat forming on my brow and eases the pounding of my heart.

"I don't know if she escaped the purge," he says quietly. "Or if she was allowed to live. Because clearly, she would not survive without a heart."

It's too much to take in. My hands close around the edge of the parchment. "Is this how she's lived for so long?"

Ryuji gives me a brief smile. "With a heart powered by arcane magic like this, yes, it's probably how. Also probably why, with this magic seeping into her bones, she passed these traits on to you."

"But metal is... *metal,* for fuck's sake." I gasp. "How can it be passed on?"

"Because the arcane magic that was used on it was living magic. Creation magic. That's why every piece of metal affected by that magic was considered extremely dangerous."

He takes the page from me and I expect him to tear it to pieces, but he scrunches it into a ball and wraps his fist around it before a brief look of concentration settles over his features.

Energy bursts around his fist, an explosion of what feels like air rushing outward, but by the time it reaches me, it's become a gentle breeze.

Ryuji opens his fist to reveal only fine grains of white dust that float away into the air.

"How did you—?"

He gleams at me. "Air, when compressed, can be deadly."

"Fucking air dragon," I whisper, trying to shake off my fears.

Fear of the unknown and unknowable.

He peers at me. "You're the first to be *born* with those claws." A faint smile ghosts around his mouth. "New life, Veda."

Like my biological mother's name.

I give a wobbly laugh. "You can't possibly be trying to convince me to forgive Galeia, can you?"

His forehead puckers. "Sometimes, to protect the ones we love, we must leave them." He sighs and whispers, "Or let them go."

Oh, there is so much that could be implied from what he said.

Maybe he's talking about Miku. Or his own decisions.

Or maybe, he's trying to ease a wound in me that I fear will never close.

Ryuji gives my hand a squeeze. "When we first met, we spoke of fear," he says, contemplating me—shockingly—without any hint of distrust. "It seems to me that the fears we all must fight are our own."

He releases my hand and takes a step back and, with a sense of finality that brings unexpected sadness, I realize we've reached the end of our conversation.

It's the end of our truce.

"We'll be gone within the hour," I say, repeating my promise to him. "You won't see us again."

Unless I somehow manage to retrieve his favorite sword—and even then, I'll find a way to get it to him that doesn't involve me returning here.

"Well, then..." He gives me a deep bow. "I wish you well."

He takes to the air with a firm sweep of his silver wings and then, he's gone.

I join my family moments later, waiting for them to gather around me—the dark elves, my dark angel brother, and the keeper, all of them carrying the weight of shadows and scars. All of them dangerous because of who and what they are.

Including me.

I close my eyes, take a deep breath, and say, "Let's go."

CHAPTER THIRTY-NINE

We step out of the keeper's transportation magic onto hard pavement.

We're completely exposed, out in the open, arriving beside a large, stone arch monument that sits at the entrance to a paved square in New York. Lucian called it the Washington Arch when he described it to the rest of us. The monument is so large that I have to crane my head back to see the top of it way above us.

Even though it's nighttime on this side of the world, and we've arrived in the shadows near the edge of the paved area, the keeper is ready with his magic to compel any passing humans to forget they saw us.

But I'm thrown when there are no people milling about. No humans. No supernaturals.

The place is unnervingly quiet and deserted.

"It's early evening," I whisper. "Shouldn't there be humans about?"

The dark elves and Lucian have immediately fanned out around me while the keeper stays close to my side.

Before we left the island, the keeper conjured sunglasses for both Lucian and me to hide our golden eyes—real sunglasses using his dark magic. He also quickly placed an illusion on the elves' ears so they appear rounded. He left their unusually-colored hair alone since Lucian was adamant that humans color their hair all different shades so it shouldn't matter.

At least, now that the elves aren't stuck in panther form, the keeper doesn't have to camouflage them as pets.

"This isn't normal," Lucian says. "Even at night, there should be people around."

The human statue carved into the nearest side of the arch seems to glare down at me from above.

"We need to leave." Anarchy's teeth are sharpening and her eyes are changing to a silver color as if she's on the verge of shifting into her panther form.

"I agree." The keeper growls. "There's magic at play here. Warlock magic. I can sense it."

I don't disagree. My skin is crawling and for once, it's nothing to do with my wings. But I spin to Lucian. "How long will it take you to find Jonah's lighter?"

When I first met Jonah, he was carrying a small, golden object with a lid that he seemed to enjoy clicking open and closed. Inside it, a tiny flame would light up that burned brightly every time.

He apparently hid that lighter here in the arch as a way for Lucian to contact him. One click of the lighter's flame and Jonah will sense it from afar. I'm not entirely sure how that magic works, and Lucian wasn't, either, but he was adamant Jonah wouldn't have lied to him about it.

"Ten seconds," Lucian replies. "I can be quicker because there aren't humans around."

"Do it."

Once we have the lighter, we can get of here and find a safer place to summon Jonah.

Lucian doesn't waste time. His wings thump out at his sides

and with a single beat, he carries himself high up near the top of the arch. He coasts there for all of three seconds before he seems to spot what he's looking for, darting forward to pluck it from between the stone crevices.

Rapidly retracting his wings, he drops to the ground again, holding the lighter up for me to see.

"Good," I say. "Let's get out of here."

The keeper's translocation magic bursts outward, ready to sweep us away, but not fast enough.

At the side of the square, only twenty paces away from our location, a male figure suddenly appears from out of nowhere.

He's in a crouched position, his hands outstretched, both palms covered in tattoos that gleam in the darkness. He's dressed in a suit, the shirt unbuttoned at the top, and has neatly-cut hair, a strong jaw, and eyes that are bright with magic.

I recognize him as the warlock named Orlan, who works for Halle.

The misty haze of transportation energy forming around the keeper streams instead toward Orlan's glowing palms. Within seconds, the warlock has sucked the magic away and continues to do so as fast as the keeper can produce more of it.

"Fuck," I whisper, since it looks like we aren't going anywhere just yet.

My family quickly forms a protective circle that fans out on either side of me, each of them facing outward.

"Okay, Orlan," I call. "What do you want?"

The warlock slowly rises to his feet, his focus on the keeper. His palms hover close together. When he used his magic on the train to produce daggers from thin air, he clapped his hands together to trigger the magic first.

"It's not what *I* want that matters," he calls back.

Before he's finished speaking, another two figures shimmer into view a few paces away from Orlan.

One of them is Halle Vanguard.

She has the ability to change her appearance at will—just as the keeper does—but it seems she's chosen to appear in a form that will ensure I recognize her. She looks as sweet as a fairy with auburn hair, bright-green eyes, and a dusting of freckles across her nose. A petite wisp of a thing, she's wearing a short, brown, plaid skirt, knee-high brown boots, and a tight, V-neck, sleeveless top in the same color as her eyes.

Beside her is Jonah, but unlike the first time I saw him, he's on his knees, blood splattered across his white collared shirt and dripping from what appears to be a fresh wound across his forehead.

I can't see much of his face, since his head is down, his ice-blond hair contrasting garishly with the blood splattered through it. For some reason, his natural healing doesn't seem to be kicking in, but then, Halle seems to have that power. Her brother wears a scar across his face that she apparently gave him when she tried to kill him.

Right now, it appears the only reason Jonah's upright in any sense is because she's gripping the back of his collar.

"Jonah!" Lucian lurches forward, but I grab him before he can surge past me. His next shout is for Halle. "What have you done to him?"

"Well, let me see," she says, calmly surveying us. "First, I followed him around and watched him stash that lighter up there. Very impressive, the way he hoisted himself all the way up there when he thought nobody was watching. And then I got Orlan to place spells around this square so that the next time there was an influx of magic here, I'd be alerted and all of the humans would suddenly experience the urge to leave.

"But it was only a few hours ago that I finally captured Jonah and, since then, he and I have been having a lovely time playing a game of question and answer." Her lips twist. "Except that he chose *not* to answer, so things got a little... unpleasant."

She lets go of Jonah's shirt and he drops to the ground,

barely breaking his fall with his hands so his head doesn't collide with the pavement.

But it seems he isn't quite as wiped out as he first appeared because his left hand darts out, his fingers wrap around Halle's ankle, and fire bursts across her boots.

The leather bursts into flames, disintegrating to reveal her leg beneath it—which blossoms with amber color, only to instantly cool to a charcoal texture.

"Oh, stop that already," she snaps down at him. "You can burn anything else you like, even my vines, but you can't burn *me*. I'm Hel, for fuck's sake, Goddess of Death and the Underworld. I'm *made* of ash."

"What is this, Hel?" I call, choosing to use her real name. "What do you want?"

"What do I *want*?" she snarls, leaving Jonah where he kneels and seeming not to care that he could attack her from behind. "I want Galeia back!"

"Then go find her," I whisper. "And leave us be."

Halle gives a cold laugh, stopping abruptly only a few paces away from me. "Oh, you think because I'm the Goddess of the Underworld that I can raise the dead? How quaint that you believe I have that power."

Inwardly, I feel weirdly sorry for her. It's clear from what Halle's saying that she believes—like I did—that my biological mother has passed away. I guess it matches with what she said the first time I fought her. She told me it wasn't she who betrayed my mother. That she would never do such a thing.

"Galeia must be incredibly cruel, even for a dark creature," I whisper. "To cause you this much pain."

Halle's forehead pinches and her lips draw back from her teeth. "Galeia was never cruel. Her only fault was to believe that light could be found in darkness. As if *love* could overcome anything."

Her eyes suddenly fill with tears, glistening as they run

down her cheeks. "Love only brings pain." She gasps for breath as she thumps her chest. "I loved her like a daughter and it only brought me pain!"

I'm shocked by the sight of Halle's tears. Also, the fact that she'd shed them so readily in front of me. Unless it's a ploy to get me to feel sorry for her.

She isn't beneath such an approach. The first time I saw her —although I didn't know it was her at the time—she was shoeless and shivering in tattered clothing, drowning her sorrows in alcohol as she slumped with her back to a tree in Central Park. It was very close to where Sosia stashed the page from *The Book of Dark Magic*.

"If you believe Galeia's dead, how does this help you?" I gesture to Jonah, who has pulled himself back into a somewhat upright position, although he remains on his knees.

Halle drags the tears away from her bottom lip with her teeth. "I want to know where my brother is. It's time for him to pay for what he did to Galeia. Now that the Ultima Nostra isn't protecting him, I can finally seek revenge."

Well, I guess we're both looking for him, then. But while she seems to want him dead, I need him alive.

"Revenge for what, exactly?" I ask. "What did he do to Galeia?"

When I first met James Vanguard, he pointed to the scar that runs down the left side of his forehead and told me it was a reminder that family will always try to end you.

But he never told me why.

"How do you not know?" The anger in Halle's eyes makes me wary. She's looking at me as if I'm some kind of traitor. I remember the way she accused me of being "on the wrong side of this" when I first fought her.

My senses are suddenly going haywire.

What does she think I know?

"Because Galeia didn't tell me anything," I snarl, breaking

away from my family to advance on her. "She certainly didn't prepare me for the shitshow I stepped into when I finally found Taiven Nostra—my father."

Not a lie since it wasn't her in the prison with me.

Halle takes a step back, her eyes widening and her focus darting from me to the others, appearing as if she's reassessing the entire situation.

In the background, Jonah's amber eyes are blazing at me. I mean, fuck, I didn't even know he existed. I didn't know that Halle and James Vanguard are old gods. And I sure as fuck didn't know my biological mother had a mechanical heart.

"I tell you what, Hel," I say to her, at the same time slowly moving my left hand behind me to gesture to my family to move back. "Now that you've chosen to be here, why don't *we* play a little game? Just you and me."

"What game?"

I wait a moment for my family to edge backward, although I don't miss the unhappy looks they're giving me. Especially the keeper, who has quickly morphed into his enenra form—the same smoke-and-ash form he previously used to survive Halle's deadly vines.

I remove my sunglasses and drop them onto the pavement with a clatter, after which I allow my claws to descend. "For every cut I make, you'll give me a truthful answer."

Her jaw clenches, but she doesn't immediately protest. "I assume that works both ways?"

I incline my head. "Indeed. For every cut you make, I'll give *you* an answer."

"Accepted," she snarls, darting toward me.

CHAPTER FORTY

lack vines shoot from Halle's fingertips as she flies across the short distance between us.

Each vine has a sharp tip and whips through the air, aimed at my face and side.

In the past, I would have cut them with my claws—and that seems to be what she's expecting, because she's clearly trying to distract me with one hand while the vines shooting from her other hand sail toward my legs.

But Anarchy taught me well.

I dart to the right and throw myself into a slide, away from the vines coming for my legs. The pavement cuts up my pants, but I'm healing even as the cuts are made. The strength of my slide takes me right up to her left leg before she can adjust her aim.

My left hand catches her ankle and with a forward push in the direction of my momentum, I upend her. A scream flies from her mouth as she lurches forward. I'm already at her back, reaching for her nearest arm and wrenching it toward me.

She has no hope of regaining her balance and she can't turn fast enough.

I catch sight of her widening eyes a second before she hits the ground, face planting on the pavement.

Oomph. I sense the air rushing from her chest as I land with my knee against her spine, pinning her down.

Before her vines can whip at me, I slice through them with two efficient cuts on either side, and then I yank her wrists together, forcing her palms flat against her lower back, immobilizing her arms and ensuring any vines she conjures now will only pierce her own body.

"Damn," she gasps against the ground, her voice breathy. "You've been practicing."

"I've used my time wisely."

In the background, Orlan has lurched forward, but Halle shouts to him, "Don't interfere."

Shifting my knee to pin one of her hands, I lean down over her shoulder to where her face is turned to the side.

Carefully, I use my free hand to very deliberately prick her cheek with the tip of my claw, drawing the tiniest spot of blood. "How did I end up in that prison?"

Her forehead creases. "What sort of question is that?"

"The I-want-to-know-where-it-all-started kind," I snap.

"Galeia was six months pregnant." Halle's voice conveys her bewilderment. "Obviously, you ended up there because she was taken there."

Okay, so at least the timing of her imprisonment was accurate.

"What do you know of her capture?"

"That's a second question," she hisses up at me.

"If you insist." I flick my claws across her face, leaving four little cuts.

"Fine!" she screams. "Cuts are not required. Ask your questions and I'll answer them."

"What happened before I was born? Tell me everything you know."

"*The Book of Dark Magic* happened," she spits. "As soon as

Taiven read the book, he changed. Until then, he was utterly in love with Galeia. Excited to be a father. But after he read it, he may as well have died right in front of her."

That's how Sosia described it to me: that Taiven died before her eyes.

Halle's face is paling, but I don't think it's because of my hold on her. "I helped Galeia disappear. I promised her we would raise you together. I would keep you both safe. We made it as far as Philadelphia, but I never dreamed that was the worst place we could go. She went to the bathroom in a café and didn't come back out." Halle sucks in a breath. "I got worried and went in after her, and the air reeked of angel. That fucking pious stench. I searched—"

Her voice chokes and she swallows. "I searched everywhere and when I found no trace of her, I stalked every angel who lived in that city, hoping to hear or see something. *Anything.* And then, finally, there was a whisper about the veil. A *prison* in the veil. That's when I knew you were both lost."

Halle shakes her head, her auburn hair catching and splaying across the pavement. "I never should have taken my eyes off her. I should have gone into that fucking bathroom stall with her."

"And then?"

Her brow furrows. "What do you mean *and then*? I descended into darkness. Nothing was the same without her."

"You seem so certain she's dead. Yet *I* escaped. Surely, she could have, too. Why have you not wondered where she is?"

Her eyes widen. "Why would you ask such a thing?"

"Just answer the question!"

Halle's lips twist. "Because the pregnancy weakened her. She didn't want anyone else to know, but she told me her mechanical heart wasn't as strong as it once was."

My ears prick at the mention of her heart—mechanical, just like Ryuji said.

"She was concerned about the amount of energy you were

taking from her," Halle continues. "She wasn't sure if she'd be able to carry you to term. When she was snatched, she was already weak! She would never have survived imprisonment. Not all these years." Halle snarls up at me. "But surely you know that already."

Before I can respond, Halle's eyes suddenly widen again. "Unless you were separated after you were born?"

And with that, she allows me to speak a truth. "Yes," I say. "We were separated."

"Dark saints, you don't know what happened to her, then?" She stumbles over her words. "Did you even know about her heart?"

I shake my head. "I don't know what really happened to her."

A sense of wariness has filled me at the way Halle described Galeia's heart as failing. I believed that the woman in the cell wasn't Galeia because she was supposedly near-immortal. But if her heart was weakened… could she have died?

But no. I remind myself: The keeper didn't tether her magic. If she'd died, even with a weakened heart, he would have remembered it.

"If you wanted answers," I say bitterly, "I don't have them."

"Well, you must be able to tell me some things." She sounds more hesitant than before. "How did you get out?"

"It was a week before you first saw me," I say. "There was some kind of battle between an angel and a dragon shifter outside my cell. Whatever happened between them, the dragon's fire broke the magical seal that kept me imprisoned."

Halle's forehead is lightly creased, but she gives a brief nod. "Dragon shifters have strong light magic that can surpass even an angel's power."

"So it seems." I ease up on her before I say, "I have one last question for you, Hel. And your answer will determine if I release you or try to kill you."

Her green eyes narrow at me. "Spit it out."

"How does your brother come into all of this?" I need to find him and I sure as fuck won't let her kill him before he leads me to *The Book of Dark Magic*.

"He betrayed me." The corners of her mouth turn down. "He stole *The Book of Dark Magic* from me."

My eyes fly wide. "*You* had the book?"

"I protected it! There are very few creatures who can look upon it and not lose their minds. My affinity with the underworld gave me the ability to resist its power."

Her face turns pale, her lips white with apparent rage. "But Jormungandr—my brother, whom you know as James Vanguard—was overcome with hubris. He took the book to Taiven. And that's when Taiven snapped."

She takes advantage of my loosening hold to lurch up beneath me, attempting to free herself. "So now you see why Jormungandr must pay!"

Oh, I really do.

I jump away from Halle, releasing her.

She rises to her feet, slightly hunched, watching me warily. The cuts on her face have healed, but I remain on the lookout for a reappearance of her vines.

Even so, my focus darts to the keeper, then to my family.

Then back to Halle. "Do you know how to find the book?"

"Of course," she snaps. "Why do you think I spent so many nights huddled in Central Park? I sensed that a page from the book was hidden there, but as soon as I saw what that page depicted, I couldn't bring myself to look at it again, so I left it there."

Halle sighs and her shoulders slump even further. "It was one last piece of Galeia's hopes and dreams that didn't belong in anyone else's hands."

I consider Halle quietly. "You let me take it."

"You're her daughter." But her glare is now accusing. "After that, I saw you working for your father and for my brother. The two men responsible for ending Galeia's life."

Oh. When I first met Halle, I *was* working with James Vanguard, protecting his son. It must have looked like I was already working for Taiven then, too.

"Fuck, no," I whisper. "I was there for revenge." But my own voice returns to a growl. "You, on the other hand, were there to kill an innocent child."

She jolts, her jaw dropping as she gasps. "I was not! I was trying to get that boy away from the fucking lot of them. It was my first and only chance to free Elijah from Taiven's clutches."

I shake my head at her. "You sent your vines after him. You killed my panther!"

Halle sniffs. "Your panther got in the way. Besides, I know a dark elf when I see one. She was going to be fine."

Her focus flickers to Anarchy and her brothers.

They're all on their front foot and I can tell they don't know if they should be stepping in or staying out of things. The keeper has folded his arms across his chest, studying me closely. Lucian, on the other hand, casts worried glances at Jonah, who is still Halle's captive.

I take a breath and then exhale into the silence.

"Let Jonah go," I say to Halle. "Jormungandr will pay for his role in what happened to me. But right now, Taiven—my father —is the greater threat."

She, too, folds her arms across her chest. "I'm listening."

"Many have tried to end Taiven's reign by assassinating him. I plan to slice his defenses away piece by piece, starting with his main obsession: *The Book of Dark Magic*. And then I'll strike again. And again. Until he has nothing left."

Her lips have parted with a quickly indrawn breath. "You speak of impossible things."

I shake my head. "All I need is for you to tell me where the book is."

I expect her to play games with me, but she answers me immediately. "It's closer than you might expect. Hidden within the catacombs beneath an old church not ten blocks south of here."

I rapidly think through the information Sosia gave me about the layout and location of Taiven's operations. As much as I need to distrust some of what she said to me, her information about places has, so far, proven to be reliable. The catacombs are a maze to navigate, but I'm generally familiar with them and I'm not deterred.

Not even when Halle continues. "Veda, trying to steal the book from your father is a guaranteed path to death."

Well, of course it won't be easy, but I'd like to know why she seems so certain it will get me killed. "Why do you say that?"

"Four weeks ago, Taiven started fortifying his defenses, mobilizing his soldiers around that area. Both humans and supernaturals now guard the buildings for two blocks in every direction."

"Do the humans know they're mixing with supernaturals?"

She grimaces. "Uncertain. In the past, there were a few human mob leaders who were aware of the Nostra Family's true nature, but Taiven likes to play his cards close to his chest." With a huff, she turns to Jonah. "Your knowledge is more recent than mine. Can you confirm?"

He wipes the blood from his forehead. "Hel's right. When it comes to humans, Taiven doesn't disclose who knows what. It keeps us walking on eggshells."

"Right," I mutter. "Then we'll need to be careful not to act in any way that reveals what we are. No wings or claws or changing forms or using magic where humans might see it."

Even so, she hasn't told me anything I didn't already anticipate.

Then she continues. "Of most concern: There's a significant influx of light magic from within the church. I don't know what's really going on in there, but even I wouldn't dare enter that place."

I chew my thoughts. "We knew we'd be stepping into a battle. If we need to fight some of Taiven's loyal soldiers along the way, then so be it. As for light magic…" I meet the keeper's gaze across the distance. "We can deal with that when we come to it."

He gives me a firm nod, his blue eyes bright in the shadows. "I can't translocate us inside the catacombs—I've only seen the outside of the church in the memories of dark creatures. But I can get us close."

"Good." Despite my certainty, I look at my family, giving them a moment to speak up, to disagree.

Anarchy lifts her hands and tips her chin at me. "Why are we still standing here?"

Her brothers grin.

Lucian gives me a firm nod.

Behind me, Jonah pulls himself upright. "I'm coming with you."

But as for Halle, she's already stepping away toward Orlan.

"This fight is not for me," she says firmly. "You'll find the book in the deepest tomb on the northern side of the catacombs. But as for your survival, well… If you make it out alive, come and find me."

There's a short, silent communication between her and the warlock, after which he lightly claps his hands, his magic flares, and in the next instant, they're gone.

I turn back to my family, but Lucian's the one suddenly speaking hurriedly, describing the internal layout of the catacombs, confirming that it's a maze, like I believed.

"I've never seen the deepest tombs, but the layout I just described should take us close," he says. "As for getting inside, there are only two entrances: the front door and a side entrance next to an alley." He turns to me. "Which do you want to take?"

Anarchy quickly interjects. "And do we go as ourselves?"

I consider for a moment the virtue of asking the keeper to create illusions that could make us look like Taiven's followers. In particular, we could mimic the male vampire, whose name is Gad, and the female berserker known as Valki, both of whom I met on the train and are part of Taiven's inner circle.

But the chances of them being present at the location are high—the most we could do is cause some momentary confusion—and the moment I use my claws, I'd give myself away.

As for trying to creep up on the place, we'll meet a lot more resistance if one of the soldiers a block away manages to sound the alarm.

"The keeper will transport us into the alley at the side of the church," I say. "He'll need to compel any human witnesses to forget the magic they saw."

My jaw clenches as I continue. "We go as ourselves. No subterfuge. We attack fast and without warning." I take a breath, remembering my vow that I will never be the version of me that Lucian saw in the book. "Each of you can decide for yourself if lethal force is required to get past those who stand in our way."

I wait a beat for my family to agree, meeting their determined eyes. "No matter what, I want everyone in the Nostra Empire to know that Taiven Nostra's lost daughter is coming for him."

CHAPTER FORTY-ONE

My heart thuds inside my chest as the keeper's mist envelops us, a swirling force that compresses my breathing.

He's standing at my shoulder where I asked him to be, a dark presence, and for a moment, it feels like it's just him and me within the white fog.

"Remember, my Veda," he rumbles at my ear. "If we get separated, I'll follow your heart." His arms wrap around me, the light kiss he drops on my cheek sending shivers to my toes. "I'll find you, wherever you are."

I exhale, knowing that this will be the last moment of calm.

Then the mist separates, bursting away from me and forming glistening droplets in the air. It's my one concession to using magic—any nearby human who inhales the mist will forget seeing us arrive this way. The supernaturals, on the other hand, will know exactly how we got here.

I find myself facing the large, wooden door on the side of the stone building, exactly where I asked the keeper to bring us. I quickly take in its arched appearance along with the neatly-kept paved alley behind me and the startled guards standing all around us.

Then my focus lands on the supernatural directly in front of me, guarding the door.

I recognize Valki, the berserker woman. She's my height with multiple piercings and she's wearing jeans with a tank top that reveals her defined biceps, along with the solid, black bracelet she's wearing around her wrist. The bracelet is attached to a thin, metal thread that winds up and around her arm to her elbow, where it's attached to another solid band.

She likes to use that wire to strangle people, but I don't intend to give her the chance to use it on me.

She jolts at my sudden appearance, her jaw drops, and she spits the gum she was chewing. "What the fuck?"

"Hey there." I leap forward, deploying a series of swift hits in a sequence Anarchy taught me, rapidly knocking Valki back against the doorframe.

Behind me, I'm aware of Lucian and the dark elves bursting into action, engaging the heavily-armed male and female guards, both humans and those with supernatural auras.

I catch flashes of steel as our opponents draw daggers and knives. Many are carrying guns, but I'm sure they won't want to use them unless they absolutely have to. Those weapons will make the kind of noise that could draw human authorities to the scene.

The dark elves are lethal shadows as they cut through the defenses around them, and Lucian quickly falls into stride with them.

I don't let Valki find her feet, extending a single claw as if it's a dagger—hopefully, it will look like one—and driving it down toward her throat.

Just before I can reach her, there's a blur of movement from the side of the alley, someone speeding toward me faster than I can follow.

All I see are brilliant, white fangs as the vampire Gad gets within inches of me, his face contorted with deadly intent.

Then—

Thump.

A mountain of muscle plows into him before he can bite me.

I catch a streak of amber light—Jonah's eyes lit up with fire—as he tackles Gad and they disappear into the shadows farther down the alleyway.

The keeper is already bending to Valki, hoisting her into the air even as the muscles in her arms are pumping up, her berserker nature triggering, her body twitching with seemingly mindless rage.

He throws her into Anarchy's path and I guess she must have given him some kind of signal because she's ready with a kick that knocks Valki into the ground.

I don't see what happens because the keeper rams open the door by throwing himself against its wooden surface and propels me through it.

"You're the only one who can safely handle the book, Veda." His hands close around my shoulders. "But never forget that it wants bloodshed. Never forget that it serves only itself."

His gaze burns into me, his angry, blue eyes becoming as dark as night, and it's with a shudder that I register the fear in his gaze.

For the last four weeks, he's repressed the feelings he first revealed to me about my quest to steal the book. His fury and pain. But I see them now in the way his features flicker and once again, I catch sight of his silver-haired form. The face that scares me.

Then he's straightening. "If this is what you must do, then go, Veda. We'll be right behind you."

I catch the clench of his jaw as he spins to face another one of Taiven's men—a supernatural with a wolf shifter aura. He quickly knocks the man down. If he could use his magic, he'd annihilate them all within seconds, but my father was clever to use humans as guards.

Racing away through the ornate room—a nave, I think it's called—with all the long chairs and the carved and painted ceiling, I head toward the altar on the dais. Lucian described a concealed door behind it, and it matches the layout Sosia made me memorize.

Carefully pushing aside the elaborate tapestry that conceals the door, I focus on everything I can feel and hear, expecting to sense guards on the other side or find some sort of magical shield at least.

I'm surprised when there isn't.

In fact, I'm surprised I haven't encountered more resistance within the church already.

I should probably be worried about that, but it doesn't change my goal.

I'll fight whatever threats I encounter when I encounter them.

Hunching to step through the small door, I find myself in a tight hallway, only wide enough for one person.

Halle said that the book is being kept in the deepest tomb on the northern side of the catacombs. Sosia's knowledge of this place stopped at the concealed door, so I follow the way that Lucian described, taking the turns left and right, heading along corridors that are thankfully wider than the first one.

I pass by stone chambers with carved walls and containing ledges filled with skulls. Sometimes, I have to stoop where the stone ceiling sits uncomfortably low. Other times, I'm squeezing through a narrow passage again.

It's completely dark, but that doesn't bother me, my sensitive eyesight proving to be an asset for once.

I stop at the point where Lucian's directions end, perplexed to find myself facing a fork in the path.

One passage veers left and the other veers right, and I can't be sure which one will take me north since either could curve back around at some point.

I close my eyes, trying to sense any kind of sound or smell that might give me a clue, only to be hit by the awareness of immense power.

It rushes across me in a wave that makes me gasp.

I'm suddenly drawn back to the moments before I looked up at the vast, night sky for the very first time.

The keeper had asked me to close my eyes while he led me down to the very first beach I ever stood on. With my eyes closed, his presence had been like a dark void next to me, a power beyond measure. It had felt to me as if his energy had been held together only by his will and the force of his crown.

What I sense now feels the same.

It can only be *The Book of Dark Magic*, drawing me toward the left-hand passageway.

Before I start down it, I extend my claws and drag them lightly along the beige stone, creating marks deep enough that my family will know which way I went.

When the corridor curves northward—at least, I hope it's northward because I can't be sure I haven't gotten turned around in this maze of corridors—the sense of power grows stronger.

Finally, a long corridor stretches ahead of me. At the end is a single, wooden door, curved in an arch at the top. The placement of the hinges tells me it opens outward.

Reaching it, I press my palms to its surface, smothering another gasp at the intensity of what I feel behind it.

It's very much like the keeper's energy, although... now that I'm closer to it... it feels different, somehow. Sharper, maybe.

I consider the possibility that there could be an army of dark creatures waiting behind this door. The power I'm detecting is obliterating my senses and I'm struggling to identify anything else.

But I reason that if this is truly where the book is being kept, then my father wouldn't allow other beings near it.

No. It's his obsession. A precious object he keeps to himself. He forces others, like Lucian, to read it only when it suits his purposes.

Taking a deep breath to calm my thudding heart, I pull open the door, bracing for what I might find.

The stone room ahead of me is circular and far larger than I was expecting. Much bigger than any of the chambers I passed along the way. At least seventy paces in each direction. In contrast to its size, the ceiling sits not far above me, certainly not high enough to fly around.

The only exit is the door I step through, which is slowly closing behind me.

It's pitch black inside, not even a beam of light, which would normally suit me, but the shadows within this room seem denser than they should be.

The hairs on the back of my neck and along my arms are rising, but not only because of the silent darkness.

In the center of the room are four statues.

They stand in a tight circle, each facing outward with their backs to each other. Even in the darkness, the color of the stone they've been carved from is apparent: one is white, the next is golden, then black, and finally crimson. The crimson color is the hardest to make out, but it appears like dark blood.

I can only see the backs of the black and crimson statues.

The one directly facing me—the golden one—is of a woman standing tall, dressed in elaborate armor and carrying a curved blade strapped to her back. She looks proud and strong, the face of a woman who has had to beat back her enemies.

Curiously, her arms are bent at the elbows, her palms turned up. Maybe in supplication. Maybe in a gesture of peace.

I dare to step farther into the room, examining my surroundings carefully, keeping my footfalls silent. As I veer to the left of the golden statue, the features of the black one become visible.

The breath leaves my chest in a *whoosh*.

What the...?

It's a statue of the keeper of dark magic. There he is, looming over me, just as he appeared when I first met him.

His long cloak drapes across his broad shoulders and covers his body from his neck to his feet while his spiked crown sits around his eyes, concealing his sight. Only the lower half of his face is visible, his lips set into an uncompromising line.

He, too, is holding out his arms, but unlike with the golden statue, a book rests in them.

A book with a black binding and golden lettering on the front.

This must be the power that drew me to this chamber.

The Book of Dark Magic.

A book so dangerous that as I reach for it, my skin crawls and shivers rush up and down my spine.

CHAPTER FORTY-TWO

$\mathcal{M}$y dark wings push and roil within my back and my claws extend and retract. Horrible, out-of-control sensations rush through me while my fingertips hover inches above the surface of the book that destroyed the life I was supposed to have.

It's finally within my reach. The first step to bringing down my father. And yet…

All I feel is dread.

An undefinable fear.

I know I should take the book and run while I can. Hell, it's been far too easy to get here and every instinct in my body is telling me I need to leave. Fast.

But my hands are shaking and my palms are sweating and by fuck, I do want run, but it's *away* from the book.

My breathing is harsh in my ears, rushing in and out of my mouth while the power within the chamber continues to press in on me, although… strangely… now that I'm standing right in front of the book…

I'm not certain that the power I feel is emanating from it.

My eyes widen with that perilous realization. My hands dart

out, but before they can close around the tome, a shadow peels away from the wall to my left.

I spin toward it, leaving the book where it rests. My claws extend as a sibilant voice sounds in the darkness.

"Not so easy, is it?" the voice whispers.

Black wings become visible within the dense shadow, parting to reveal my father leaning against the wall, his arms folded across his chest.

"I couldn't open it at first," he says calmly, not a hint of shame in his voice despite his admission. "But I'm glad I did."

He considers me with golden eyes made so much brighter by his luminescent skin. Every angle of his face and cheekbones and tall physique is perfectly balanced. Perfectly beautiful, as angels are. He tucks his wings away, and I remind myself how dangerous it would be to allow my own wings to extend, since he could try to use my feathers against me again.

Golden light glimmers around his hands, the threat of light magic only seconds away. Magic that can break my bones and burn my skin.

My focus flickers to the book, but I don't move closer to it.

The moment I reach for it, I'm certain that Taiven will unleash his power on me.

I need to time my actions. Let him get close to where I can use my claws and all the skills Anarchy taught me.

Taiven paces to the right, veering closer to me with every step, not taking his eyes off me. "I heard a whisper that the old wolves in Portland didn't kill you when they had the chance, and I thought, surely, that can't be true because they would never let a dark creature like you live."

He must be talking about the powerful wolves in the forest where the keeper healed me.

"Then I heard another, even more unbelievable rumor, that the dragon masters gave you safe haven. *Impossible*. Or so I thought."

He studies me in the way my jailer, the angel Zadkiel, used to look at me, as if I'm some sort of specimen to be dissected into my various parts.

"I was so unsettled that I consulted the book, even though I know its contents front to back," he says. "And that's when it showed me something new." His lips rise into a cold smile. "Something you will want to see, Daughter."

My focus darts to the book, my forehead creasing, but when I don't respond, Taiven's eyebrows rise.

"Isn't that why you're here?" he asks. "To understand your past and know your future? Well, go ahead. Read it. I won't stop you."

Surprised, I narrow my eyes at him, intensely wary of his invitation to lay my hands on the book.

Then, I remember what Lucian said about the fist you don't see coming.

Maybe Taiven is trying to lure me into a false sense of safety. Or he thinks the book will break my mind and, once I'm vulnerable, he can easily end me. He can't know that this book won't corrupt me. I know I can read it without harm.

I have nothing to fear in this moment except the pain Taiven might inflict on me with his light magic.

"Read it, Daughter," he whispers as he draws to a halt. "Go on. I'm giving you this one chance."

I have absolutely no intention of opening it, but I'll sure as hell take it from him.

Reaching for the book, I fight every instinct within my body that warns me to leave the tome where it lies. I tell myself over and over that stealing it will destroy my father, not me.

At the moment before my hands would slip around the book's edges, rapid footfalls reach me from the corridor outside the chamber and the balance of power in the air around me shifts.

The keeper's approaching presence is as vast and massive as

the energy I sensed in this room before I entered it, an opposing force that pushes at my mind and body in a dark swell.

He bursts through the door, black scales rushing across his visible skin and his eyes turning a fiery golden. Flames lick at his hands and a dragon's roar leaves his lips. "My Veda! Leave the book and run!"

His wild eyes meet mine as he storms toward me and the fear in his voice is like icy water. "Run for your life."

Ahead of me, my father is suddenly laughing. Cold, awful laughter as golden light bursts around his palms and outward.

His light magic explodes across the room, a wash of bright energy that knocks into the keeper and casts every small detail around me into sharp relief.

In that blink, that infinitesimal second before the energy hits me and I'm thrown backward, the silhouette of another creature becomes visible.

A woman stands against the wall behind my father, her head bowed, her knees slightly bent, and her shoulders slumped. She's dressed in golden armor and carries a curved blade at her back, and I wouldn't even know who she was if I hadn't hit the ground right in front of her statue.

What the...?

Only a few paces away from me, the keeper has dug in his heels, leaning into the explosion, his dragon wings extended, cutting through the magic and forming a shield between me and my father.

The keeper's dark magic billows outward, a storm of fire and malice, beating back the deadly light.

He's shouting and I can barely make out his words above the maelstrom. "Your father has a keeper! He controls the keeper of light magic!"

In the distance, the woman's silhouette disappears, like some kind of ghost melting back into the stonework, but the power my father wields is all too real.

How? Did he free her like I freed the keeper of dark magic? Or did he somehow invade her realm?

I have no answers.

All I know in this moment is that I'm lucky to be alive.

I'm doubled over, lying on my side, suddenly aware of another force around me. Some kind of... sphere... against which the raging light magic is swirling and swelling.

For a moment, I think the keeper—my keeper—must have placed a shield around me and then I become aware, with a sinking stomach, of the hard edges of the object pressed to my chest.

The Book of Dark Magic.

My fingertips had touched it just before Taiven's magic exploded and now, I'm clutching it to my chest.

I try to right myself, making it up onto my knees as the fight rages in front of me, my keeper and my father locked in battle.

The book's outer cover, where my arms are closed around it, is tugging violently against my hold. When I try to keep it shut, its edges sharpen, slicing across my arms and drawing blood.

In pure reflex, my arms open and the book *thuds* to the floor in front of me.

"Read it!" My father's shout reaches me above the storm of power raging around the room. "See who your real enemy is."

Before I can jump to my feet, the sphere around me glimmers, solidifying where I kneel. My back collides with it, a solid force that bites me with sharp energy, sending me to my knees.

At the same moment, the book's binding unravels into ropes that whip around my wrists, yanking my hands flat to the floor beneath its lower edge.

I struggle against the ropes, trying to free my claws to cut the restraints apart. When I can't, I duck my head toward them, aiming to sever them with my teeth.

My mouth closes around the ropes, only to encounter

sudden spikes, sharp needles that shred the roof of my mouth and my tongue.

I jolt backward in shock, spitting blood as more of the book's binding unravels, another thicker rope shooting upward and wrapping around my throat. Its front section solidifies between the book and my neck into a pole that stops me from darting forward again, lest I ram it through my own throat. A second later, I sense it split down my back, ropes rushing around and around my torso.

I scream and thrash, but the restraints only tighten, constricting my breathing while the sharp end of the pole slices across the front of my throat. Warm blood sprays across the floor and the exposed blank front page of the book.

My black blood soaks into the dark paper, the droplets disappearing as fast as they can fall, the paper appearing instantly dry again. Thirsty.

This book wants blood.

With a sob, I stop struggling, aware of my keeper's furious shout as the book opens and there's nothing I can do to stop it.

CHAPTER FORTY-THREE

Images leap up from the page, moving across the black parchment in front of me.

My younger self is huddled on the floor of my cell, my filthy hair clumped down my back, my dress not so short as it was when I escaped ten years later.

Tear tracks cut through the film of dirt on my young face.

I'm holding Sosia in my arms, her head resting in the crook of my elbow, her body laid across my legs.

I'm trying to get her to drink a few droplets of water, but she refuses. "Don't waste water on me now, Daughter," she says, her voice a rasp across her cracked lips.

She lifts her hand to my face, her arm trembling with the effort as she brushes away my tears.

"You will escape this place." There's a desperate plea in her eyes as her voice becomes fainter and harder to hear. "Go to Central Park. You remember it... Remember the places I told you about... Go to the statue of the toadstool..."

She gasps and shivers in my young arms.

"I've hidden something there. It's important. Promise me,

Daughter…" She closes her eyes, her breathing shaky. "Promise me you'll find it and always remember… We were loved."

Outside of the image, where I kneel, I close my eyes, not wanting to see again the moment when the only mother I knew died, but the image keeps playing in front of my closed eyelids, defying my wish to look away.

"Mother?" my younger self whispers as I wait… and wait… and wait…

"Mother?"

Her vacant eyes stare upward and her chest has fallen still.

"Mother!"

I remember how heavy she was in my arms in that moment and how badly my heart was breaking and how much I wanted to scream.

A wail breaks out of my mouth and I can't tell if it comes from me or my younger self. In the image, I'm doubled over, holding on tightly to a body that no longer houses the only person who had ever loved me.

There's a sudden rush of air, seeming to chill my skin even now, as the angel Zadkiel bursts through the cell door.

He rushes into the darkness, drops to his knees opposite the younger me, and he's cursing over and over, words that shouldn't pass an angel's lips.

He snatches Sosia out of my hold, lifting her so abruptly that her arms and legs dangle and her head lolls.

Younger me lurches forward, claws out, screaming at him to leave her alone.

He nearly drops Sosia's body to extend his right hand, a slap of light magic burning across my younger self's shoulder, sending my thin form flying across the floor. It gives him enough space to rush out of the cage and close the door behind himself.

My younger self leaps after him, screaming and beating my

fists and claws against the closed door, my wails shrieking from the pages of the book.

The sound echoes around me, fading as the image leaves my younger self behind, focusing on Zadkiel as he rushes along the wide corridor between the cages—these ones made out of bars, including the one where the panthers were being kept.

He makes it to the door at the end of the dark corridor and pauses there, Sosia held tightly to his chest, with his ear turned toward the door and his head tilted for a long moment before he opens it.

When I escaped from my cell, I couldn't look at what lay beyond that door because the environment was too bright for my eyes. I was aware of steps—the panthers helped me navigate them upward—and when I reached the top of them, I somehow fell into the keeper's realm.

Now, even though it's still bright within the image, I can see what I missed before.

A spiral staircase hangs in the air, a seemingly impossible structure with no visible supports around it. It doesn't have railings, but as Zadkiel rapidly ascends it, doors appear on both sides of each step. And then disappear again as he takes the next step up.

The uppermost step doesn't seem to lead anywhere, but he heads toward it instead of going through any of the doors.

When he reaches the top, he glances around, and then—

I'm shocked when he opens his arms and dumps Sosia's body into the empty space in front of him.

Her frail form plummets for a brief second before the bright air swallows her and her body simply disappears.

My hands flex against the floor where they're bound, as if I could catch her from outside the book.

Then the image leaves Zadkiel and rushes down after her.

Down into a sudden darkness that couldn't be seen from the staircase.

Her body becomes visible again as she plummets through that darkness, her descent slowing until she floats to a stop, and her body settles onto the same gleaming, black surface on which I landed.

It's the floor of the keeper's realm.

Zadkiel threw her into it, the same way I fell into it from the top of the staircase.

I hold my breath, my mind consumed by the pure black of the keeper's realm, the cold, gleaming surfaces, only vaguely aware now of the battle that continues to rage around my present self—the flashes of light and dark, the beat of dragon's wings, the cut of bright blades…

From within the pages in front of me comes the swishing of the keeper's cloak dragging across the floor. No doubt he's coming to take the dark magic from Sosia's bones and tether it.

I never asked him about the moment he took *her* magic. Assuming she was a creature with little power, he probably wouldn't even remember it amid all of the dark creatures whose magic he tethered over millennia.

He appears within the image as an inky silhouette, his figure tall, shoulders broad, his body obscured by his cape and his eyes covered by his crown where it used to sit low around his head.

Desperately, I wish I could shut off the images, because I don't want to watch him take whatever's left of her.

He bends to Sosia's body, crouching beside her, his hands closing around her shoulders.

That's when she opens her eyes.

CHAPTER FORTY-FOUR

scream passes my lips as Sosia gasps for breath within the image, dragging air into her chest as she stares upward, directly into me, as if she can see me outside the pages of this book and she's trying to tear the heart out of me.

I wrench again at the ropes that hold me in place, sending fresh blood splattering through the image to the paper beneath it. As much as I struggle to free myself, it does me no good.

Sosia's hand has flown to her chest, pressing so hard that it looks like she's about to tear through her own skin and flesh. She could if she released the claws she was cursed to have.

"How...?" Her whisper reaches me a moment before her focus shifts to the keeper where he kneels beside her, still gripping her shoulders, his cloak spread out across the floor behind him.

I expect her to be afraid or confused, but her expression settles, a softness coming over it that freezes me to the spot.

"Oh." She exhales as softly as a breeze before she reaches up with her free hand to brush her fingertips across his jaw. A touch that appears as gentle as the one she pressed to my younger self's cheek. "It's you."

I'm certain he says something back to her, but he's leaning over her and I can't see his face or his mouth and suddenly, my ears are buzzing and the sounds from within the book are muffled.

Her mouth moves. She's speaking again, and I wish I could read her lips because I can't hear what she says—or if he replies to her.

For a full minute, the sounds are warped, muffled, buzzing, and I risk impaling my throat when I strain forward in an effort to hear them.

Then a look of resignation settles over Sosia's features and suddenly, the buzzing clears, her voice cutting back in so clearly that it's almost like a shout in my ears.

"Will you take my claws now?" she asks.

His response is cold and empty. "I will take everything."

There's a blur of movement.

His left hand darts down, plunging into her chest, ripping through flesh and bone before his fist tears upward again, covered in blood.

A scream of shock rests on my lips. My eyes are wide as I follow the dripping blood from his fist down to her broken body.

Her eyes are still open.

She's still alive and focused on him, her lips parting softly, her final words spoken on a quiet exhale. "My daughter..."

Then her features smooth out.

The life leaves her eyes, she lies still on the black marble floor, and I know that this time, she won't wake up.

I can't breathe as the image continues to play out in front of me, the keeper drawing back, opening his fist to reveal the still-beating organ gripped within his fingers.

No.

A scream tears out of me.

Please, no.

A heart rests in his bloody palm, its fleshy parts crushed while its metallic plates and delicate, interlocking parts continue to move in perfect harmony.

A mechanical heart that continues beating in my hearing.

Thud-thud. Thud-thud.

Slower and slower until the mechanism stops and then the metal becomes dull and lifeless.

A shriek of horror and rage and denial breaks across me. My scream, torn from my chest.

Because Galeia—my biological mother—had a mechanical heart. A heart that nobody else could have had.

My mother… *My mother…*

I'm suddenly aware that silence has fallen around me.

The dark sphere that surrounded me is peeling away, curling like paper in a fire, while the ropes that bound me are fraying and the pole that threatened to impale my throat is crumbling into ash that falls onto the pages.

All of the dust and blood gathers together, reforming the book's cover until it lies silent and still on the floor in front of me, leaving me cold and broken.

"Lies," I whisper.

It must be lies.

The keeper told me he hadn't tethered Galeia's magic. He wouldn't have lied about that, not when he knew the pain it would cause me.

My focus is drawn to him now.

He's on his knees, his scales torn across his face and arms, his dragon wings drooping at his sides, his shoulders stooped so low that his fists rest on the floor in front of him, but somehow, his eyes are raised to mine.

My father looms over him, light flickering around his palms and making his skin glow. "You gave him the power in your heart, didn't you, Daughter?"

The smile on Taiven's face makes my blood run cold.

"Your heart is breaking now," Taiven continues. "And thus, he too will break."

This is what my father wanted.

To destroy me and the keeper of dark magic with me.

In the background, the light magic keeper has become visible again. She's slumped against the stone wall, her eyes empty, golden orbs, her arms hanging at her sides, the weapon at her back scraping against the stone with every breath she takes, a horrible, rasping sound in the silence.

"Do you see now who your real enemy is, Daughter?" Taiven asks.

I drag a shaky breath into my chest, clinging to a shred of hope anchored in the beliefs that *The Book of Dark Magic* turns love to hate and only serves itself and is full of lies, so many lies.

"Did you do it?" I whisper, my focus on my keeper, willing him to tell me that he didn't. That he doesn't even know what I'm talking about.

His gaze doesn't waver, his soft murmur barely audible. "Don't break, my Veda."

A little piece of my heart crumbles.

"Don't break," he whispers.

And then another piece, fracturing and shattering.

I remember his fury when I talked of stealing the book. I remember the way he told me that the book would destroy me.

My furious scream echoes around the stone chamber. *"Did you kill her?"*

I stumble to my feet, scooping up the book and carrying it with me, holding it close to my chest.

It no longer feels dangerous to me, no longer repels me.

Accusations tear from my mouth as I advance on him. "Did you rip out her heart? Did you take my mother from me and then lie about it? *Did you betray me?*"

"Don't break, my Veda," he says, shaking his head, fresh

blood spilling from the cuts across his face and chest where his clothing is torn.

"She was alive. She was free. She could have come back for me." My cries are full of pain, all the pain that didn't have to be mine. "She could have freed me."

"It isn't that simple—"

"Oh, but it is." I'm only three paces away from my keeper now and I close the gap within seconds, dropping to my knees beside him, letting the book *thud* to the floor beside us as I reach for his face.

I press my palms to his torn skin—the coldness of his cheeks, the warmth of his fresh blood, because his strength comes from my heart and my heart is breaking. "Did you lie to me?"

His lips turn down. His arms rise around me, his hand tight against the back of my neck.

"I warned you, my Veda." His voice is raw. With agony or fury, I can't tell which. "I warned you that I'd betray you." Dark light glimmers at the edge of my vision, glittering around the crown that took the power from my mother's heart. "I told you I'd lie."

He presses his forehead to mine, closing his eyes.

"My Veda," he whispers.

I lean in and kiss him with all the rage and hatred in my soul, a clash of mouths and teeth and souls.

"I know your name now," I murmur against his lips.

Because names have power. The power to determine our destiny, define our intentions, or destroy our hearts.

He grips my head, his breathing ragged. "Name me, my Veda. Tear back the layers and tell me who I am."

"*Emil*," I whisper. "*Enemy*. You were always my enemy. I just didn't know it."

His eyes slowly darken with the power of a thousand souls. "Yes. I am. But the real question, my Veda... My conqueror...

My beautiful, dark love... The real question is: Will you have your revenge?"

Find out how Veda and the keeper's story ends in
Crown of Fate,
the final book with no cliffhanger.

If you'd like to know all about the Vandawolf and the magic that created Galeia's heart, check out The Kingdom of Betrayal series.

CROWN OF FATE

(DARK MAGIC SHIFTERS #3)

His dark soul will be my ruin...

Content information: Crown of Fate is a dark paranormal romance, the third in the Dark Magic Shifters series.

Recommended reading age is 18+ for sex scenes, mature themes, violence, and language.

NO cliffhanger.

Get your copy of Crown of Fate.

ALSO BY EVERLY FROST

DARK MAGIC SHIFTERS

(Dark Urban Fantasy Romance)

1. Wolf of Ashes

2. Bond of Flames

3. Crown of Fate

KINGDOM OF BETRAYAL

(Fantasy Romance)

1. A Sky Like Blood

2. A Sin Like Fire

3. A Storm Like Iron

4. A Soul Like Glass

BRIGHT WICKED - COMPLETE

(Fantasy Romance)

1. Bright Wicked

2. Radiant Fierce

3. Infernal Dark

STORM PRINCESS - COMPLETE

(Fantasy Romance)

1. Book 1

2. Book 2

3. Book 3

ASSASSIN'S MAGIC - COMPLETE

(Urban Fantasy Romance)

1. Assassin's Magic

2. Assassin's Mask

3. Assassin's Menace

4. Assassin's Maze

5. Rebels

6. Revenge

7. Rogue

8. Assassin's Match

SOUL BITTEN SHIFTER - COMPLETE

(Dark Urban Fantasy Romance)

1. This Dark Wolf

2. This Broken Wolf

3. This Caged Wolf

4. This Cruel Blood

SUPERNATURAL LEGACY - COMPLETE

(Angels and Dragon Shifters)

1. Hunt the Night

2. Chase the Shadows

3. Slay the Dawn

4. Claim the Light

DEMON PACK - COMPLETE

(Dark Paranormal Romance)

1. Demon Pack

2. Demon Pack: Elimination

3. Demon Pack: Eternal

MORTALITY - COMPLETE

(Science-Fantasy Romance)

Mortality Complete Set: Books 1 to 4

1. Beyond the Ever Reach

2. Beneath the Guarding Stars

3. By the Icy Wild

4. Before the Raging Lion

<u>Stand-alone fiction - dark romance</u>

Corrupt Me: Immortal Vices and Virtues

ABOUT THE AUTHOR

Everly Frost is the USA Today Bestselling author of fantasy romance, urban fantasy and paranormal romance novels. She spent her childhood dreaming of other worlds and scribbling stories on the leftover blank pages at the back of school notebooks. She lives in Brisbane, Australia with her husband and two children.

- amazon.com/author/everlyfrost
- facebook.com/everlyfrost
- instagram.com/everlyfrost
- bookbub.com/authors/everly-frost
- goodreads.com/everlyfrost